The Invasion

Lady Victoria March congratulated herself on escaping the vulgar throng in the country inn where she was stranded. She had managed to engage the inn's only private drawing room to take her repast in precious privacy.

But now that privacy had been invaded. First by the innkeeper, who rudely informed her that a fine lord was about to enter—no matter how she might protest. And now by that lord himself.

Stunned, Victoria listened as the most magnificently magnetic man she had ever met said softly, "Permit me to make known to you Lord Damion St. Claire."

Victoria realized that he awaited her reaction to his name. "Forgive me, my lord. I am not familiar with your reputation. I have but recently returned to England."

Lord Damion's mouth slowly curled into a grin of startling charm. "Allow me to inform you, madame, that you are alone with the most notorious rake in England. . . ."

SUITABLE MATCHES

The
Demon Rake

Gayle Buck

A SIGNET BOOK

NEW AMERICAN LIBRARY

Copyright © 1986 by Gayle Buck

SIGNET TRADEMARK REG. U.S. PAT. OFF. AND FOREIGN COUNTRIES
REGISTERED TRADEMARK—MARCA REGISTRADA
HECHO EN CHICAGO, U.S.A.

SIGNET, SIGNET CLASSIC, MENTOR, ONYX, PLUME, MERIDIAN AND
NAL BOOKS are published by New American Library,
1633 Broadway, New York, New York 10019

First Printing, December, 1986

1 2 3 4 5 6 7 8 9

PRINTED IN THE UNITED STATES OF AMERICA

One

Lady Victoria March stood at the parlor window overlooking the small inn yard, watching the misting rain with a frown. She was thoroughly disenchanted with the unceasing wet weather that had marked her journey through England. She had always heard that the peaks and dales of Derbyshire were beautiful, but she had been able to see little of the countryside these past days.

A private chaise-and-four swept into sight, mud spraying from its iron tires, and stopped beneath her window. The driver sprang down from the box to let down the step. From the door emerged a figure known to have turned the most absorbing thoughts from a feminine mind. Victoria was diverted, but it was not necessarily the handsome breadth of the gentleman's shoulders that first caught her attention. Drawing on a lifetime of experience as a soldier's daughter in Portugal, she immediately recognized a touch of the military in his bearing. As the British army hounding Napoleon's armies in Portugal were a close-knit group, Victoria wondered idly if she had ever met the gentleman. But she could not clearly make out his face because the tall beaver he wore was pulled low across his brow to protect him from rain.

The gentleman leisurely descended to the soggy ground and with a slight nod acknowledged the fawning innkeeper. Although a portly man, the master of the inn bobbed low at the waist, rubbing his hands together. Victoria smiled as she recalled her own cool reception when he realized that she was traveling alone and would not order more than tea.

Still bowing, the innkeeper ushered his distinguished guest ahead of him out of the weather. Then he bellowed toward the stables in a voice that Victoria could hear even through the leaded glass window. "Hie there! See to his lordship's cattle!" Two ostlers slowly emerged from the stables, their shoulders hunched against the rain. Satisfied, the innkeeper disappeared into the inn.

Victoria's thoughts returned to the conclusion of her journey. The innkeeper had grudgingly admitted that her destination, Belingham Manor, lay within easy distance. If the weather did not worsen she could reach the estate before nightfall.

Victoria thought that was fortunate. Her good friend, Sir Harry Belingham, had pressed on her an extra sum when he saw her off on the packet from Portugal to England, and Victoria had thought she had more than ample funds for her journey and whatever miscellaneous expenses she might have while at Belingham Manor, but now she was not so certain. She had found it far more dear to travel in England than in Portugal. The tab was likely to be outrageous for the late afternoon tea she had ordered, but she had not wanted to impose on her hostess by arriving light-headed and in need of dinner. She decided she would write her banker in London for funds as soon as she was settled in at Belingham Manor. Then she would pay a visit to her father-in-law, who lived within a short distance of the Belingham estate.

There was a knock on the parlor door and she turned away from the window, anticipating the tea she had ordered. "Please enter, waiter." To her surprise, the innkeeper himself entered the parlor. His bow to her was barely civil. "Forgive this intrusion, madame," he said without visible penance. "There is a gentleman, wishing to be private as it were, and there being no other available parlors—" He paused, shrugging his shoulders.

With a flicker of outrage, Victoria realized the

man meant to turn her out. She knew that he would not have dared to impose on her if she had arrived in proper style with a maid or companion. "I take it the gentleman is a singularly favored guest!"

"Mine host puts himself badly, ma'am. I fear my credit will be beyond repair if left in his clumsy hands."

The innkeeper started. His eyes rolled back in dismay, and past his shoulder Victoria saw the tall gentleman who had alighted from the maroon chaise. He was unknown to her after all, and in appearance quite different from the military set she was used to. His fashionable buff pantaloons were smoothed without a crease into topboots of a mirror finish, setting off muscular legs, and his broad shoulders were shown to advantage by the superb cut of his fawn coat. The gentleman's lean and somewhat browned countenance reminded her forcibly of a proud Spanish hawk, at once haughty and compelling.

Upon meeting the amusement in his cool gray eyes, Victoria realized that she was staring and a faint flush rose in her face. She said quietly, "I fear my company manners have grown sadly shabby. Pray will you not join me, sir?"

"It will be my pleasure, ma'am," said the gentleman gently. He turned to the discomfited innkeeper and his voice grew markedly hard. "I will have a cold collation with a bottle of your finest claret. I assume the lady has ordered tea. Oblige me by giving her your first consideration."

Victoria thought to herself that the gentleman's arrogance carried him too far. But the wooden-faced innkeeper merely bowed and retreated from the room.

The gentleman glanced across at her with an unreadable expression, then tossed the greatcoat that lay over his arm onto a rush-bottomed chair and sent his beaver spinning after it. "I apologize for any distress you may have suffered on my account, ma'am," he said softly, smoothing a wrinkle from his sleeve.

"Pray do not apologize," said Victoria, thinking that he must be of a singularly quixotic nature to have mixed himself in her business so thoroughly. "Indeed, it was not necessary—"

"On the contrary, it was most necessary," he interrupted. "The man is rag-mannered and a rascal." His voice was polite but it brooked no argument. "It was mere whimsey that I took a dislike to the tap room and followed after our fine host. Consider yourself fortunate that you are not now ensconced in the public coffee room, madame."

Disconcerted by the force of his opinion, Victoria thought it prudent to say nothing. The gentleman obviously possessed a quick temper.

A striped sofa was conveniently at hand and she seated herself with the unconscious grace natural to her.

In silence the gentleman strolled across the room, bowing slightly as he passed her, and went to the darkening window. Resting one hand on the sill, he stared out at the lingering shadows. Victoria was thus afforded the opportunity to study his sharp profile unobtrusively. She was again struck by something soldierly in his bearing. He spoke and carried himself as though accustomed to command, she thought.

Glimpsing his frown, Victoria could not imagine him joining in the easy comaraderie that was habitual among the younger men of her acquaintance. Indeed, her late husband Charles and his friend Harry would no doubt have pronounced him a dull dog.

Her companion remarked casually, "It appears that we will have a thunderstorm by nightfall."

"Oh, do not say so!" exclaimed Victoria.

He turned, astonished by her vehemence, and raised a thin brow. Victoria colored faintly under his stare, but her eyes gleamed with rueful humor. "Pray do not heed me, sir. Simply put, my journey has been plagued by rain. I had hoped for a clearing sky this evening to mark its end."

"I, too, find it unappealing weather," said the

stranger. He gestured at her lavender pelisse. "You are in mourning. Pray accept my condolences." Silently Victoria inclined her head. "I am somewhat acquainted with the neighborhood," he said. "Do you visit relations?"

Victoria hesitated to reply. She was uncertain why she should feel reluctant to divulge her destination, but experience had taught her to trust her instincts. Quietly she sidestepped his curiosity. "I am staying with friends," she said briefly. He looked mildly surprised by her evasion but made no comment.

After a quick knock a waiter entered the parlor with a tea tray. The innkeeper followed, bearing a dusty bottle of wine cradled in his arm. While the waiter set out Victoria's tea and a plate of thinly sliced cold beef sandwiches, the innkeeper carefully uncorked the bottle. "A sample from my best private stock, m'lord," he said, pouring out a glass. With a deferential bow he offered the stemmed glass to the gentleman.

Victoria watched with quiet amusement as her companion tasted the red wine with exaggerated care. The innkeeper watched him with an anxious air. "Excellent, mine host," said the gentleman gravely. "Your palate astonished me."

The innkeeper's expression eased into a jovial smile. He returned the glass to the table. "Will there be aught else, m'lord?"

"For the moment, no," the gentleman said crushingly. "However, after I have supped I will require my carriage. I will not be spending the night."

The innkeeper bowed with obvious disappointment. "Very good, m'lord." He muttered sharply at the lingering waiter and hurried the man out of the room.

"We are served, ma'am," said the gentleman as he offered his arm to Victoria. She rose gracefully to her feet and discovered that the gentleman was a good head taller than herself. After the slightest hesitation she placed her fingers lightly on his elbow. It had been a long time since she had been so formally escorted to dinner. Raising her eyes, she again encountered cool amusement in the gentleman's gaze.

He seated her at the table, murmuring, "Our host has a remarkably loose tongue." He took a chair across from her, his expression sardonic. Victoria found the careless glint in his eyes disturbingly familiar. "Permit me to make known to you Lord Damion St. Claire," he said softly.

The silence was expectant. Victoria realized that he awaited her reaction to his name. "Forgive me, my lord. I am not familiar with your reputation. I have but recently come to England."

Lord Damion stared at her in astonishment. His mouth slowly curled in a grin of startling charm. "My arrogance is well served! Allow me to inform you, madame, that you dine with the Demon, a most notorious rake."

Victoria threw him an interested glance as she picked up the china teapot and poured the steaming tea. "I am certain you exaggerate, my lord. To my mind a rake is hardly a gentleman, which you have certainly proven yourself to be."

Cynicism chilled his expression, turning his eyes to hard agate. "Do not be so certain, madame. A gentleman born may play the rake better than any." He leaned back in his chair and idly swirled the claret in his glass. "But I do not know your story. I believe you mentioned having but just come to England?"

Victoria took time to sip her tea and choose her words carefully. She decided it would be best if she did not make herself known to Lord Damion. In this neighborhood even a chance acquaintance could know of the March family, and given her relationship with her late husband's family, Victoria infinitely preferred that they not know of her arrival until she was ready to announce herself. "Yes. I have been in Portugal. My husband was with the cavalry until he was killed." She considered the plate of sandwiches and took one.

Lord Damion frowned. "Forgive me. It was not my intention to touch upon a painful memory."

Victoria met his eyes. "My lord, I realized very early in my marriage that I might one day face his death. My husband's nature thrived on unpredictability and danger." She paused and a fleeting smile lighted her face. "Indeed, Charles was terribly rackety until he was assigned to detached duty for the cartographers. He sketched amazingly well, and very swiftly, so that he was often sent through the French lines to scout the country."

"Hardly what I would call an enviable task. The country is impossible," said Lord Damion, studying her with interest. The dove-gray bonnet she wore threw shadows under her long-lashed golden brown eyes and prominent cheekbones. Her face was too thin and unfashionably browned for his taste. Except for her grace of manner and obvious breeding, he thought her looks unremarkable until the quick smile flitted once more into her expressive eyes.

"You speak as though from firsthand experience," said Victoria, brushing crumbs from her slender fingers.

"I was with Sir John Moore in '09," said Lord Damion. His mouth thinned a moment, then he smiled. "I well remember the life. It could hardly have been a comfortable existence for you, ma'am."

"I have known little else. My father was a soldier, you see." She paused, then said softly, "It was a decent life, my lord. I shall miss it in many ways."

"I hope the future will prove as rewarding," said Lord Damion, his unreadable eyes on her face. An improbable thought struck him. But the lady had chosen not to honor him with her name and he could only speculate.

"And I also, my lord," said Victoria with a little laugh. An unlikely vision of her husband's family welcoming her with open arms caused her lips to curl upward in amusement. She had never met the Marches, and Charles had mentioned little enough about any member of his family except his stern father. But Victoria rather thought that the family would take their cue from Lord Robert, the Earl of

March. And what she had heard of that gentleman led her to believe that he would find little to approve in her. After all, her upbringing had not been typically English. Her father had been a younger son of an impoverished country lord who had chosen to make his home and his fortune in a foreign land because his beloved Portuguese bride could not bear to be separated from her family.

But at least she need not make more than a token visit to the Crossing, her husband's ancestral home, before truly settling in at Belingham Manor, where she was certain of a cordial reception. Lady Belingham had sent a reply immediately upon receipt of Harry's letter that assured Victoria that she was welcome to stay as long as she cared to and certainly through Christmas. Remembering the warmth of Lady Belingham's invitation, Victoria smiled again. She did not notice the look of speculation in Lord Damion's eyes as he watched her expressive face.

A silence fell while Victoria finished her sandwiches and Lord Damion addressed his wine. Both were absorbed in their own thoughts.

There was a diffident knock on the parlor door. Lord Damion laid an arm over the chair back, half turning in his seat. "Enter."

The door creaked open and the innkeeper stepped in. His beady eyes shot to each of their faces before he made a low bow. "Begging your pardon, m'lord," he said, folding his hands over his stomach. "But I 'ave come to inform m'lady that her chaise is standing ready."

Lord Damion cocked his brow at her. Victoria placed her napkin beside her plate. "Your company has been most agreeable, Lord Damion. But I fear I must be on my way," she said.

Lord Damion rose from the table and accompanied Victoria across the room. "I find that a most regrettable circumstance. I should have liked to have deepened our acquaintance."

At the door Victoria turned to give her gloved hand to him. He held it a moment longer than necessary. His gray eyes glinted down at her and Victoria realized with surprise that he was deliberately trying to disconcert her. "I bid you fair weather, madame," said Lord Damion softly.

"Thank you, my lord, and good-bye," said Victoria, disengaging her fingers from his. She turned quickly and caught the innkeeper's knowing expression before he could smooth it away. She pretended not to notice. "I will wish to depart immediately."

The innkeeper bowed deeply. "This way, m'lady," he said respectfully, and led her down the dim narrow hall. Victoria was torn between annoyance and amusement by the man's changed attitude. Her consequence was obviously much heightened since she had shared a private parlor with Lord Damion St. Claire. She thought whimsically that she might make a practice of dining with rakes if it guaranteed her such exceptional service.

Two

The innkeeper did not pause in the public tap room but ushered Victoria directly to the heavy plank door to the innyard. Victoria saw that her chaise stood waiting with a restive team of four. The bay leader shook its mane, setting the traces to jingling. She knew immediately that this team was the best that she had yet had hitched to her hired carriage.

With misgivings Victoria opened the corded reticule dangling from her wrist to take out her purse and settled the tab. The innkeeper jingled the coins in his palm. Victoria braced herself, prepared to haggle with the man. She was surprised when he fished out a few coins and gave them back to her with a bow. "It was a pleasure to serve m'lady. I could not accept such a handsome tip," said the innkeeper.

Victoria did not believe him and she was further convinced when the man threw an upward glance at the window above them. She smiled, realizing that they must have an audience. Again Lord Damion's consequence was at work on her behalf. She knew the wily innkeeper would not lose a tuppence when it came time to figure his lordship's bill. A man hunched in a frieze coat pushed past them in the doorway, shouldering Victoria rudely against the plank door. He hurried on, mumbling indistinctively, while the innkeeper helped her to regain her balance. "Pay 'im no heed, m'lady. A pint too much, he 'ad," said the innkeeper dismissively.

"Obviously," said Victoria dryly. She lifted the long hem of her pelisse before stepping down into the churned mud of the yard. The damp air smelled of horseflesh and hay. She breathed deeply, reminded sharply of Portugal. She promised herself that she would return quickly to Lisbon, to the home which she and Charles had made and which she now managed for herself. The army would naturally march again in the spring and she would lose the company of her English acquaintances. But she would still have her Portuguese friends and the stable that was slowly gaining in reputation for well-blooded stock.

A low rumbling turned her gaze to the late afternoon skies, where sullen clouds rolled ominously across the horizon. It appeared that Lord Damion had been right in his weather prediction. Behind her, the innkeeper unknowingly echoed her thoughts. "This curst rain!" he exclaimed.

The postilion jumped down from his perch beside the coachman and unlatched the chaise door for her. Victoria mounted the iron step and ducked quickly into the chaise. The door was latched behind her as she took the seat facing the horses.

A whip cracked. The chaise lurched forward, axles squealing in protest. The wheels slowly gathered speed and settled into a dull humming complaint. Victoria leaned toward the window. A fine drizzle was falling but she glimpsed the innkeeper's back as he disappeared through the inn door. He had stayed only long enough to be certain of her swift departure, thought Victoria wryly. She looked up at the parlor window and made out a tall figure. She thought that he raised his hand in farewell, but she couldn't be certain. The trees bordering the inn yard quickly obliterated any view of the hostelry.

Victoria sat back against the musty seat squabs. Her brows furrowed as she pondered Lord Damion St. Claire. She had found him to be disturbingly attractive and her response was due to more than his strong lean looks. In his company she had felt the stirring of an old excitement that she had been certain had died with Charles.

Victoria loosened the ribbons under her chin so that she could put back her bonnet. Lord Damion had called himself a rake and Victoria could well imagine that his aloof amusement fascinated many women. She herself was not immune to him. Victoria caught her thoughts lingering on the impenetrable expression that had been in Lord Damion's eyes when they had rested on her. With unwonted energy she ran her fingers through her flattened curls. "Don't be foolish!" she said aloud.

Yet Victoria knew, however she might wish it, that she would not soon forget Lord Damion's disturbing effect on her. Charles March, for all his engaging charm, had never caused her to stare like an awkward schoolgirl on first meeting.

On the contrary, she had tried to lash him with her riding crop for his impudence in catching up her bridle and thus ending an impromptu race across the plain. She smiled, remembering. It had been a stormy introduction but Charles March had soon had her laughing with him.

When she and Charles had returned to the stables that day, Victoria had been surprised to find her uncle, Carlos Silva y Montoya, waiting for them.

Carlos had not often intruded on her riding hours and she wondered what could be so important. But her uncle had not come to meet her.

Charles March had kicked out of his stirrups to land agilely on his feet beside the older man. The two men embraced as only comrades-in-arms can. With open astonishment Victoria watched the meeting between her uncle and the young Englishman.

"So, young Carlos, you have come at last. I expected you earlier," Carlos had said. Victoria regarded the young Englishman with new eyes, for her uncle's warm reception of him spoke volumes about his character. Carlos Silva y Montoya was reputed to be a man of action who had little time for less hardy souls. During the war he acted at times as a guide and an informant for the British army. Victoria wondered how someone like Charles March could possibly have become his friend.

"I had a rare bit of action to attend to first," Charles March had said with a flashing grin. His lively gaze turned toward Victoria, who had dismounted and joined them. "But as it happens I am happy to have been delayed until this morning, or I would not have made the acquaintance of this charming lady." He bowed low to Victoria.

Carlos drew his niece's gloved hand through the crook of his elbow and gave Victoria's fingers an affectionate squeeze. "Your eye is a discerning one. My niece is as a rare jewel. She came to me when her father died two years ago and I have seen her become a beautiful woman. So, Victoria, what do you think of my young friend?"

"I suspect that he could charm the birds from the sky if he wished. And you are yourself no sluggard, Carlos," Victoria said, her eyes dancing.

The two men laughed. Carlos Silva y Montoya clapped the young Englishman on the shoulder. "You shall stay with us when you can, young Carlos."

"I shall be happy to do so, sir," Charles March said. His admiring eyes met and held Victoria's glance.

Victoria could scarcely recall a moment afterwards

that Charles had not figured in her life. Since his death, she found herself to be incredibly lonely though she was still surrounded by their mutual friends.

Victoria did not know what she might have done if she had not had her young daughter to look after.

The chaise suddenly bounded into the air, jolting Victoria from her bittersweet memories. The carriage landed hard with a sharp crack and slewed. Victoria grabbed the hand strap set in the ceiling even as the chaise crashed over. She was flung from the seat and lay still a moment, stunned.

The door above her jerked open and she looked up into the coachman's weathered face. His head and shoulders almost obliterated the fast waning afternoon sun. "Be ye all right, m'lady?" he asked anxiously.

Victoria groped and found her reticule, then put her hand on the door beneath her to steady herself as she sat up. Under her flattened fingers broken glass shifted. She raised her hand to inspect the thin ribbon of blood traced across her palm. "Yes, I am perfectly fine," she said calmly, plucking out the minute sliver of window glass.

"If ye give me your hand, m'lady, I can pull ye out," said the coachman. Victoria stood up and discovered that her shoulders topped the side of the chaise. With the coachman's solicitous help she scrambled over the side of the chaise to the road.

Victoria stood on the damp gravel and surveyed the scene. The uneasy team shifted, hooves clopping softly the soaked ground. One of her portmanteaus had been thrown from the chaise and opened on impact. White shifts had tumbled in the damp roadway. The chaise itself lay on its side and even her untutored eye found the cause of the accident. A large rock sat behind the off wheel of the chaise.

The coachman joined her a brief moment. "The axle is broken in two, m'lady," he said regretfully.

"We shall have to return to the inn, of course," said Victoria resignedly.

"Aye. Or mayhap ye would prefer to wait here

with the lad while I ride one of the leaders to Belingham Manor for help," said the coachman.

Victoria bit her lip, scanning the overcast sky. The trees crowded close, looming across the narrow section of road. The wind rustled through the branches overhead and tugged at her skirts. She wondered if the weather would hold. It was not to her liking to be caught out at night in a downpour without better shelter than the disabled chaise. It occurred to her that she had not seen the postilion since the accident. "Where is the boy now? Is he all right?"

"Eh, Jem was thrown and he is a bit shaken, m'lady. But he will protect ye, never fear. I'll just leave the blunderbuss with him," said the coachman comfortably.

"Very well, then," said Victoria, deciding quickly. "The boy and I shall await your return from Belingham."

The coachman nodded and walked over to the team, at the same time calling to the postilion, who came slowly from around the chaise and abruptly sat down, holding his head. The coachman shook his head and clucked soothingly at the horses as he began to undo the traces.

A swiftly moving chaise-and-four swept around the bend in the road. The sun's dying rays illuminated the scene of the accident and the sharp-eyed driver pulled on his reins. A passenger thrust his head out the carriage window, his dark hair wild in the swift passage of the wind.

Victoria drew a thankful breath at sight of the slowing vehicle. She moved out of the roadway to stand in the deepening shadows at the road's edge and brushed a loose curl back from her brow. All at once she felt somehow foolish to be found in such straits.

The chaise-and-four had not come completely to a stop before its door was flung open and a man swathed in a greatcoat leaped out. The stranger strode swiftly in her direction. "Have you been injured?" he called sharply.

Victoria started, recognizing the deep voice. She sighed, thinking that it was simply too provoking to be rescued by the same man twice in the same evening. She stepped out of the tree shadows and met him as he came up. "I am perfectly well," she said calmly, though she still felt unnerved. "Once more I owe you thanks for your timely appearance, my lord."

"It appears to be one of my better habits this evening," said Lord Damion dryly. He seized the opportunity to satisfy his earlier curiosity. "Forgive me, but my memory seems to have deserted me. I have forgotten your name, madame."

"I am Lady Victoria March," Victoria said without thinking as she readjusted her bonnet over her hair.

"The devil you say!" There was a mixture of animosity and distaste in Lord Damion's voice.

Victoria steeled herself against his unfriendly tone, realizing that her prior instincts had been correct. Coolly she looked up at him. "Indeed the devil it is." She noticed that the coachman was bent over the postilion and heard a low exchange between them. Dismissing Lord Damion's displeasure as unimportant, she joined the coachman. "Is the boy hurt badly?"

The coachman pulled the boy up, supporting him around the waist when he was on his feet. "Naught wrong with Jem but a sore head and a cracked shoulder, m'lady," said the coachman cheerfully. "A pint or two and the sawbones in to him will set him up in a trice. Eh, Jem?"

"Aye," whispered the postilion manfully, his pale young face pinched with pain.

Victoria heard Lord Damion's step beside her. "Get him on one of the horses before he faints," he ordered the coachman. "I will send my man over with a flask. He'll need a stiff swallow to get him over these abominable roads."

"Aye, he will at that, m'lord," said the coachman. With the postilion sagging against him, he made his way over to the patient team. Lord Damion turned to Victoria. The dim light seemed to lend a hardness to his expression. "I beg you will accept a seat in my chaise, Lady Victoria. The postilion will feel easier if he does not need to put on a brave front for your benefit."

Though surprised by his offer, Victoria nodded her acceptance. She was again impressed by the humane side of Lord Damion's nature. Not everyone would consider the postilion's feelings. "Thank you, my lord," she said, smiling.

He did not return her smile and said brusquely, "I will arrange matters." He strode away with long strides that carried him swiftly to his driver's side. He gave his orders in a clipped manner that left the man wooden-faced.

Victoria sighed, feeling a lowering of spirits. Lord Damion's instantaneous change toward her once he was aware of her identity confirmed her suspicions that there would be difficulties with Charles's family. Lord Damion was obviously aware of the family's opinion of Charles, and by extension herself.

Victoria shrugged off her oppression with the thought that at least she was sufficiently warned. Matter-of-factly she went to retrieve her portmanteau and knelt on her heels to gather her scattered belongings. A couple of the shifts were streaked with mud. She would ask to have them laundered as soon as she was settled at Belingham Manor.

She pulled tight the leather straps on the portmanteau and rose to her feet with it. The portmanteau was gently taken from her by Lord Damion's driver. "Allow me, m'lady," he said, saluting her by a touch of his hat. "His lordship's compliments and would m'lady do him the honor of joining him in his carriage?" Privately Victoria was not at all certain that she wished to, but she nodded. The driver accompanied her to the chaise.

Lord Damion waited beside the open door. "That will be all, William," he said, and gestured for Victoria to precede him. She gathered her skirts and stepped up into the carriage, seating herself on the opposite side of the chaise to leave room for her companion.

The chaise swayed under Lord Damion's weight as he followed her inside and latched the door behind him. He seated himself and almost immediately the well-sprung chaise rocked forward.

Victoria glanced at her companion. The dusk made it difficult to be certain but she thought she detected a certain grim set to his features.

Lord Damion laid his beaver on the seat between them and stretched out at his ease. "I believe it is time for plain speaking between us," he said shortly. "I wondered about your identity at the inn. The coincidences were too striking. But I dismissed my suspicions as impossible until now. I should tell you that I am intimately acquainted with the Marches and their affairs. Your presence here will certainly be unwelcome, madame."

Victoria was taken aback for only a moment by his breach of conduct. "Lord Damion, I accepted a place in your carriage. That does not give you leave to pry into what does not concern you," she said firmly.

Lord Damion ignored her snub. He shot her a measuring glance. "I confess that I am astounded. Charles March seems to have had more sense than he was credited with. I have no idea of your antecedents, nor do I care, but you at least bear all the appearance of being a lady. That in itself will prove a surprise to the family."

Victoria discovered that her fingers were clenched tight in the folds of her pelisse. She wondered how she had ever thought Lord Damion likable. "If you truly stand on intimate acquaintance with the Marches, then you must be aware that the family cast Charles off years ago. As a consequence, their speculations are of complete indifference to me!" she said coldly.

His lordship gave a crack of cynical laughter. "Yet you are here. In the end it comes down to the same, my lady. I have known females of your stripe before. You have but come for your pound of flesh."

Victoria controlled her anger with difficulty. It was not her intention to quarrel with every ill-bred person who crossed her path. "You will have the goodness to set me down, sir. I would far rather ride one of my jobbers than to remain here with insult."

"No, madame, I will not," said Lord Damion. "We will arrive at the Crossing together. That is my destination also, you see. If I mistake not, the scene will be one which I shall not want to forgo. Believe me when I say that you will find cold welcome this night, Lady Victoria."

"You mistake my destination, Lord Damion. I am expected at Belingham Manor," Victoria said crushingly. "I have no wish to expose myself to March hospitality if your lack of breeding is any example of what I may expect." Her words were punctuated by a deafening crack of thunder.

Three

Rain drummed like pebbles on the chaise roof. Lord Damion raised his voice above the sudden onslaught and Victoria was infuriated to hear a tremor of laughter in his tone. "Your choices seem somewhat limited, Lady Victoria. The road will be a quagmire by the time we reach the Crossing and I fear that to attempt Belingham Manor tonight would be the height of folly. But I leave the decision to you, madame."

Victoria looked out the window and she could not deny the truth of what he said. A sheet of rain slapped the pane and lightning crackled blue-white in the sky, dazzling her. Her journey had been bedeviled by the weather from the outset. Now because of it she would be forced to endure the unexpectedly obnoxious Lord Damion St. Claire and the March clan.

Victoria lifted her chin. She was a soldier's daughter, born and bred. She refused to quake at the first sign of hostility. It was only what she had anticipated, after all. But the Marches and their circle would not easily forget Lady Victoria March when she returned to Lisbon, she thought. "I am certain that I shall find a stay at the Crossing most instructive, my lord," she said, her voice faintly acid.

"Excellent," said Lord Damion blandly.

Victoria turned her attention once more to the rain, disdaining any further communication with him. Lord Damion was apparently of like mind, for he did not attempt to address her.

They had been sitting in silence for several minutes when the chaise's movement slowed. Lord Damion remarked, "I believe we have nearly arrived." Victoria shot an alert look at the dark figure sprawled in the far corner, then leaned closer to the window. But she could make nothing out through the rivulets of rain.

A few moments later the chaise came to a stop. Lord Damion roused himself and put on his beaver. "I will see that we are expected," he said, and twisted the latch on the door. Rain swirled in briefly, then he was gone. Victoria waited, listening to the furious rain.

A minute later, the door beside her was wrenched open. Victoria stifled a scream. Strong fingers caught her by the arm. "Fainthearted, ma'am?" shouted Lord Damion above the rolling thunder. He stood in the open door, rain coursing down his greatcoat. The beaver was jammed tight over his eyes and a steady stream of water flowed from the curved brim.

Victoria raised her voice. "I count it a misfortune to have met you, Lord Damion!"

"I daresay. However, this is hardly the place to discuss it," said Lord Damion, lifting her bodily from the seat. Victoria gasped in shocked outrage, but he gave her no chance to object.

Lord Damion swung her out of the chaise and set her down hard on her heels. A vicious blast of wind billowed Victoria's skirts and flung her against him. He swore impatiently, the wind snatching away his words. Thinking only of the need to get them both quickly out of the fury of the storm, he picked her up in his arms and started away from the chaise. Blinded by the driving-rain, Victoria pressed her face against his broad shoulder. She felt his arms tighten as he climbed upward. Abruptly the rain ceased beating around them and she heard the slamming of a heavy door. "You may let go my coat," breathed Lord Damion's amused voice in her ear.

Victoria snatched her fingers from his lapel as though burnt. He set her down none too gently and steadied her with an impersonal hand under her elbow. She looked up, wordless with anger. The mockery in his gray eyes suddenly changed to laughter. She realized how ridiculous she must appear. As though I were a drowned tabby cat, she thought furiously, aware that she was flushing. Water dripped down her nose and hastily she brushed it away, looking daggers at Lord Damion.

"My dear Damion!"

Lord Damion stepped quickly past Victoria, a warm look transforming his lean face. Victoria turned to stare at the silver-haired man who took his outstretched hand. The old gentleman was tall and bore himself with an elegant ease that made the cane he leaned on seem merely decorative. The two men gripped hands with an obvious affection for one another.

"How are you, sir?" asked Lord Damion.

"I live," retorted the older man shortly. He stepped back from Lord Damion with a pleased smile on his heavily lined face. "James told me but a moment ago of your arrival." His glance fell on Victoria and his voice perceptively chilled. He had obviously witnessed her rather compromising entrance in the arms of Lord Damion. "You have brought a friend, Damion?"

The old gentleman's frosty eyes raked over Victoria. She put up her chin defiantly and ignored the steady drip from her garments to the marble tiles.

The gentleman's gaze came to rest on her face and she returned his measuring look fearlessly.

"I bring you a new member of our family," said Lord Damion, handing his curly beaver to a footman. "Allow me to present Lady Victoria March, who has just journeyed from Portugal for a visit with us."

The hall was suddenly electric with tension. A faint grin curled Lord Damion's mouth as he directed a mocking glance into Victoria's dark eyes. "Lady Victoria, you have the honor of making the acquaintance of Sir Aubrey St. Claire, uncle both to Charles March and myself."

Silence greeted his introduction. Victoria sought something to say that would break the horrible, lengthening suspense. Sir Aubrey recovered from his stupefaction and without hesitation took Victoria's hand. "My dear, you are most welcome," he said. "I only wish that Lord Robert could have been here to greet you as well. But I must tell you that the earl died in his sleep these two days past."

The news staggered Victoria, for it had been at the invitation of Lord Robert, the Earl of March, that she had come to England. "I am deeply sorry, sir," she said quietly, thinking that Sir Aubrey little knew how dismayed she was. "I understand that it must be a very awkward time for a visitor to arrive, so I shall remove to Belingham Manor at first light."

"Nonsense, my dear. You'll stay a few days at least, and then we shall see how the weather is shaping," said Sir Aubrey. "I would not want a valued new member of our family to be mired on the road."

Victoria saw Lord Damion's brows shoot up and his obvious surprise helped to restore her balance. "Thank you, sir, but really there is no need to put you out. I actually had no intention of intruding upon the family. I am expected at Belingham Manor, you see." Her eyes took on a dangerous sparkle. "Lord Damion—"

Sir Aubrey interrupted firmly. "Damion persuaded you to come here instead. I would not hear of it

25

otherwise. But we will speak more on the morrow. You must be fatigued from your trip. I shall ask that the housekeeper show you to a room." He turned to a footman and briefly addressed him, then raised a thin brow in inquiry. "May I offer you refreshment, Lady Victoria?"

"Thank you, Sir Aubrey, but no," said Victoria. "I supped earlier at the inn." It was obvious to her that Sir Aubrey did not wish for a scene of any sort before the servants. She felt a small thrill of satisfaction that Lord Damion had been denied his entertainment for tonight.

A plump woman joined them. "Ah, there you are, Mrs. Lummington," said Sir Aubrey. "Pray have the goodness to show Lady Victoria to a room. She is fatigued after her long journey."

The housekeeper curtsied. "This way, my lady."

Victoria dropped a slight curtsy to Sir Aubrey and murmured good night before she turned to follow the housekeeper to the grand sweep of the ornamented staircase. As they ascended the wide carpeted stairs, she head Sir Aubrey's suddenly cold voice. "You will do me the honor of joining me in the study, Damion."

Victoria's face burned. It was obvious to her that the old gentleman had preferred to smooth things over for the benefit of the servants, but his private opinion would no doubt differ from his expressions of welcome. Sir Aubrey was likely questioning Lord Damion even now about the circumstances of their acquaintance, and deprived once of his amusement, Lord Damion would no doubt make certain that his uncle realized the folly of greeting her with such cordiality.

Lord Damion was abominable, thought Victoria. She could bear his contempt for what he assumed to be the object of her visit, but she found it difficult to forgive his deliberate attempt to humiliate her. Sir Aubrey was every inch the austere patrician. Victoria was unpleasantly aware that to him she must have appeared the very essence of an army baggage when Lord Damion had dumped her so unceremoniously in the hall. It was not the impression she had wished to create upon first meeting a member of Charles's family.

"Here we are, my lady," said Mrs. Lummington. "It was Lord Robert's wish that a number of the rooms should always be ready for company. I hope the room is to your liking."

Victoria shook herself free of her reverie to find that they had traversed a long hall. The housekeeper was holding open a stout door. Within, Victoria could see a fire laid in a stone fireplace. Sparing the rest of the bedroom hardly a glance, she crossed to the grate to spread her fingers to the welcome warmth. She had not realized before how chilled she had become.

Behind her, Mrs. Lummington bustled around the four-poster bed. "I shouldn't think you would care for a tub this late, my lady, so I shall just help you out of them wet things and directly into this shift," she said.

Victoria reluctantly turned away from the friendly heat. The canopied bed was turned down to expose inviting linen sheets. A cambric nightshift lay neatly folded across the foot of the bed. The housekeeper was briskly sliding a warming pan under the coverlet.

Mrs. Lummington's offer to help her undress surprised Victoria. "Thank you, Mrs. Lummington. You are very kind, but I can make do."

"Now, that you can't, my lady," said Mrs. Lummington, shooting a comprehensive glance at her tired face. "The old gentleman would fair have me hide if I left you to struggle with those heavy wet skirts, and you worn out. You just undo those lovely pearl buttons while I finish with the warming pan and then I'll have you popped into bed before you know it."

Victoria laughed at the housekeeper's motherly bullying and obediently began unfastening the mother-of-pearl buttons that closed the front of her pelisse.

Mrs. Lummington was as good as her word. Before Victoria realized it she was under the coverlets, warm and snug. The housekeeper closed the door softly behind her, leaving the room silently warmed by the fire's dying red coals. Victoria sighed and turned her face into the feather pillow.

Four

The breakfast room was empty when Victoria entered, but she was not unhappy to find herself alone. She had woken with a sense of well-being she was loath to have spoiled so early in the day by the inevitable tensions her arrival would cause.

The morning's chill penetrated her long-sleeved muslin gown and she drew over her slim shoulders a Kashmir shawl bordered in red and gold. The rich motif contrasted vividly with the subdued mourning color of her gown, but Victoria had unpacked it when her trunks were brought up earlier. The shawl had been an extravagant gift from Charles March and in some fashion it seemed to lend her courage.

Tall narrow windows shed pale sunlight across the mahogany breakfast table laden with covered dishes. Victoria seated herself in a highbacked chair and lifted the silver covers from the dishes. Small clouds of steam rose, enticing her with fragrant aromas. The healthy appetite that she thought she had lost forever during the rough passage across the English Channel was suddenly revived. She reached out for the serving spoon to a dish of bacon and poached eggs.

A browned masculine hand was before her. Victoria looked up to meet Lord Damion's sardonic gaze. "Allow me," he said with just the proper touch of civility. Victoria threw him an unfriendly glance before lowering her lashes. Deftly Lord Damion served her and himself. He seated himself on her left and with a glance at her composed expression asked blandly, "Marmalade, Lady Victoria?"

"Thank you, no," said Victoria coolly.

"Come now, it is really quite excellent." Lord Damion snapped his fingers as though in sudden inspiration. "Or perhaps you would prefer the honey?"

Victoria contemplated him for a long moment. His exaggerated anxiety to please her contrasted sharply with the devilish laughter lurking in his eyes. Wary of him, she summoned up a smile and said demurely, "Your recommendation persuades me in favor of the marmalade, my lord."

Without a word Lord Damion passed the serving bowl to her. He sat back and watched while she spooned marmalade onto her plate. His gaze remained fixed on her as she prepared a biscuit. By the time Victoria had finished eating the biscuit, she was beginning to be made nervous by his undivided attention. She picked up her fork and cast a casual glance toward the breakfast-room door. Surely Sir Aubrey would soon put in an appearance.

Lord Damion laughed softly. "My dear Lady Victoria, you must be content with me. My mother, Lady Hortense, does not rise until noon. And as for Sir Aubrey, he is an unsociable devil in the morning and prefers to take his breakfast in his room."

Victoria gave him the briefest glance before she plied her fork. Mimicking his tone, she said, "My dear Lord Damion, I can well conceive why Sir Aubrey prefers solitude to the company of those possessing strange humors." Immediately she was annoyed with herself for allowing him to provoke her. Her vexation was too apparent, for Lord Damion smiled faintly and turned his attention to his plate.

The ensuing silence was broken by little more than the clatter of cutlery and Lord Damion's request for the salt. Once he stared over at her with a familiar dancing glint in his eyes and Victoria readied herself for a snub, but he made only a banal observation on the weather.

Victoria did not think that her temper could support Lord Damion's sole company for much longer. She knew that he needled her deliberately. If he had been Charles March, she would have ripped up at him long before. But Victoria was well aware that she dealt with a different sort of man in Lord Damion St. Claire. She sensed a steeliness in him that she was wary of and she decided that it would be wise to wait until she knew him better before she challenged him.

Lord Damion made a hearty meal of the biscuits and eggs and finished off with steak and kidneys. But Victoria found her own appetite quite flown and picked at her plate. As soon as civility would allow her, she rose from the table, intending to return to her room until either Lady Hortense or Sir Aubrey sent for her.

She hoped the summons would come from Sir Aubrey. She had been surprised by Lord Damion's mention of his mother and she shuddered to think what Lady Hortense must be like if she at all resembled her obnoxious son. Victoria felt far more capable of dealing with Sir Aubrey, whom she had at least met.

Before she could retreat, her elbow was caught in a strong grip. She looked up in indignation. Lord Damion stood beside her and the hard glint in his gray eyes warned her to silence. A manservant had entered the room and began to clear the table. He was apparently absorbed in his task, but Victoria saw his eyes flicker toward Lord Damion and herself.

"Perhaps you would care for a turn about the gardens, Lady Victoria?" Lord Damion inquired in a civil tone. The grip on her elbow left her in little doubt of what he expected her answer should be

Victoria's temper rose, burning away her caution. Staring up at the arrogant face above her, she thought it was past time that Lord Damion learned in no uncertain terms her opinion of his character and manners. He was obviously correct that private conversation would be difficult in a household where the servants moved so freely. Victoria thought the gardens would suit her purpose admirably. Her eyes were bright as she bestowed a smile on him. "I believe I would enjoy a stroll, my lord!"

Lord Damion bowed and led her through french doors to a flagstone terrace blown with leaves. Releasing her arm, he turned to latch the doors securely behind them and effectively shut off the manservant's curiosity.

Victoria felt the tug of a cool wind and hugged her shawl closer. She stared in dismay at the storm-torn grounds. The sculpted hedges had a curiously flattened look and the trim beds were choked with snapped branches. The graveled walks among the hedges and trees were littered with soggy leaves.

Victoria changed her mind about a walk in the gardens. She turned to tell her companion so, but Lord Damion ignored her movement back toward the french door. He again took her elbow and propelled her down the wide stone steps to the walkway. Victoria had no choice but to accompany him unless she wished to struggle, which she felt would be humiliating.

"The walkways should be free of water further on," said Lord Damion. He looked around. "I imagine the gardeners are indoors drowning their sorrows."

Victoria read the determination in his face and silently allowed herself to be drawn on. Their pace was outwardly companionable but there was no mistaking the compelling force of Lord Damion's fingers on her elbow. Too late Victoria attempted to sidestep a rivulet of mud. She jerked up her muslin skirt and saw with annoyance that the hem was stained. "I assume there is a particularly lovely stretch you wish to show me?" she asked with exaggerated politeness.

Lord Damion glanced down at her, amused by her irony. "Can you doubt it?"

"In a word, yes." said Victoria. She suddenly felt her shoes soaking through. "And it is too wet!"

He burst out laughing. "You should have thought

how thin your shoes were before we left the break-fast room, my girl!"

"You sir, are by far too familiar," said Victoria evenly. "And you have used me abominably."

Lord Damion glanced down at her as he guided her into an arbor trailing forlorn vinery. His fingers loosened and Victoria shook herself free of his heavy hand. He leaned a broad shoulder against the arbor's stone support and looked into her smoldering eyes. "My apologies," he said with an ironic smile. "Indeed, after you had retired yesterday evening I was treated to a fine trimming by my uncle for my sad lack of manners."

Victoria took care not to allow her astonishment to show. "You certainly did me no favors last night, St. Claire," she said, deliberately neglecting his title to emphasize her displeasure. "I dare not imagine what Sir Aubrey thought. You handled me as— "

"As a soldier handles a camp follower." The curl of his lips was unpleasant. "Isn't that how you trapped my cousin Charles? I imagine an earl's son, however penniless he was at the time, seemed a worthy enough investment."

Victoria struck out at him. He caught her wrist in a bone-crushing grip. "An open palm stings, but you would do well to remember that it has never proven effective with the Demon, my girl!" he said harshly.

"Let me go, St. Claire!" She did not deign to struggle against his cruel fingers but stood looking up at him with contemptuous eyes.

Lord Damion coolly studied the angry flush in her cheeks. "Not quite yet," he said, and put his free hand into his coat pocket. He brought out a small trim pistol that Victoria immediately recognized. He observed her gasp with grim satisfaction. "What, pray, had you planned to accomplish with this trifling toy?"

"Do you often search women's bags, St. Claire?" asked Victoria coldly.

"There was little need to search." Lord Damion returned the firearm to his wide pocket. "The driver found it as he was removing your things from his seedy vehicle. He was naturally puzzled and gave it to me when I settled his account."

"You have paid off my chaise?" repeated Victoria in astonishment. Her wide mouth tightened. "You have taken an insufferable liberty, my lord. I shall appreciate it if in future you will tend your own business rather than mine!"

"At the moment you are my business." Lord Damion smiled with open mockery. "Need I tell you how mulish you appear? Your determination is futile, Lady Victoria. This journey shall not profit you in any way, I can promise you."

"I should like my pistol back, Lord Damion," said Victoria, making an effort to speak with civility. "I shall not encroach any longer on the family's hospitality. I shall depart immediately for Belingham Manor."

Lord Damion raised a dubious brow, certain that she was making an idle declaration. He released her bruised wrist and leaned back against the vine-covered stone with his arms crossed, eyeing her in amusement. "My dear girl, you have no choice but to stay. You cannot possibly mean to walk."

"I am certain that Sir Aubrey will be good enough to order out a carriage," said Victoria. Her smile held a little mockery of its own. "You have yourself informed me of your dire reputation. I have but to say that I found the Demon's proximity too upsetting for words."

Lord Damion's jaw tightened. He was no longer amused. "You little witch," he said softly, dangerously.

Victoria did not heed his hawkish expression. "I suppose that is a compliment of sorts, coming as it does from a man who delights only in insult," she said scathingly.

Without warning Lord Damion jerked her to him. A ruthless arm pinned her against him and her chin was caught up in a vise. His breath was warm on her shocked face. "You are so wrong, my girl." The icy glitter in his eyes was frightening. "I delight in much more!"

He lowered his head to take her mouth with brutal lips. Victoria struggled wildly, beating him with her fists. His hard fingers bit deep into her shoulders, arching her backward. His mouth was scalding, merciless. Her senses suddenly reeled. She shuddered, her lips parting under his. Immediately the pressure of his mouth gentled. She felt his arms loosen. His hands shifted to explore, tracing fire.

Sudden fear leaped to life within her. Victoria groped for his pocket and her fingers closed on the pistol. With unexpected strength she twisted free, the cold ivory-handled firearm firmly in her hand. She trained it on the second shining brass button of Lord Damion's coat, her breath coming quickly.

Lord Damion went white under his tan. He stretched out his hand. "Give it to me, please. It is loaded."

Victoria's laugh quivered in her throat. A stirring of wind blew a truant curl over her wary eyes. "Do not tempt me. You are a fortunate man, Lord Damion. If Charles were here, he would not hesitate." She half turned, lowering the pistol.

Lord Damion caught her by the shoulder and spun her around. He wrenched the pistol out of her hand and threw it into a barren flower bed. His fingers bruised her arms and Victoria cried out, less in pain than in anger.

"Oh consummate, Lady Victoria," he said thinly. "I applaud the perfect blend of fear and outrage." His eyes raked over her with contempt. "And I have yet to compliment you on your attire. Charles died two years ago and you are yet in widow's weeds. Very affecting, believe me!"

"You are abominable," breathed Victoria.

"Your opinions are of no interest to me," snapped Lord Damion. "I feel certain you were not unaware that you come at an extremely propitious time. The reading of Lord Robert's will is to take place in a few days. How is it you knew to come? What is it you hope to gain, madame?"

"It is none of my making, Lord Damion," said Victoria with tight anger. "I received an invitation from Lord Robert some months ago. I chose to honor it. Until last night I did not know that he had died."

Lord Damion released her with undisguised contempt. "You disappoint me, Lady Victoria. I expected a more plausible story from a woman of your obvious intelligence."

Victoria swept him an exaggerated curtsy. "Your high opinion of me is overwhelming, my lord. I am persuaded I must join the legions of females gratified by your least attention!" She saw the leap of hot anger in his eyes and realized that she had once more gone too far. Victoria avoided his outstretched hand and fled back to the doubtful sanctuary of the Crossing.

Five

Victoria glanced back once as she flew up the terrace steps. She saw through the hedges Lord Damion's rapidly approaching figure. His dark hawkish face looked forbidding as he slipped her pistol into his pocket. When he glanced up and caught sight of her, his mouth tightened in grim fury.

Victoria did not wait, but nipped neatly through the french doors into the breakfast room. Swiftly she went around the long table and into the hall. Another tête-à-tête with Lord Damion was not to her liking, not while the pulse jumped in her throat and her limbs shook like so many leaves. It was beyond her comprehension why he should have affected her so.

Without taking notice of the footmen's curious glances, Victoria picked up her skirt and started up the stairs. She intended to take refuge in her room and so avoid Lord Damion's unwelcome attentions until she was summoned to an audience by Sir Aubrey. If she had a few minutes alone, she could regain her composure.

"There you are, my dear." Victoria whirled on the stair with a gasp. Sir Aubrey paused, taking in at a glance Victoria's heightened color and her muddied hem. His world-weary eyes lighted in knowing amusement. "Forgive me. I did not mean to startle you, Lady Victoria."

"It is of no consequence, sir," said Victoria. Her fingers trembled slightly as she drew up her shawl. She wondered how she could gracefully escape before Lord Damion appeared. She placed no confidence in him not to rejoin battle before the household and the thought of such a scene was distasteful to her.

"I see that you have dared the gardens this morning," said Sir Aubrey with a nod at her stained skirt. "Naturally you are chilled. Come, Lady Victoria. There is a fire in the sitting room and I have much to discuss with you."

At Victoria's expression, Sir Aubrey chuckled. He said dryly, "It is either I or Damion. Quite frankly, you would do better with me. My nephew is a devil when he is crossed."

Victoria was fully aware of the truth of Sir Aubrey's observation. She guessed that Lord Damion must have reached the stone terrace. She could not now escape to her room before he caught up with her. Deciding quickly, Victoria joined the old gentleman at the bottom of the stairs. "You persuade me, Sir Aubrey."

"Indeed, I hope to do so," he murmured as he ushered Victoria into the sitting room. He closed the oak door softly behind them and motioned her to a striped silk wingchair before the hearth. "I prefer that Damion not join us just yet. He will naturally assume that you fled in terror to your room and it will be a short time before he discovers otherwise."

Stung, Victoria said quickly, "I assure you that I do

not fear Lord Damion." The memory of his burning kiss rose unbidden and she resolutely thrust it away.

Sir Aubrey took the wingchair opposite her. His cool eyes were penetrating. "Curious how one can be mistaken. I was certain that Damion and his love-making brought a catch to your lovely throat that frightened you very much."

A tide of hot color swept Victoria's face. Monstrous that Lord Damion had taken liberties with her at all, but for Charles's uncle to guess it was to complete her humiliation. She said in a mortified voice, "I cannot pretend to misunderstand you, Sir Aubrey. I can only assure you that I did not seek, nor did I wish for, Lord Damion's attentions!"

The old gentleman chuckled gently. "How wise of you not to deny the obvious, my dear. In truth, I am well acquainted with Damion's character. I did not think that you had ventured into the gardens this morning without compelling reason."

"In my few dealings with him, Lord Damion has rarely given me much freedom of choice," said Victoria shortly.

Sir Aubrey regarded her with curiosity. "Do you dislike him so much, then?"

Victoria's breast rose in indignation. She said hastily, "He is insufferable!"

"How thoroughly refreshing. I assure you that is not usually the case," said Sir Aubrey dryly.

"So I am given to understand. Lord Damion took pains to inform me of his fatal reputation upon our first meeting," said Victoria disdainfully.

"Did he," murmured Sir Aubrey, an appreciative gleam lighting his eyes. "It is true that he is called the Demon, and for just cause. However, you must understand that he has grown into his cynicism quite naturally. The foolish creatures will throw themselves at him."

Victoria's brown eyes flashed molten gold sparks. "But I have not, so I fail to see why I am subjected to such familiarities. In all frankness, Sir Aubrey, I find Lord Damion's behavior unpardonable."

"I quite agree with you, my dear. Indeed, I am unable to account for Damion's unusual conduct. He does not make a habit of abducting females or pressing his suit where it is not wanted. You can only have set up his back in some fashion, for I assure you Damion can be a perfect gentleman when he so chooses." Sir Aubrey eyed Victoria speculatively. "However, I did not ask for this interview to discuss Damion's character, or lack of it. I assume that Charles did not inform you that he wrote to Lord Robert's solicitor?"

Victoria stared at him, taken aback. Sir Aubrey smiled thinly. "I see that he did not. There were apparently very few letters, but the solicitor was able to tell Lord Robert of Charles's marriage. Naturally the earl requested to see the letters. He remained interested in Charles's life though he never himself approached his son. Lord Robert confided much in me in those days. He informed me that he had changed his will and had added a codicil that pertained to you. Do you believe in fate, my dear?"

"I believe more in relying upon God and one's own abilities," said Victoria, still disconcerted. Charles had never mentioned such lengthy correspondence. Victoria now wondered if Charles had not had a premonition of his own death and attempted a reconciliation with his father. Whatever else Charles had meant to do, he had kindled Lord Robert's interest in his marriage, thought Victoria.

Sir Aubrey nodded in satisfaction. "You are very much as Charles described—practical, spirited, and well bred. I believe you will suit Damion admirably."

Victoria started. She looked at Sir Aubrey's calm expression and hoped that she had misunderstood him. "Surely I have mistaken your meaning, sir."

Sir Aubrey raised his thin brows. "I did not take you to be dense, my dear. Pray allow me to clarify myself. I am proposing that you wed my rakehell nephew, Lord Damion St. Claire."

Victoria let out her breath slowly. "You jest, Sir Aubrey."

"I assure you that I am quite sober, Lady Victoria," said Sir Aubrey. "Lord Robert privately discussed this possibility with me after Charles's death and again on his deathbed. The codicil I spoke of will provide a substantial allowance entailed solely to you and your children if you become the next Countess of March. You see, he wanted both to provide for you and, if possible, to bring Charles back to the family through you."

"I understand, I think. But it is truly too absurd a notion to contemplate." Victoria respected Sir Aubrey for attempting to discharge a dying man's wishes, but she was not prepared to sacrifice her own independence.

"But why should it be absurd?" Sir Aubrey leaned toward her, his expression earnest. "You have the fire that Damion likes, my dear. No simpering miss will do for him. He needs to be challenged. And St. Claire is a very wealthy young man in his own right, besides being Lord Robert's heir. What could be more advantageous than a match between you?"

Victoria stared at him incredulous. It was almost comical that Lord Damion's uncle should approach her for such a reason. "Lord Damion strikes me as quite capable of choosing his own bride. And since it is obvious that he has taken the greatest dislike to me, I doubt that I would be his most likely choice."

Sir Aubrey impatiently waved aside her observation. "Nonsense! Still your doubts on that head. Damion has come to realize the importance of setting up a nursery since he will now be the head of the family. And he will be guided by me in making the most suitable match."

Remembering the implacable expression in Lord Damion's eyes, Victoria could not imagine anything less likely. She suddenly pitied Sir Aubrey. Lord Damion's rakehell life must greatly trouble the older man if it compelled him to search for a bride for his nephew. Sir Aubrey's efforts were doomed in her case. Even if she were to consider such an outrageous proposal, Lord Damion's reputation alone would give her pause. One certainly could not expect him to be a compatible or faithful mate. Moreover, she had herself found him to be arrogant, ruthless, and overbearing. Victoria said gently, "Sir Aubrey, what you propose is impossible. Lord Damion and I would never suit. I am sorry."

"I do not propose a love match, but a marriage of convenience!" said Sir Aubrey, mistaking the cause of her lack of enthusiasm. "Pray allow me to speak frankly, Lady Victoria. Such a marriage will make you secure for your lifetime, with position and every imaginable comfort. Every door in society will be open to you and that, my lady, counts for much in this world. As for Damion, the acquisition of a wife will lend him respectability. He will more than likely continue to keep his mistresses, but that need not concern you once you have produced an heir. Damion would not have any objection to your own affairs, of course, as long as you exercised discretion."

Victoria made a strangled sound and threw up her hand for him to stop. Sir Aubrey snorted. "After tagging after an army I did not expect you to be missish, girl!"

Laughter threatened to overcome her and Victoria was forced to exert all her will to remain sober. She found difficulty in speaking, but managed to say, "Forgive me, sir. But I could not countenance, even for a moment—"

"Damion is naturally aware that a marriage of convenience is hardly the stuff of romantic fancy for a young woman. But you are particularly well suited for such an arrangement, my dear. A widow has few illusions about conjugal bliss. And Damion would feel deeply in debt to whomever he married for agreeing to amiable cohabitation. I hardly feel it necessary to point out that can only be an advantage to his lady."

Victoria's amusement was swiftly dissipating. "Sir Aubrey—"

He overbore her attempt to interrupt him. "Lady Victoria, his lordship was my dear friend as well as my brother-in-law. I respect the hope behind his expressed wishes, which was the desire to keep the March family line linked with the earldom in some fashion. Having met you, Lady Victoria, I am persuaded that were you to fill the role of Damion's wife, you would be a credit both to him and to the March family."

Victoria shook her head. "Sir Aubrey, I am sorry to disappoint you. I am flattered by your favorable impression of me, but truly—"

Sir Aubrey laughed. "My dear, I am a cynic regarding women and their natures. You appear to be a cut above some and that was the deciding point in your favor." He allowed his voice to reflect impatience. "I am an old man with little time left to me, Lady Victoria. Pray leave off the ladylike demurrals and give me a straight answer."

"Indeed, I am trying to," said Victoria.

"My dear, you must see that time is of the essence. You are here and the opportunity to snare Damion before he returns to London, where there will be countless others to vie for his favor, is not to brushed lightly aside. In short, you would be a great fool not to take advantage of it."

Victoria saw that it was impossible to gracefully decline Sir Aubrey's audacious proposal. He was determined that she would consent. "Then I am a fool, Sir Aubrey," said Victoria bluntly. "I am sorry to wound you, sir, but there is no point in pursuing this absurd conversation further. I have no intention of being a party to this scheme. I do not anticipate remarriage at all, and especially not to Lord Damion St. Claire."

Sir Aubrey shrugged. He said cynically, "I have found nearly all women alike in the end. You married once for position and you will again. It might as well be Damion."

Victoria went white. She had to fight back the sharp retort that rose to her lips. Sir Aubrey was accusing her of being an opportunist of the worst kind. She could scarcely believe that he had indeed been told the details of any correspondence from her husband. Charles could not have hidden the happiness they had found in their short marriage. Surely Lord Robert would have commented on that to his confidant.

Victoria wondered if Lord Damion was a party to his uncle's strange scheme. She knew him to be head-strong and arrogant but he had not yet impressed her as dishonest. Surely he did not countenance Sir Aubrey's scheme. "Is Lord Damion aware of your fantastic proposal to me?"

Sir Aubrey's heavy lids hooded the expression in his eyes. "My dear Lady Victoria, does it matter?" He seemed impatient at her naiveté.

"I suppose that it doesn't," said Victoria. Suddenly she felt oddly disappointed and looked at Sir Aubrey with dislike. "I will be obliged to you to immediately call out a carriage. I will be setting out for Belingham Manor within the hour."

"Ah, that spirited temper which Charles wrote of so expressively at last comes to the fore. Lord Robert was particularly struck by those passages, you know." Sir Aubrey was gently mocking. "Believe me, my dear, I admire your control. You make it quite plain that at this moment you wish me to the devil and my demon of a nephew along with me."

"I have no intention of bandying words with you, Sir Aubrey," said Victoria firmly. "At this point I wish only for a carriage."

He smoothed his coat sleeve meticulously. "I fear that you must bear with us for a while yet. This morning at first light I sent to Belingham Manor to inquire whether Lady Belingham and her daughter have returned from Bath. Regrettably they have not."

Victoria gazed at him with some suspicion. "Surely there is some mistake. I am expected."

"I am sorry, my lady. I believe it was an unexpected trip made to whisk that wild child out of the clutches of an ineligible suitor," said Sir Aubrey. At her expression of dismay, a faint complacement smile curled his thin mouth. "You are naturally quite welcome to extend your stay here as long as you wish."

Sir Aubrey's explanation closely echoed Sir Harry Belingham's own comments about his younger sister's willful nature. Reluctantly Victoria relinquished the notion that Sir Aubrey was attempting to fob her off.

Yet to continue under the same roof with Sir Aubrey and Lord Damion after having been made aware of their monstrously insulting plans for her was repugnant. She heartily wished that she could sweep from the room and with towering hauteur order a carriage from the nearest village. But she knew her immediate finances would not allow her that luxury. Briefly Victoria contemplated an immediate withdrawal to a certain Anglican bishop's home, where she had left her daughter Jessica, but as swiftly discarded it. She had not yet accomplished her purpose for coming to England and that goal now appeared dependent on Lord Robert's will, which meant that she needed to remain in the neighborhood until the reading. She hated the thought of being away from Jessica for longer than she had planned, but it was better than subjecting her daughter to the rude treatment she was encountering. In the meantime she would notify her banker of her whereabouts so that she would not again be caught in the same trap.

When she again met Sir Aubrey's gaze, Victoria's eyes smoldered dangerously. "It is with the greatest reluctance that I am forced to accept your continued hospitality, Sir Aubrey. Pray do not think that this means I acquiesce in your abominable scheme or that I shall meekly accept further insult!"

Sir Aubrey appeared affronted. "My dear Lady Victoria—"

The oak door was suddenly thrust open. Lord Damion's eyes flicked over Victoria before he addressed Sir Aubrey. "I must beg the honor of Lady Victoria's private company, sir. We left our conversation this morning unfinished."

Sir Aubrey deliberately ignored his hard tone. "My

dear Damion, pray do join us. My delightful new niece and I have been discussing the future."

Victoria stiffened in her chair. Lord Damion closed the door with a snap and his eyes remained fixed on Victoria's still face as he approached. His walk reminded her forcibly of a large cat, at once lithe and dangerous. A shiver raced down her spine. She had already had a taste of his unpredictability.

"Indeed? Pray enlighten me, Uncle." Lord Damion's voice was silken. Gently he swung a beribboned fob from between his long browned fingers.

"Ah, you must wait for the will to be read to satisfy your curiosity, Damion. I am positive that we shall all find it of paramount interest," said Sir Aubrey. His smile was malicious as his eyes flickered toward Victoria. "I cannot convey how delighted I am that you accepted Lord Robert's invitation, Lady Victoria. Since he told me of it I have been truly agog to get your measure."

With a muffled exclamation Victoria jumped to her feet and stood at the grate with her back to the two men. She clasped her hands together tightly, inwardly raging. She could see now that Lord Robert had an ulterior motive for asking her to the Crossing and it galled her that she had been so manipulated.

Lord Damion let drop the eyeglass that was suspended by a black riband at his waist and regarded Victoria with a frown. So she had told him the truth about receiving an invitation from Lord Robert. He suddenly felt very foolish. He had always prided himself on being an accurate judge of character, but he had been entirely in the wrong about Lady Victoria. And as a consequence he had treated her with abominable disrespect.

Sir Aubrey observed them with satisfaction. He rose from the chair with the help of his cane. "You may now resume your discourse, Damion."

Six

Lord Damion bowed slightly to his uncle as the older man left the room. He closed the door and with his hand still on the knob looked meditatively across at Victoria, who had turned to face him. Remembering vividly the emotions he had evoked in her and what she had but moments before learned of his character, Victoria met his eyes with proud defiance. "I assume that you have come to belabor me further. Or shall you put a period to my unwelcome existence with my own pistol?"

Lord Damion's keen eyes narrowed. "I wish to do neither," he said, crossing the room to stand next to her. He laid a long arm along the top of the mantel. Acutely aware of his eyes on her, Victoria averted her own. Lord Damion said quietly, "My uncle made mention of Lord Robert's will. Though his lordship did not take me wholly into his confidence, I may guess at Sir Aubrey's revelations. He was privy to a great deal and has no doubt apprised you of the way things stand."

Victoria gave an angry laugh. "Oh yes, he certainly did that!"

"I know that it must have come as an unpleasant surprise to you. Believe me, I would never have countenanced Sir Aubrey's confidences if I had guessed what he meant to do," said Lord Damion quietly. He abhorred the harshness his uncle had obviously seen fit to employ with Lady Victoria, especially since she was proven a legitimate guest of the family. "I hope you will disregard his abominable lack of tact."

Victoria looked up at him in astonishment. His tone was not friendly but it was sincere. He even appeared discomfited by his uncle's absurd suggestion. Victoria felt a rush of happy relief that he had not after all been party to Sir Aubrey's proposition. He was not the cold opportunist Sir Aubrey had led her to believe him. She smiled tentatively at him. "Thank you for your understanding, my lord. I promise you that it is already forgotten."

Lord Damion felt a resurgence of his initial liking for her. He had been struck then by her well-bred air and he had to admire her present fortitude in the face of her disappointment. Sir Aubrey had undoubtedly been ruthless in squelching any hopes she may have had about Lord Robert's will. "I regret the discomfiture you have been subjected to, not the least of which has been at my hands," he said with civility. "I should not have doubted your word that you had received an invitation to visit the Crossing. Pray accept my sincere apologies. I shall in future remember to treat you with the respect due to a lady."

Victoria was unexpectedly affected by this fresh illustration of his kindness and felt a sudden prick of tears. Blinking unsuccessfully, she said, "So foolish. I fear this morning has proven singularly unsettling."

"I quite understand, ma'am." Lord Damion offered his handkerchief to her and Victoria dabbed at her eyes with the fine lawn. "You will naturally wish to join your friends at Belingham Manor with all speed. Have you spoken to my uncle of your departure?"

"Yes, but Sir Aubrey learned only this morning that Lady Belingham and her daughter are not at home. They have made an unexpected trip to Bath and it is apparently not known when they will return," said Victoria. "Sir Aubrey has offered to put me up until their return. I hope that you have no objections?"

"My objections no longer exist. I hope our understanding is such that we may forget the past, if you agree," said Lord Damion. He held out the pistol to her.

"Of course." Victoria, accepted the small firearm and put it in her pocket. She smiled again, unaware of the unusual effect her fine brown eyes were having on him. Glancing down at her stained hem, she said, "If you will excuse me, I'll repair to my room and make myself presentable once more."

"I will ask that a maid be sent to you immediately." Lord Damion walked with her to the door and opened it for her.

Pausing only to send a footman with a message to the housekeeper, Lord Damion accompanied Victoria across the hall to the foot of the stairs. As she ascended the first step, he detained her with a light touch on her elbow. "I have an engagement this morning with the steward, but perhaps later you will allow me the pleasure of acting the proper host and show you the gallery, where hang several portraits of Charles's ancestors, illustrious and otherwise, as well as some of my own."

Standing as she was on the first stair, Victoria found that she was almost at a level with him. She caught her breath at the familiar glint in his eyes. Surely Charles had looked at her just so. Without being conscious of it, Victoria drew away from him. "Thank—thank you, my lord. I should enjoy it above all things," she stammered, and went quickly up the stairs.

Surprised by her emotion, Lord Damion looked after her with a faint frown. Dismissing it with a shrug, he turned away and walked to the study where the steward would already be waiting for him.

Victoria reached her room and closed the door behind her. She leaned against it, hands pressed to her warm cheeks. The look in Lord Damion's eyes, his nearness, had brought a breathless excitement to her that she had not felt in a long time. Vividly she felt again his hard arms and demanding lips.

Victoria shook herself, dispelling the memory with a shiver, and moved away from the door. She put the pistol away in its case. The look in Lord Damion's eyes reminded her of Charles and only that. She had been too long alone. That was why her breath would catch when she was around Lord Damion. It had little to do with his lovemaking this morning. He simply reminded her too sharply of Charles. With unwarranted irritation Victoria began to undo the buttons on her gown.

A discreet knock came at the door and a maid entered on Victoria's hail. She bobbed a respectful curtsy. "I am called Mary, an' it please m'lady. Mrs. Lummington has sent me to wait on your ladyship until your own ladies' maid should be arranged for." She came forward to nimbly finish unbuttoning the back of Victoria's gown.

"I know that you will do very well for my needs, Mary," said Victoria, omitting that she would not be residing at the Crossing long enough to warrant a dresser. It would be only a few days until the will was read. Then she and her daughter would be together again. And if Lord Robert had written the truth in his letter, little Jessica would be established without question as a March and with every right to her English heritage. But Victoria vowed to herself that if there appeared to be the slightest chance that Jessica would be slighted, she would never tell Charles's relations of her existence.

"Why, thank you for saying so, m'lady," said the maid, gratified. She helped Victoria out of the gown and clucked her tongue over the soiled hem. "Proper filthy, it is. Begging your pardon, m'lady, I'm sure."

Standing in only her thin shift and stockings, Victoria poured water from a pitcher into a hand basin so she could splash her arms and face. "I fear I must agree, Mary. And you will find almost everything in the small portmanteau in the same state. I did not even bother to unpack it. My carriage broke down late yesterday evening and the portmanteau flew into the road, tumbling everything in top the mud," she said as she dried her hands with a soft towel.

The maid pursed her mouth. "Proper shocking, I

say. To think of your intimates scattered over the countryside. I will have every last stitch of it laundered, m'lady!"

Victoria laughed in genuine amusement. "Oh, there was no lasting harm done. However, if Lord Damion had not arrived in good time before the downpour, it might have proven far worse. I would now be nursing a putrid throat, I am sure."

"Aye, for all he's so cold, m'lord Damion is a proper Christian gentleman," said the maid. She was lifting the lid on Victoria's larger trunk and so did not see her new mistress's look of astonishment. "When the old lord, m'lord March that would be, suffered with his attack, he couldn't properly move nor talk anymore, leastways so a body could understand him. Oh, didn't he get fierce when he couldn't make hisself understood the first time! That was when m'lord Damion began to come for days at a time to help his lordship run this great house. It were his heart, the doctor said, and nothing to be done for it." The maid drew out a dove-gray gown and shook out the creases. "Here we are, m'lady, this one will do the trick. The others need a bit of pressing."

She threw the gown over Victoria's head and smoothed it into place. Victoria began to button the narrow cuffs while the maid did up the back. "How long ago was this?" she asked, curious. Charles had spoken so rarely of the family he had left behind and then had dwelt only on his father's strict notions of family honor. Victoria had never quite understood why Lord Robert should have cast off his only son and heir for joining the army. But then she had come of yeoman stock and her father, having taken up a military career when young, had chosen to settle in Portugal rather than return to the isle of his birth. His had been a restless mind, open to change, and Victoria had inherited much of his resilience.

"Before ever I came to the Crossing, m'lady. Mrs. Lummington, she could say for certain, but I heard tell it was right after Master Charles ran off to join the army," said Mary cheerfully. "It tore the old lord up something fierce, but it were the news that Master Charles was dead that brought on his worse attack. He fell over cold as stone and didn't wake for ever so long."

Victoria stared at her pale reflection in a tall mirror. Oh Charles! she thought unhappily.

"That were a bad day, no one knowing where to turn until m'lord Damion was sent for," said Mary. Frowning, she twitched at a stubborn crease in Victoria's skirt. "It needs a bit of pressing, too, after being folded so long, m'lady."

"It shall have to do for now," said Victoria, picking up a hairbrush and giving her curls swift attention. "But I hope that you may have my other gowns and shifts done soon or I shall truly be sunk in disgrace."

"Do not be worrying your head over that, m'lady. They'll be clean and pressed before ever the others arrive," said the maid reassuringly. She handed the cashmere shawl to Victoria. "My, isn't it a lovely thing!"

Victoria draped the shawl around her shoulders so that it lay in graceful folds. "Before the others arrive? Who might that be?"

The maid looked at her in surprise. "Why, Master Evelyn and his lady and the lawyer, to be sure. Oh, I am forgetting that you have just come." She glanced around as if afraid of being overhead and lowered her voice to a conspiratorial whisper. "The talk is that his lordship did favor m'lord Damion over Master Evelyn something awful. Well, and why shouldn't he when m'lord Damion is the elder? At all events, everything will surely go to m'lord Damion and won't Master Evelyn be in a proper taking! He is filled with vile envy for his cousin m'lord Damion. It's said we'll see violence before all is done."

Victoria now regretted encouraging the maid's gossip. "Nonsense! I am certain the speculation is greatly exaggerated. Master Evelyn must surely hold his cousin in proper esteem."

"Yes, m'lady," said Mary dubiously. "Will there be aught else, m'lady?"

"Thank you, no. That will be all, Mary," said Victoria. The maid curtsied and turned her attention to Victoria's trunks.

Victoria gave a last glance in the mirror and swept out of the room. On her way to the stairs she wondered how much reliance could be placed in the servants' gossip. Surely it was not such a desperate case with Evelyn St. Claire as the maid had made out. Yet after her experiences with Lord Damion and Sir Aubrey it would not surprise her in the least to discover that another of Charles's relations possessed a devilish temper. Victoria was fast coming to the conclusion that it was a family trait. At times Charles himself had been wildly unpredictable. Even Harry Belingham, who had been his friend from boyhood, had more than once commented on what he called Charles's freakish starts.

At the thought of Sir Harry Belingham, Victoria remembered that he did not know of her awkward situation. She had promised to write him and now she could tell him of his parent's unexpected absence and her own plight. And while she was at it, she would write her banker and her daughter Jessica as well. When Victoria reached the bottom of the stairs she inquired of a footman the location of the library.

Under his directions, Victoria soon found the room she sought. The shelves stretched upward to a high plastered ceiling. Tall velvet-draped windows that Victoria guessed must look onto the garden ran across one wall and a stone fireplace stood at the far end of the narrow room. A snapping yellow fire was laid in the grate and before the welcome warmth were set two highbacked reading chairs. To one side beneath one of the windows was a cherrywood desk and chair.

Victoria went to the desk and discovered all the necessary supplies she needed to write her letters. She seated herself in the cushioned chair and pulled a sheet of paper across the desk to her. Dipping a pen in the inkwell, she began her missive to Sir Harry Belingham.

She briefly explained her situation to Sir Harry, but was careful to keep her tone cheerful. She hesitated over what she should say about Lord Damion and finally decided that it would be best to leave well enough alone. She concluded the letter and lightly sanded it before sealing it in an envelope with wax. She then penned a short note to her banker requesting that funds be forwarded to her at the Crossing and wrote letters to a couple of Portuguese friends. Her last letter was addressed to a Miss Rebecca Webster, who had been her companion on the passage from Portugal and who was now watching over Jessica while residing with her brother, Bishop Horace Webster, only fifty miles away.

Victoria was sealing this last missive when she heard a distant bell. "It cannot be time for luncheon already!" she exclaimed aloud. Surprised, she looked up at the mantel clock and saw that it was indeed one o'clock.

Seven

Victoria rose from the desk and left the library with her letters, intending to ask a footman to post them for her. She met Lord Damion in the hall, and while exchanging civil greetings, he offered to frank her letters for her. "And I shall make certain that in future there is always a sum in the desk for your use," he said.

"Thank you, my lord," said Victoria as she handed the envelopes to him. "I was surprised to find it so late. The morning quite slipped away while I did my correspondence."

"I, too, have spent a pleasant morning," said Lord Damion. He put the letters into his coat pocket and then offered his arm to her. "May I escort you in to luncheon, Lady Victoria?"

Victoria accepted his arm and accompanied him into the dining room. Sir Aubrey was standing beside the table. He wore an impatient expression that did not ease when he saw them. "You have certainly taken your time about it."

An older woman who was already seated remonstrated with him softly. "Mind your manners, Aubrey."

Lord Damion held a chair for Victoria and over her head greeted the woman. "Good afternoon, Mama." He went around the table to bestow a light kiss on her plump cheek. She smiled up at him as he took a chair beside her.

Victoria glanced across at Lady Hortense curiously, recollecting suddenly that Charles had spoken once of his aunt, and with affection. Though gray liberally streaked her soft brown hair, Lady Hortense appeared younger than her years. Victoria decided that her cheerful expression was the reason. She hoped that Lady Hortense was as kind as she appeared. It would be refreshing to meet someone with normal kindness after her experiences with the male members of the family.

"Lady Hortense, allow me to present Lady Victoria," said Sir Aubrey shortly, taking his seat. He grimaced as he shifted his weight. "Damned gout."

Victoria nodded respectfully to Lady Hortense and wished both her and Sir Aubrey a good day. Sir Aubrey stared at her with wintery eyes. "Have the decency to refrain from good cheer in my presence, madame."

"You can be such a bear at times, Aubrey. Pay him no heed, Lady Victoria. He soon quietens if he is not the center of attention," said Lady Hortense. She feigned not to see Sir Aubrey's baleful glare. "We are all family, so I shall not stand on ceremony. I am delighted that you are visiting us. Dear Charles was a great favorite of mine and I hope to find a friend in his lovely wife."

Victoria was charmed by her easy friendliness. "Thank you, ma'am. I truly appreciate your welcome, especially when it is such an awkward time."

Lady Hortense's expression saddened and she sighed. "It is difficult on us all, of course, but we shall weather it."

"How are you holding up, dear ma'am?" asked Lord Damion gently, his eyes on his mother's face.

She summoned up a smile for him. "I'm doing very well, Damion. I'm told that your uncle did not suffer and for that I'm grateful. Sir Aubrey saw to all of the necessary arrangements and the chapel service was beautiful. Reverend Pherson is such a dear, sensitive man," she said. "I'm now free to remember Robert in better days and to become acquainted with Lady Victoria while she is with us. Do you make a long stay, my dear?"

"I had not planned to, ma'am. I am expected later at Belingham Manor," said Victoria.

"It could be in Lady Victoria's interests to be here for the reading, of course," said Sir Aubrey, shooting a meaningful glance at Victoria as he spooned his soup. She knew that he referred to their earlier conversation. The man had no shame, she decided furiously, and wondered that he dared to bring up the topic before his nephew and Lady Hortense.

Lady Hortense frowned at her brother-in-law. "Really, Aubrey, you can be so indelicate on occasion." Sir Aubrey gave a bark of laughter.

"However badly my uncle puts himself, I believe that we can assure my new cousin of some sort of future provision," said Lord Damion quietly, his eyes resting on Victoria's face. He had seen her flush and, in an effort to spare her, changed the subject. "Has there been any word of Evelyn and Doro?"

Sir Aubrey's expression soured. "Oh aye. I heard yesterday. He and that puling girl-child will be here for the reading. Doubtless Evelyn cherishes hopes of Lord Robert's affections."

"That is unworthy of you, Aubrey, and I believe you know it," said Lady Hortense quietly.

Sir Aubrey did not deign to reply. He testily addressed the footman, instructing him to leave off serving the rest of the meal and not to disturb them again until called for.

Lord Damion looked across at Victoria, a glint of humor in his eyes. "Pray tell us about Portugal, Lady Victoria. My mother is positively eaten with curiosity but too well bred to show it."

"Damion, you rogue!" Lady Hortense laughed. "But it is true. He knows me so well. But truly, you and Charles must have led a most extraordinary life. I cannot imagine ever sleeping soundly with those marauding French over the next hill."

Victoria laughed, shaking her head. "It was not so bad as that. The French have never come into Lisbon. When the army marches out each spring, those of us who are left behind are anxious, of course, but the best antidote we have found is to keep ourselves employed."

"It does help when one can remain busy," agreed Lady Hortense sympathetically. "Did you go about society much, then?"

"Oh yes, but the entertainment is sadly deflated after the military leave. The officers are a merry lot. It is rather dull without them," said Victoria. "But the Portuguese enjoy life and we soon have picnics and assemblies to attend, besides riding and the coursing of rabbits. I myself am always in the saddle."

"My dear! Isn't that rather dangerous with the war? I have heard such tales about the French soldiers," Lady Hortense said, faintly horrified.

Sir Aubrey snorted. "Nonsense, Hortense. She is more at risk should her mount step in a damned rabbit hole and she is thrown than she is of running into a French patrol that near to Lisbon."

"I gather that you have an interest in horses, Lady Victoria," said Lord Damion. He wondered why she should look so startled by his comment. "Have you heard in Lisbon if the army's mounts are at last adapting to the country? I understood that there was some hope that a change in feed was the answer."

Victoria shook her head. "The stock brought from England still sicken and die in the Portuguese climate, my lord. Indeed, I was informed that the cavalry is yet in dire need of extra mounts. But for most of the army's purposes the native Portuguese stock will be found to be more than adequate."

"You are obviously knowledgeable, Lady Victoria," said Lord Damion, somewhat surprised by the note of authority in her voice.

Victoria hesitated a second. "My father, in addition to serving in the army, bred horses outside of Lisbon. Some of my earliest memories are of the foaling season."

"This morning the steward mentioned to me that the stable master is concerned about a brood mare that is foaling out of season. Perhaps you would care to accompany me later when I go to inspect her?" asked Lord Damion.

"I should like it very much, my lord," said Victoria, and went on to ask for particulars of the mare's condition. Lord Damion repeated what he had gleaned from the steward.

Sitting back in his chair and observing them, Sir Aubrey smiled faintly. He was pleased with the girl. She was going to work just right for Lord Damion. Sir Aubrey was content to let things ride. He turned to his sister-in-law. "Well, Hortense, how is the altar cloth coming?"

Lady Hortense, who had been listening benignly to her son and Lady Victoria, looked at him in surprise. He did not usually express interest in her little projects. "It is coming along very nicely, Aubrey. The design is beginning to take shape."

"Good, good," said Sir Aubrey, casting a glance at his nephew and Lady Victoria, who were still discussing horseflesh.

The footman suddenly entered. Sir Aubrey looked

up, a blistering reprimand on his lips. The footman hurried into speech. "Pardon this intrusion, sir. My Lord Damion is wanted—"

An angry voice said, "Never mind, I shall announce myself!" The man was pushed unceremoniously aside and the owner of the voice came into view.

Sir Aubrey's mouth tightened. "Evelyn!"

Victoria realized that this must be the gentleman whom her maid had said was of a violent nature and she examined him with unfeigned interest. Evelyn St. Claire was a young man of stocky build and medium height. He was attired in a wet greatcoat and muddied riding breeches and boots. Observing his flushed face and smouldering blue eyes, Victoria could well believe the maid's assessment.

"You're a ragmannered whelp, sirruh," snapped Sir Aubrey. "How dare you appear before the ladies in your dirt?"

Evelyn ignored his fathers' admonition. He acknowledged Lady Hortense with a short bow, but his angry glance passed over Sir Aubrey and Victoria to fasten on Lord Damion. He said abruptly, "St. Claire! You are the one I wish to see." Dull red stained Sir Aubrey's weathered cheeks.

Lord Damion chose to appear unaware of his cousin's discourtesy. "Of course, Evelyn. In a moment. Pray sit down and join us," he said calmly.

"There is no time, St. Claire. Dorothea and my precious sister-in-law are trapped in our carriage down at the crossing," snapped Evelyn.

Lady Hortense gasped in concern. "My dear! Are they all right?"

"Yes, for the moment, Aunt," said Evelyn.

"What happened?" asked Lord Damion. Victoria observed that Evelyn's tight face relaxed slightly.

"I was riding beside the carriage. We have a new driver. Before I could stop him, the cow-handed fool tried to take the carriage across the low place. It floundered and is now up to its axles," said Evelyn swiftly.

Lord Damion was rising even as his cousin finished. "Has the vehicle tipped over?"

Evelyn shook his head. "But we could not cut the horses free. Without their weight to act as a counterbalance, I feared that the entire equipage would roll over." His voice sharpened with ragged fear. "You know how that crossing is after this kind of rain. The water is higher than I have ever seen it. St. Claire, if we linger much longer—"

"I will come at once. Call for horses and the men, Eve," said Lord Damion. His cousin turned on his heel, setting up a shout in the hall. Lord Damion turned to the others sitting silently at the table. "I expect that we shall return shortly. If you would, Mama, pray alert Mrs. Lummington of our errand."

"Of course, Damion." Lady Hortense rose immediately, glad of something to do. She paused beside her son and reached up to place her hand against his hard cheek. "Pray take care, Damion."

He smiled and placed a quick kiss in her palm. "I always do, Mama." She nodded and hurried from the room.

Sir Aubrey waved his hand at Lord Damion. "Well, do not just stand there. Go, go. We will see to what needs to be done at this end."

Lord Damion nodded and left the room. Evelyn met him outside the door, and as Lord Damion joined him, Victoria caught his hurried voice. ". . . she's in the family way . . . insisted upon coming . . ."

"Well, well." Sir Aubrey drummed his fingertips on the table. "Evelyn has managed to make a botch of it, as is his usual custom, and Damion needs must run to the rescue."

Victoria looked at him. She thought his contempt for his son was out of place under the circumstances. She did not bother to hide her disapprobation as she rose from her seat. "I will join Lady Hortense and Mrs. Lummington in preparing for their return."

Sir Aubrey looked up at her, a thin smile on his lips. "I see that you disapprove of me, my lady, but I make no bones about whom I dislike. My son Evelyn is a damned puppy. He is not worth the salt in that shaker, my lady, and so you'll find."

"I know that you will excuse me, Sir Aubrey," Victoria said quietly. She exited the dining room, followed by the gentleman's snort of derision.

Eight

Victoria saw the housekeeper beginning to ascend the stairs and called to her. Mrs. Lummington paused, impatience and curiosity warring in her expression. Victoria quickly asked if Lady Hortense had already informed her of the crisis.

"Aye, we've heard of it. The crossing is a treacherous spot, but with m'lord Damion in charge they'll make all right and tight," said Mrs. Lummington. "Her ladyship is already gone upstairs to see that the beds are warmed properly and I've set Cook to making up hot toddies for the ladies when they come."

"We may need more than warm beds and hot toddies, Mrs. Lummington," said Victoria. "I overheard Master Evelyn express concern for his wife because she is in the family way."

Mrs. Lummington blew out her cheeks thoughtfully. "I catch your meaning, my lady. I will see that a man is sent for the physician directly we know if he is needed."

"You might as well send for the sawbones now, Mrs. Lummington." The two women turned at Sir Aubrey's harsh voice. He leaned on his cane in the dining-room doorway. "Think, woman. In this infernal weather it will take the man a good two hours at best to reach Chatworth."

"Aye, Sir Aubrey, You may rely on me, sir. I will

attend to the matter immediately," said Mrs. Lummington, curtsying.

"See that you do," said Sir Aubrey. When the housekeeper had left, he turned hard eyes on Victoria. "We've time on our hands, Lady Victoria. Indulge me in a rubber or two of whist. You do play, of course?"

At Victoria's nod, he ordered tapers to be brought to the sitting room. While he was engaged in shuffling the cards, Lady Hortense came in with her embroidery basket and settled herself on the settee. "I can never resist bright light," she said humorously as she began plying her needle.

Victoria laughed, and as she admired the brightly colored altar cloth Lady Hortense was working on, she said, "It is beautiful, ma'am. I myself am but a tolerable needlewoman and I envy those with more talented fingers."

"Thank you, my dear." Lady Hortense glanced over at her brother-in-law. "Aubrey, Mrs. Lummington informs me that dear Doro is in the family way. Why ever did you not tell me?"

"Evelyn does not confide in me, Hortense," said Sir Aubrey harshly. "Come, Lady Victoria. I am done with the cards." As Lady Hortense shook her head, Victoria took her place at the card table.

Nearly an hour passed while Sir Aubrey satisfied himself that Victoria was a worthy opponent. "You have played whist often, I see," he commented finally, watching as Victoria expertly shuffled.

"Charles loved gaming and I thus gained more than a passing familiarity with the pasteboards," said Victoria. "He was forever betting on something and won more often than not."

Sir Aubrey smiled. "He became a hardened gamester, did he? I had always a taste for the gaming hells myself. Charles was a scapegrace, but I understood him. He was more like my own son than his cousin Evelyn could ever hope to be." There was an old bitterness in his voice that Victoria was quick to detect. Beyond them, Lady Hortense firmly pressed her lips together, determined not to involve herself.

"I expect Master Evelyn will be grateful for your forethought in sending for the doctor, Sir Aubrey," said Victoria.

Sir Aubrey cracked a laugh. "That's rich, 'pon my word! My son would as lief spit me on his sword than admit a drop of gratitude to me, my lady. He does not easily forget that he is descended from the wrong side of the blanket."

"Now that is quite enough, Aubrey," said Lady Hortense firmly. "You do not need to rake up the buried past."

"Do I not? She should know about the family she is allied with." Sir Aubrey threw an unreadable glance at Victoria from beneath half-hooded eyes. "I am the bastard of the St. Claire clan, Lady Victoria. Lord Damion's father, the Viscount St. Claire, was my half-brother. The viscount's mother was Lady Amelia. Mine was the blacksmith's daughter."

He stared at her fiercely and Victoria finally felt compelled to comment. "I did not know," she said lamely.

"Then Charles had less brains than I gave him credit for. He should have prepared you for the worst, my dear." Sir Aubrey's smile was a shade malicious. "By nature passions run deep in the March and St. Claire clans. Lord Robert's will shall undoubtedly act as a catalyst of sorts. The title goes to the St. Claire family if Charles died without an heir. In that event, as his widow you will inherit what is undoubtedly a mere pittance. But I credit you with a sharp wit. I assume that a brat of suitable age will be brought forward at the appropriate time to confound us all."

"Aubrey! How dare you treat that girl in such a base fashion," exclaimed Lady Hortense, bright patches of color in her cheeks. She pulled at her thread which she had knotted in her agitation.

Sir Aubrey spared her a glance. "Pray recall that I

am a bastard, my lady. I may be excused much that is base."

Victoria regarded the old gentleman with mounting anger. She said coldly, "I consider your accusation a vile impertinence, sir!"

Sir Aubrey chuckled, delighted that he had been able to rouse her temper. "Aye, play your cards close, my dear. I have no objection. But we shall see if I am not right."

Victoria was trembling. He sat opposite her with the ghost of a superior smile on his thin mouth. She wanted nothing better than to toss her glass of wine at his head, but she forced herself to concentrate on her cards instead. Carefully, deliberately, she laid down the pasteboards and looked across at him.

Sir Aubrey glanced at her revealed hand and his brows rose. "Well done, Lady Victoria. You have beat me all hollow."

"Pray take care that you do not underestimate me again, Sir Aubrey," said Victoria levelly.

Sir Aubrey's look was sharp. "I wonder if I have not?"

"Oh bravo, my dear," said Lady Hortense softly.

The sound of voices raised in the hall brought all three to their feet. "If I am not mistaken, the rescue party has returned," said Sir Aubrey as he went to the sitting-room door. Victoria followed close behind him. Lady Hortense flung down her embroidery and clutched Victoria's arm.

Lord Damion entered the hall carrying a woman in his arms. Her head was cradled against his broad shoulder and her heavy raven tresses, loose from their pins, cascaded over his sleeve. Lord Damion was giving terse instructions to the butler, who nodded his understanding.

Behind him stood his cousin. Evelyn protectively supported a drooping young woman whose face was deathly pale. His eyes were shadowed with worry and he snapped at no one in particular, "Where is Mrs. Lummington?"

Lord Damion turned to him. "I've had her sent for, Eve. She will come directly."

Sir Aubrey advanced on them, leaning on his cane. "I perceive that the ladies are the worse for their experience."

"Dorothea is having pains before her time, sir. Mrs. Giddings has but fainted," said Lord Damion. There was a note of impatience in his voice as he glanced down at his fair burden.

The woman in his arms stirred and sighed. Slowly she opened her startlingly violet eyes. "Oh, my—my lord!" she said in pretty confusion.

"Can you stand?" asked Lord Damion.

"I believe so," she said, though there was a note of doubt in her voice. Lord Damion set her carefully on her feet. She swayed against him and he lent her the support of his arm.

Evelyn looked down at his wife's utterly white face. "St Claire, we need a doctor." There was tension in his voice. "Dorothea—"

"I had Chatworth sent for an hour or more ago," said Sir Aubrey. "The manservant ought to return with him before much longer."

Evelyn looked at his father frowningly, hardly seeing him. "Much obliged, sir." His wife stifled a moan and turned her face into his sleeve. "Where the devil is Mrs. Lummington?" asked Evelyn angrily.

Victoria went to him. "Mrs. Lummington is undoubtedly preparing a room for your wife, who shall be more comfortable once she is settled in bed. Pray allow me to accompany you and Mrs. St. Claire upstairs now, sir. I am no stranger to childbearing women and I may be of assistance." Evelyn nodded curtly and picked up his wife in his arms.

He and Victoria started up the stairs, closely followed by Lady Hortense. The housekeeper appeared on the landing as they reached it. "Master Evelyn, I've a bed ready for the mistress. Follow me straightaway, sir."

As Evelyn obeyed, he asked, "Have you had any word on the physician, Mrs. Lummington?"

"I'm sorry, Master Evelyn." Mrs. Lummington shook her head regretfully.

From below Sir Aubrey watched the small group's swift progress. "Lady Victoria is no stranger to childbearing, heh?" he repeated softly, and smiled.

Lord Damion ushered Mrs. Giddings to a chair against the wainscoting. She sank onto it and smiled gratefully at him. Her fingers pressed his forearm briefly. "Thank you, my lord," she said huskily.

Lord Damion bowed and gently extricated himself from her grasp. "The honor was mine, madame. I have asked for a woman to attend you." He turned to a waiting footman and handed his beaver to him before he began unbuttoning his greatcoat.

"What happened, Damion?" asked Sir Aubrey.

Lord Damion glanced at him as he divested himself of the soaked greatcoat. "It was much as Evelyn said. In addition, some of the stones seem to have washed out of the low place and made it twice as treacherous. The hole was large enough to catch one of the front carriage wheels so that it came perilously close to overturning. As it was, the carriage was nearly lying on its side with the ladies trapped inside. The water was rising, but we were able to remove the ladies to safety before we attempted to pull the carriage out of the current."

"It was much too horrible for words!" exclaimed Mrs. Giddings, not liking to be overlooked. She had stripped off her soft kid gloves and now pressed them to her lips as though remembering a nightmare. "I could see the water rushing by the carriage window. Dorothea had hysterics and the horses were giving the most bloodcurdling screams—"

'What of the horses, Damion?' interjected Sir Aubrey. He bowed in apology to Mrs. Giddings for interrupting her, but her beautifully molded mouth still tightened in irritation.

"The team was in remarkably good condition for all that they had tangled in the traces and had to be cut free. The leader has a bruised fetlock, but that was the worst injury," said Lord Damion. "I give

Evelyn's driver credit for keeping his head despite his very real fear and calming them as best he could."

Sir Aubrey nodded. "The mark of a good man, that."

"A good man! The idiot should be horsewhipped for his stupidity. Anyone with eyes could see that the water was too high," said Mrs. Giddings. She signaled imperiously for a footman to take her sodden cloak. The gentlemen exchanged a long look.

Accompanied by a housemaid, Victoria descended the stairs. As she reached the bottom step, Lord Damion immediately went to her. "How did you leave Mrs. St. Claire, ma'am?"

"She is resting comfortably for the moment, my lord. Lady Hortense is staying beside her for a time." Victoria looked up at him searchingly. "I assume that the doctor has not yet arrived?" Lord Damion shook his head, frowning.

Sir Aubrey tapped his cane loudly on the tiles. "Out with it, my girl. Will Dorothea drop that whelp before her time?"

"I am no midwife, sir. I shall simply rest easier with a physician's opinion," said Victoria.

"Damnation!" exclaimed Sir Aubrey, reading evasion into her reply.

"Doro is hardier than she appears," said Mr. Giddings, engaged in coiling her heavy dark hair over a slim shoulder.

Sir Aubrey glanced at her with acute dislike. When he spoke his tone was deceptively contrite. "Forgive me, Margaret. I have passed over your own appalling experience. Your sensibilities must be aggravated beyond bearing."

"To be sure, my nerves are sadly overwrought," said Margaret, her violet eyes sliding in soft appeal to Lord Damion.

"Then I must certainly accept your excuses and bid you good night, my dear," said Sir Aubrey briefly. He indicated the maid standing quietly behind Victoria. "This young woman will show you to your room."

Margaret stared at him agape. She recovered quickly and said, "I fear I am yet too shaky to negotiate the stairs alone, Sir Aubrey. Perhaps if I had assistance—" Her eyes again sought Lord Damion and her smile beckoned.

"Of course, madame. I know that William will ably assist you," said Lord Damion unfeelingly. He had never cared to be manipulated by a woman. He beckoned toward one of the footmen.

"That will not be necessary," said Margaret, much annoyed. She flounced to the stairs and tossed her gloves at Victoria, who instinctively caught them. "Here, girl, you may carry these."

Victoria's brows rose in astonishment. The maid gently took the kid gloves from her, curtsying, and hurried after Margaret Giddings, who was already ascending the stairs.

Margaret met Evelyn St. Claire coming down but she swept past him without a word. He turned around on the step to watch her, then continued his descent. "What has gotten into Margaret now?" he asked cheerfully. Sir Aubrey snorted in disgust and Evelyn laughed.

Lord Damion had observed two footmen carrying serving trays into the sitting room and suggested that they quit the hall. "For I ordered a cold collation earlier and I for one could do with a sandwich," said Lord Damion, offering his arm to Victoria. She accepted his escort, amused by the unusual warmth of his gaze. Sir Aubrey and Evelyn followed them into the sitting room.

Victoria quietly thanked Lord Damion when he had seated her on the sofa, expecting him to withdraw. Instead he asked, "May I fix you a plate, my lady?" A smile lurked at the corner of his sensual mouth that Victoria found difficult to ignore.

She glanced over at the buffet that the footmen had set out before silently exiting. The sight of cold jellies, meats, and cheeses awakened a rumbling in her stomach. She realized with surprise that it was far past the dinner hour. "I would be most grateful, my lord," she said.

Lord Damion served a plate for himself and another for Victoria, then returned. Victoria accepted the plate piled high with food and a glass of wine. "Thank you, my lord, but I hardly know where to begin," she said with a laugh.

"It is likely all we will get this night, my lady," said Lord Damion warningly. Victoria was astonished when he elected to sit beside her on the sofa. She could not imagine why he had suddenly attached himself to her.

Sir Aubrey settled stiffly into a wingback chair while Evelyn chose to stand at the mantel, where he began eating with great gusto. Sir Aubrey watched him with glowering eyes. "Well, sirruh, what do you mean by traveling with that puling wife of yours in the family way?" he demanded.

Evelyn threw back his head defensively, his expression darkening. But before he could reply, Lord Damion said smoothly, "Dorothea is willful in her own quiet fashion, sir, as well you know. Evelyn, how was Doro when you left her?"

"She was resting. The pains are gone," said Evelyn shortly. He threw his father a darkling look. "My aunt, who is staying beside her tonight, seems to think that Doro will be fine."

"I am certain that the doctor will confirm her opinion when he arrives," said Lord Damion. He suddenly smiled at Victoria and she felt a momentary leap in her pulses. "Forgive my manners, Lady Victoria. I do not believe that you have been properly introduced to my cousin."

"We have met. My aunt made a rather hurried introduction and mentioned how you . . . befriended the lady." Evelyn nodded stiffly to Victoria. She saw his glance travel to Lord Damion before returning to her and she was startled by the unfriendliness in his stare. "I stand in your debt for your support to my wife, madame. However, I find St. Claire's decision in bringing your person to a family gathering both ill-timed and insulting."

Nine

Victoria was taken aback by Evelyn St. Claire's attack. Then she understood that he had mistaken her for Lord Damion's mistress and swift blood rose in her face.

The others apparently had no difficulty deciphering his meaning either. "Evelyn!" thundered Sir Aubrey. He half rose from his chair, his face purpled with rage.

Even through her embarrassment, Victoria could still look at Sir Aubrey in surprise. He had had no compunction about insulting her himself and she found it paradoxical that he should protest when someone else did so.

"You have mistaken the matter, Evelyn," said Lord Damion in a hard voice. "Lady Victoria is Charles's widow. She is in England to visit the Belinghams, only to find them away from home. She has graciously accepted our uncle's invitation to reside at the Crossing until their return and allow us the opportunity to come to know her."

"Nevertheless the lady arrived in your company, cousin, and that must make any explanation suspect," said Evelyn.

"You damned insulting—You've all the manners of a mongrel whelp, sirruh!" exclaimed Sir Aubrey harshly.

Evelyn's lip curled. He shot back quickly, "It is hardly any secret from whom I have inherited the mongrel!"

Victoria rose hastily. "I think it past time for me to retire. Good night, gentlemen." She made for the door and her escape, only to find Lord Damion beside her. She turned toward him, her chin lifting.

He opened the door. "Allow me to escort you, Lady Victoria," said Lord Damion.

'Pray do not, my lord." Victoria left the sitting room.

As Lord Damion turned from the door, he eyed his young cousin with a grim expression. "Evelyn, I believe it is time for you and me to have a discussion."

Victoria entered her room, her shoulders drooping with fatigue. She saw that the fire was banked in the grate and the bedcovers had been turned back invitingly. She signed with weary appreciation. There were advantages to having a lady's maid. She let the cashmere shawl slide to the floor and unbuttoned her cuffs as she approached the bed.

A movement in the dark corner of the room brought her up short. A woman stepped out of the shadows. Victoria recognized her with amazement. "Mrs. Giddings!"

Her visitor laughed softly. "I hope I did not startle you overmuch, Lady Victoria. My room is close by and I thought I would step in for a chat with you before I retired."

Victoria had had time to absorb the woman's revealing silk and lace peignoir and the long plait of black hair laid artistically over a slim shoulder. Victoria doubted that the charming effect was for her benefit. "I hope that I have not kept you waiting long," said Victoria dryly, and thought it was a wonder the woman's teeth were not chattering with cold.

Mrs. Giddings smiled and with languid familiarity caressed the corner post of the bed. "I do hope that you will forgive my faux pas earlier this evening in mistaking you for a servant. I understand from my maid that you actually arrived with Lord Damion." She looked Victoria up and down before saying insultingly, "His taste has dramatically changed."

Victoria stiffened. "You have mistaken the matter, Mrs. Giddings."

Margaret laughed softly, watching as her fingers

moved slowly over the bedpost. "Oh, I think not. Lord Damion does not travel with female boon companions. No, you are one of his fancies or soon will be."

"Really, Mrs. Giddings!"

Her hand dropping from the post, the woman turned suddenly on Victoria. Dying firelight reflected the bright hardness of her eyes. "Allow me to deliver a friendly word of advice, Lady Victoria, or however you choose to style yourself. The Demon is accustomed to fire and beauty in his women. For the sake of your pride, leave the Crossing before he discovers how bored he is by you. For believe me, he will be!"

Victoria had had enough. She went to the bedroom door and wrenched it open. "Pray leave my room, Mrs. Giddings."

Margaret regarded Victoria for a moment, amused by her obvious anger. She walked to the door, only to pause on the threshold to caress the cool silk covering her firm breast. "Do you not think rose becomes me? It is Damion's favorite color, you know," she said softly. Then she walked away.

Victoria was stunned by the woman's blatant rudeness. She closed the door with a snap and leaned against it a moment, trying to collect herself. Her glance fell on the bed and she came away from the door. It was certainly of no benefit to stand here all night. Victoria stripped to her chemise and slid into bed.

But sleep eluded her as her thoughts returned again and again to her experiences of the last two days. She realized that from the moment she made herself known to Lord Damion she had been subjected to abuse and outrageous conduct by members of Charles's family. Lord Damion and Sir Aubrey thought of her as a fortune hunter, to be manipulated as it pleased them. Evelyn St. Claire had instantly leaped to the conclusion that she was his cousin's mistress, an opinion shared by Margaret Giddings who obviously saw her as a rival for Lord Damion's favors. Victoria thought that probably even kind Lady Hortense assumed that she had come to the Crossing to demand that provision be made for her support.

It particularly disgusted Victoria that the male members of the family had assumed that once she was exposed to Lord Damion's charm she would be more than willing to tumble into bed with him. Lord Damion himself apparently believed in his own reputation. Victoria recalled that he had been astonished at their first meeting when she did not react immediately to his name. She wondered what exactly he had anticipated and a vision of Margaret Giddings came to mind. Victoria grimaced to herself.

The one member of the family who had treated her with any degree of unsuspicion had been Dorothea, who had wanly accepted her support and thanked her for her concern. Victoria wondered somewhat bitterly if that lady's sweet temper would disappear as she regained her strength. She was, after all, Margaret Giddings's sister.

Victoria wished there were some means she could use to show them all up for fools. If she could but prove that she was not interested in Lord Damion or his position, that alone would suffice to disconcert the gentlemen and Mrs. Giddings.

Victoria stared at the ceiling. She could easily prove it if she pretended to fall in with Sir Aubrey's scheme. With that one stroke all concerned would believe that they had been correct about her character.

Halfway believing that she could hear Charles's hearty amusement at her thoughts, Victoria smiled to herself in the dark. She was tired and thinking foolishly. She stretched her arms over her head and snuggled deeper into the pillow.

Ten

Victoria and Margaret Giddings met on the stairs on their way to breakfast. They exchanged cool nods but neither felt inclined to start up a conversation.

When they entered the breakfast room, they discovered Evelyn and a gentleman in a black frock coat already seated at the table, addressing steaming mugs of coffee while they conversed in low voices.

Evelyn looked up and gave the ladies a general greeting. "And see, here is good Chatworth at last. He has already been up to see Doro and pronounces her right as rain."

The physician rose to bow to the ladies as they seated themselves, then turned to remonstrate with Evelyn. "Master Evelyn, pray recall that I also prescribed quiet and no strenuous activity for your young wife."

"She shan't like that part above half, you know," said Evelyn.

"Come, Evelyn! Such a regimen will pose little difficulty for Doro. She has never liked excitement," said Margaret as she made her selections from the plate of sweet biscuits. "Doro prizes the country and her little dogs above all else. I have often wondered how she bears such a boring existence."

Evelyn flushed and Victoria quickly interposed. "I am happy that it has all turned out for the best. I see that your coat is still damp, Dr. Chatworth. Was it raining again when you came?"

The physician laughed. "I am not damp from rain, my lady, but the dunking I took at the crossing. I fear that I am not an accomplished horseman. My brute slipped and over I went."

"Is the stream still so flooded then?" asked Victoria with surprise. "I had quite thought it would have begun to subside by now."

"It is usually a couple of days before the low place is down. We won't see anyone from the village besides Chatworth for at least that long," said Evelyn.

"Evelyn, do you mean that I am stranded here for yet two days more without my dresser? How am I to go on, pray? The stupid girl I have been given is a clumsy fool. She twice pulled my hair while brushing it this morning," said Margaret.

"You are well enough, Margaret," Evelyn said, and then somewhat clumsily attempted a reassuring compliment. "Indeed, rusticating seems to become you."

"Pray do not be an ass, Evelyn," said Margaret crushingly.

Dr. Chatworth coughed and discreetly excused himself, saying that Sir Aubrey had requested that he look in on him before his departure. When he left the room, Evelyn addressed his sister-in-law. "Do you know, Margaret, if you were not Doro's sister, I would swiftly drop you from my circle of acquaintances. You have never met Chatworth in your life and you go out of your way to prove yourself a shrew."

Margaret gave a peal of laughter. "Why should I care what a country quack may think?" she said scornfully. "And you flatter yourself, Evelyn. It is I who suffer the connection between us. Believe me, I don't care two sticks for your opinion."

Evelyn leaned back in his chair. Victoria, observing the sudden cynicism that chilled his eyes, was struck by his strong resemblance to Sir Aubrey. "Well I know whose opinion you do care for, Margaret. It was not sisterly concern that decided you to quit London and accompany us, as Doro prefers to believe, but whom you might encounter here at the Crossing."

Margaret stiffened and threw a swift glance in

Victoria's direction. "That is quite enough nonsense, Evelyn. We are in company."

Evelyn turned to Victoria. "Cousin Victoria, my dear sister-in-law grows restless with her widowed state and I suspect that she has designs on poor Cousin Damion. Should we warn him, do you think?"

"Evelyn, I believe you are upsetting Mrs. Giddings," said Victoria, taking note of their companion's whitened face.

Margaret rounded on her. "I hardly need your championship, my fine lady. As for you, Evelyn, you show lack of breeding with every breath." She threw down her napkin and sailed to the door.

"By the by, St. Claire usually rises an hour earlier," called Evelyn. His sister-in-law checked herself in midstep, then whisked out of the room.

Chuckling, Evelyn turned back to meet Victoria's steady gaze. Immediately he became shamefaced. "My pardon, Lady Victoria, for my behavior last night. After you had retired, St. Claire made everything quite clear how you came to be in his company. I could scarcely credit that he had abducted you. His conduct was outrageous, even for the Demon. I made certain he understood my feelings about that, believe me. At all events, my own assumptions were totally unwarranted. I hope you will accept my humble apology."

"I don't know that I should," said Victoria frankly.

"I realize the light in which I appear. I didn't believe St. Claire at the first because— The thing of it is, I thought it all a hum that Cousin Charles had married. Indeed, with his shocking reputation . . . but Charles was a smashing fellow. I only wish that I had known him better," said Evelyn, his bright blue eyes sincere.

Victoria felt herself slightly mollified by his ingenuous explanation. "I appreciate your apology, Mr. St. Claire."

Evelyn recognized that he had almost won her over. "Pray call me cousin. We are family now, after all," he said, real warmth in his voice. A boyish grin lightened his too serious countenance. "Please, Lady Victoria."

"Very well," said Victoria, letting go her reluctance to trust him. The St. Claires could be charming when they chose to exert themselves, she thought. She smiled at Evelyn. "I shall if you will address me as Victoria."

"Done, Cousin Victoria," said Evelyn promptly. They smiled at one another, both relieved to have the misunderstanding cleared up and in the past.

"But I must tell you that you can be an extremely ill-mannered young man. And just now I quite felt for Mrs. Giddings," said Victoria.

Evelyn's expression darkened. "It is only certain people who set me off, you know, and Margaret is one of the worst. I can't abide her. She is sweetness itself when it suits her purposes, but only let someone come between her and her desires. Then she is a raging vixen."

"I can well believe it," said Victoria dryly, remembering her nocturnal visit.

Evelyn eyed her curiously. "You are not at all as I pictured Charles's wife should be. You are quieter than ever he was. And you don't fly into a pucker even when there is good reason."

Victoria laughed at him. "You are a great too nonsensical for your own good, Evelyn. Spouses are rarely alike, and what has temper to do with anything?"

"Cousin Victoria, to survive in this family you must possess a hardy temper," said Evelyn with a half smile.

"I am a survivor, Evelyn, never fear," said Victoria. "But what of Lady Hortense? Surely she—"

"Believe me, for all my aunt's good nature I have seen her cut up pretty stiff," said Evelyn. "But now I am curious to hear what you have concluded about us, cousin. What do you think of St. Claire? Is he as arrogant as he pretends, do you think?"

"That topic I shan't touch," said Victoria, pouring herself another cup of coffee.

"Very wise of you, Lady Victoria," said Lord

Damion as he came up behind them. When they turned, he was satisfied by their expressions that Evelyn had made things right between them. He took the chair opposite Victoria. "One moment more and I might have heard something to my discredit."

"Never to your discredit, my lord, but perhaps to your dismay," said Victoria quickly, a hint of mischief in her brown eyes.

Evelyn whistled appreciatively. "You are well served, St. Claire!"

"But we shall see who has the last word, Evelyn," promised Lord Damion. His young cousin gave a rude hoot and he laughed. "I feel unaccountably under siege. Allow me to gently disengage and tell you the reason I originally joined you. I intend to pay a visit to the brood mare that I mentioned to you yesterday, Lady Victoria, and I came to invite you to accompany me to the stables."

"I would be honored, my lord. Give me but a few moments to put on my walking boots and I shall join you in the hall," said Victoria, rising from the table. Evelyn and Lord Damion rose with her and bowed as she left the room.

Lord Damion looked at his cousin. "You are welcome to join us, Evelyn. It is one of Black Son's mares."

Evelyn shook his head, unsmiling. "I am no puppy to tag after you, St. Claire."

"I did not think you were. I was under the impression that Black Son was one of your favorites," said Lord Damion quietly, preparing to quit the breakfast room.

Evelyn instantly regretted his discourtesy. "St. Claire," he began. Lord Damion turned and raised his brows. Under his dispassionate gaze Evelyn felt himself redden. He said brusquely, "Chatworth has seen Doro this morning and pronounces her in fine shape. Much obliged for your help yesterday."

"I am happy to hear it, Evelyn." Lord Damion bowed and continued on his way.

Evelyn St. Claire stared broodingly at the door

where his tall cousin had disappeared. He did not understand why Lord Damion should set up his back, but he had always felt the same antagonism for his elder cousin.

He heard Lord Damion's deep voice, answered by Lady Victoria's quieter tones. Evelyn smiled, a wicked light leaping into his blue eyes. "Won't Margaret be in a passion, though," he remarked aloud, and began to whistle cheerfully.

When Victoria joined Lord Damion in the hall, she was wearing a heavy woolen cloak and sturdy boots. A footman had fetched an overcoat and a low-crowned beaver for Lord Damion and it was not long before he inquired if she were ready. Victoria assented and together they left the hall by way of a narrow side passageway. As they reached an outside door that led onto the back of the manor, Lord Damion remarked that the old structure was something of a rabbit warren.

He and Victoria made their way across the muddy yard to the stables. Inside the well-built stone building, the stable master was waiting. He touched his forehead in respect. "I thought ye might come, m'lord," he said with a thick country accent. He glanced at Victoria.

"John, this is Master Charles's wife, Lady Victoria. Her ladyship's father bred horses when she was a girl, and when I told her of our patient, she expressed an interest in coming," said Lord Damion.

The stable master nodded. "The mare be this way, m'lord." He showed them to a stall where a big-bellied mare with a drooping head stood. The horse raised her nose at their approach, blowing anxiously.

"Oh you beauty!" Victoria reached out to scratch the mare's white blaze. She crooned softly to the beast and after a moment's hesitation the mare allowed her muzzle to settle near Victoria's shoulder, her ears swiveling to catch the soft Portuguese endearments.

Lord Damion's brows rose in surprise at Lady Victoria's fluid Portuguese. She sounded almost like a native to his untutored ears. But it was her instant rapport with the mare that astonished him most. "You have made a conquest, Lady Victoria," he said softly.

"Aye, that she has," agreed John, grudging respect on his craggy face.

Lord Damion turned to the stable master to confer on the mare's condition. As he listened to John's assessment, he watched while Lady Victoria looked the mare over, even checking her mouth and legs. He was amazed by her attentiveness and her ease of manner with the animal. He was intrigued by her skill and for the first time wondered about her background, for it was patent that she had spent much time around horses. He could not help but think that she'd surely had an odd upbringing for a gentlewoman.

"Aye, m'lord. She'll drop the foal late in the week, I expect," said John.

Victoria, who had listened with only half an ear to the men's conversation, said, "I think it will be sooner. And unless I miss my guess she will have difficulties, for there is something about her stance and the passive expression in her eyes that bothers me," she said, dusting off her hands as she came out of the stall. She saw their surprise and skepticism and smiled. "Believe me, gentlemen, I've experience enough to know. My earliest memories are of the foaling season and I have never yet missed a spring." The stable master looked sharply at her, then at the mare.

Though he remained skeptical, Lord Damion acknowledged her with a bow. "Then all the more reason to keep a close watch on Starfire. I shall want word at the first signs, John."

"Aye, m'lord." The stable master touched his forehead and watched as Lord Damion escorted the stranger from the stables. He turned to stare speculatively at the mare. "For all she's a female, her ladyship looked a knowing one. Mayhap ye told her ladyship someit ye kept from me, heh?"

Eleven

As Lord Damion and Victoria left the stables, she said, "The mare is obviously bred for speed and her foals must surely reflect that. I should very much like to see the stud if I may."

"Black Son is kept in the west field. We will ride out one day to watch him. He, too, is a swift animal." Lord Damion glanced down at her. "I am impressed, my lady. Your father obviously taught you well and instilled in you a great love for horses."

"He was a remarkable man. And he had able help in his friend, Carlos Silva y Montoya," said Victoria.

Lord Damion thought he detected a note of warmth in her voice. "Were you close to this Carlos Silva y Montoya?" he asked curiously.

"Carlos was my guardian after Father died. I met Charles through him," said Victoria. Her companion raised startled brows. She saw that they were not returning directly to the manor house. "Where are we going, my lord?"

"I wished to determine if the flood has dropped since yesterday. We will be able to see the crossing once we are clear of these trees." Lord Damion did not add that he was reluctant to return directly to the manor because he had an overwhelming desire to be alone a little while longer in her company. She interested him as no other woman had done for some time and Lord Damion was in the habit of indulging his own whims.

They soon emerged from the shelter of the trees that protected the manor house. The wind was brisker in the open and Victoria was glad of her heavy cloak.

She and Lord Damion stood at the top of an incline. The ground before them sloped away to meet a rolling brown stream swollen past its banks. On her left the carriage track curved away from the manor down to the stream, where it abruptly disappeared and then reappeared on the far side. Victoria realized that this must be the infamous crossing.

Lord Damion was examining the same point with keen eyes. He remarked, "I spoke several times to the earl of putting down a short bridge at that point. But he was adamant against it. He said that he preferred the old ways best, even if it meant needless inconvenience."

"Charles gave me to understand that his father could be difficult," said Victoria delicately.

Lord Damion threw her a glance, understanding that she was recalling more than one past statement. "Perhaps, but you must also realize that there was wrong on both sides. Even before Charles left to join the army he and his father often had falling outs. I was already with Sir John Moore when the break between them began to occur, but my mother wrote me about it. Apparently Charles inherited much of his father's strength of will and that, coupled with a wild streak, did much to divide them. Yet Lord Robert remained sincerely attached to his son."

"Yes. And I know Charles, too, felt keenly for his father. Even in his blackest moments he had a grudging respect for him. But pride forbade him to return as a supplicant for Lord Robert's forgiveness," said Victoria. "I believe that must be why Charles corresponded with his lordship's solicitor. He knew that the solicitor would pass on the contents of the letters and it was his way of giving a glimpse of his life to Lord Robert."

Lord Damion stared at her. "I did not know that Charles corresponded with anyone here in England."

"I am not at all surprised. I did not learn of it until yesterday when Sir Aubrey informed me of Charles's correspondence," said Victoria. "I was naturally amazed, for Charles never mentioned it."

"My uncle has a disconcerting habit of learning more than he ought, and he sometimes uses his knowledge for his own ends," said Lord Damion dryly. Victoria threw him a startled glance, wondering if he referred to Sir Aubrey's avowed familiarity with Lord Robert's will and his scheme to have them marry.

Lord Damion was unaware of her surprise. His attention was trained on a lone horseman following the track below. "Brave Chatworth. I fear the crossing is still too flooded for any but those on horseback. I'll wager that we do not see the solicitor for some days yet."

"I suppose Mrs. Giddings's dresser will also not be seen for yet a while," said Victoria, thinking of that lady's ill humor.

"The second carriage bearing the ladies' maids and their baggage, not to mention Doro's two little dogs, turned back last night for the village. After witnessing their mistresses' plight I doubt that they will be in any great hurry to brave the crossing," said Lord Damion. He grinned suddenly at Victoria. "May I assume that Margaret was distressed by her maid's continued absence?"

Victoria chuckled and a mischievous twinkle lit her dark eyes. "Quite, my lord. And Evelyn's odd sense of gallantry did not make matters better. He remarked that rusticating became her."

Lord Damion gave a shout of laughter. "Breakfasting early has its advantages," he observed. He noticed that she shivered. "I believe the wind is growing stronger. Shall we return to the manor, Lady Victoria?"

Victoria agreed to it and they walked back in companionable silence. She felt more in charity with him than she had at any time since their first meeting. She glanced up at his lean face. Victoria thought it would not be difficult to like Lord Damion if he were to remain as approachable as he had been that morning.

When she and Lord Damion reentered the hall,

they found Sir Aubrey setting up a shout. He glared at Lord Damion. "There you are, sirruh! I was just sending for you." He thrust a crumpled sheet at his nephew. "Chatworth brought that around with him. I have but just finished it. What do you make of it?"

Lord Damion calmly scanned the closely written sheet and looked up. "It appears straightforward enough. The solicitor writes us that he will join us when he is able."

Evelyn, Margaret, and Lady Hortense had all been brought to the hall by Sir Aubrey's angry voice. Margaret spared a dagger glance for Victoria when she saw her with Lord Damion and quickly positioned herself near that gentleman's elbow.

Sir Aubrey pointed a shaking finger at the offending letter. "The solictor mentions another beneficiary to Lord Robert's estate in his letter, Damion. And he proposes to contact this upstart before he comes to preside over the reading. The only heirs to Lord Robert are already gathered under this roof!" There were general exclamations and excited speculations.

Amid the confusion Victoria quietly excused herself to Lord Damion and made her way upstairs to change out of her boots. Lord Damion looked after her thoughtfully, puzzled by her seeming lack of interest in the situation when even Margaret Giddings, who had nothing to gain, was expressing an opinion.

When Victoria returned downstairs some minutes later, she found Lady Hortense alone in the sitting room, quietly embroidering her altar cloth. Lady Hortense smiled at her in welcome. "We have had such excitement, have we not? At the last Evelyn could stand no more and has gone out riding and Margaret went up to sit with Doro. As for poor Sir Aubrey, he is still beside himself. I was never more grateful than when Damion took him off to the library for private speech."

"Lord Damion appears well able to handle any disturbance with a calming authority," said Victoria, sitting down beside her on the sofa. She picked up the yarns to hold them so that they would not tangle. Lady Hortense nodded to her in appreciation.

"I daresay it is Damion's military training. The army steadied him amazingly, I am happy to say," said Lady Hortense. "You would never have recognized him a few years ago. Damion was a wild young man of a very quick temper, very much like your Charles was."

"Forgive me for saying so, ma'am, but I have observed that a hasty temper is a common trait in this family," said Victoria dryly. "And I have yet to see any member bother to bridle it."

"Oh, I think it nearly impossible to bridle it, my dear. And only Evelyn seems to have escaped what I call the heart of fire. Of us all, he is least likely to burn those around him," said Lady Hortense placidly.

Victoria stared at her in astonishment. "Dear lady, surely you jest. Evelyn is as bad as the others."

"Oh no." Lady Hortense glanced at her. "You are doubtless confusing Evelyn's fits of temper with the true March rage. You see, the families have been connected through several generations and it is always this one trait from the March side which seems to crop up. You may see it in Sir Aubrey. But Evelyn's anger passes off quickly and then he is as agreeable as one could wish. I believe he inherited his mother's sweetness of disposition but he deliberately takes care to hide it from Sir Aubrey."

"I had noticed that Evelyn and Sir Aubrey do not care overmuch for one another," said Victoria.

Lady Hortense sighed. "Evelyn resents his father and I cannot find it in my heart to blame him. Sir Aubrey married late in life, and though he loved Amanda, his habits were too well established for him to give up his pleasures in London. Amanda preferred the country estate and that was where Evelyn was raised. He saw his father but rarely, and Sir Aubrey was not the sort of man to easily endear himself to a small boy."

"That I can well believe," said Victoria, a twinkle in her eyes.

Lady Hortense laughed, then said, "When Amanda died a few years ago, I believe Sir Aubrey deeply regretted his neglect of his family and tried to make amends with Evelyn. But of course Evelyn had become a grown man and it was too late. Now Evelyn will have little to do with him and I fear that Sir Aubrey feels it most grievously."

"How sadly ironic," murmured Victoria.

Margaret entered the room. She acknowledged Victoria's presence with a bare nod before turning her attention to Lady Hortense. "Doro asked me to convey her regards, my lady. She intends to join us for luncheon today."

"I am so glad. Dorothea is such a dear little creature. I have missed her gentle company," said Lady Hortense.

Margaret seated herself in a silk-covered chair and began to flip through a ladies' magazine. "Indeed, we shall be quite the family when we sit down at luncheon. You must not be shy, Lady Victoria." Her smile was sweet and she said softly, "But then I cannot imagine you have a retiring nature at all for you seem to get along so well, and particularly with the gentlemen."

Victoria smiled faintly at the woman's barbed words. "I have found that a gracious manner will always gain one respectful attention."

Though attentive to her embroidery, Lady Hortense was aware of the undercurrents in the younger women's exchange and wondered at it. "Quite true, my dear. I can yet recall my own mother instructing me on the virtues of proper deportment and easy conversation. I doubt that the demands of society have changed much since my day. Margaret, how did you leave London? Were there many still in town?"

Balked of her prey, Margaret turned her shoulder on Victoria to reply to Lady Hortense.

Victoria rose to go to the pianoforte in the corner. She trailed her fingers idly over the ivory keys and glanced over the music sheets laying on top of the instrument.

"Oh, do you play, Lady Victoria? Somehow I did not expect living with the army would encourage the polite arts," said Margaret with a tinkling laugh.

Lady Hortense contemplated Margaret gravely for a moment, wondering at her inexplicable antagonism toward Victoria. She had never known Margaret Giddings to be so discourteous. Turning to Victoria, Lady Hortense said gently, "Pray favor us with a tune, Lady Victoria. I for one find music most enjoyable."

"Certainly, my lady," said Victoria. She seated herself at the pianoforte and began to play softly from memory so that she did not intrude upon her companions' conversation. As always, she quickly became caught up in the music. Victoria lost touch with her surroundings and in her thoughts she was playing for Charles as she had done so often in the evenings when he was at home.

A hand was laid gently on her shoulder. Victoria looked up, half expecting to see Charles, and with a stab of disappointment returned to the present.

"I am most reluctant to stop you, Lady Victoria," said Lady Hortense, withdrawing her hand. "We have sat idle these past twenty minutes in absolute wonder. You have a marvelous gift for music, my dear. Does she not, Margaret?"

"Oh, quite marvelous," said Margaret with a brittle smile.

Lady Hortense abandoned Margaret as an ally. "But here are Sir Aubrey and Damion to escort us in to luncheon."

Victoria rose from the pianoforte bench. She met Lord Damion's thoughtful gaze and inexplicably colored. She addressed herself to Lady Hortense. "Thank you for your kind words, my lady. I apologize if I have kept you waiting. I seem to lose all sense of time when I play."

"Quite all right, my dear. We are not usually so formal about luncheon or I would have let you continue. But it is a rare occurrence to have the whole family together," said Lady Hortense, giving Victoria a warm smile. Her inclusion of Victoria as one of the family was obvious and Victoria returned her smile.

Sir Aubrey claimed Victoria's arm, leaving Lord Damion to escort his mother and Margaret. As they went into the dining room, Sir Aubrey murmured, "I must again revise my original opinion about you, Lady Victoria. Your performance at the pianoforte must lay to rest any doubts I may have had about your upbringing. I approve of good breeding."

"I am overwhelmed, Sir Aubrey,," said Victoria with a touch of sarcasm. He let out a bark of laugher, admiring her spirit.

Margaret made certain that she had a place next to Lord Damion. She was pleased when Victoria was seated somewhat down the table. Anticipating the opportunity to claim Lord Damion's attention for herself, she was prepared to enjoy the meal.

When Sir Aubrey had seated Victoria, he glanced around and testily demanded, "Where is Evelyn? If we are to have a damned formal luncheon, the least he—"

"I am here, sir. And I have brought Doro with me." Evelyn tenderly seated a small young woman whose slim figure was slightly thickened with her pregnancy. He took his place beside her. Sir Aubrey stared at them, his ire cut off in midstream. His daughter-in-law greeted the gathering in her soft pleasant voice and he snorted.

Twelve

Victoria curiously studied the young woman and thought she had never seen anyone who better fitted the description of an angel. Dorothea St. Claire had soft brown hair and a fawn's gentle brown eyes. Her face was heart-shaped and her hands and wrists were delicately formed.

She apparently felt Victoria's regard and turned to her with a smile. "I must thank you once more for your encouragement last evening, Cousin Victoria. It meant much to me and to Eve. I hope that we may become much better acquainted while we are both here."

"I would like that, Mrs. St. Claire," said Victoria, warmed by the girl's genuine friendliness.

"Pray call me Doro. Everyone does, you know," said Dorothea.

"I shall remember to do so," said Victoria.

Sir Aubrey leaned toward them. "I am happy that you are well enough to join us, girl. You've a bit of healthy color in your cheeks today. I am glad to see it."

"Thank you, sir," said Dorothea softly. Evelyn drew her attention to the soup and vegetables. She nodded, allowing him to serve her. When he pressed her too hard to accept greater portions, she stopped him with a gentle word.

Evelyn eventually left Doro to her meal and leaned past her to talk to Victoria. "What did you think of Starfire, cousin?"

"She is a beauty," said Victoria with quick enthusiasm. "I only wish that I could see her in action."

Catching their conversation, Lord Damion said, "Lady Victoria has won over John Dickens, Evelyn. That should tell you something about her knowledge of horses."

"I should say it does! Why, crusty old John detests women anywhere near his stables," exclaimed Evelyn in awe.

"A triumph indeed, my dear," said Lady Hortense humorously, raising a general laugh.

Margaret was piqued that Victoria had suddenly become the center of attention, and especially that Lord Damion's eye should rest so warmly on her. She leaned forward. "I did not realize that you were such an animal enthusiast, Lady Victoria. But I suppose that is a requirement when one is raised in the tail of the army."

Evelyn reddened and started to rise, but Dorothea stayed him with a firm hand on his arm. "Let our cousin handle Margaret," she whispered.

Victoria was calm. "Good horseflesh has always been of concern in military circles, Mrs. Giddings, and so to me."

"Indeed. Your devotion is admirable," Margaret said with amused superiority. "I would not be at all surprised to learn that you had gone down to the stables even before breakfast. For my part, I could not have swallowed a morsel after tramping through a smelly stable." She shuddered fastidiously.

"I had quite finished breakfast when Lord Damion offered to show the mare to me," said Victoria easily. She had the satisfaction of seeing a spark of vivid anger flare in Margaret Giddings's eyes.

Evelyn relaxed in his chair, grinning. Doro was right, he thought. Cousin Victoria would do. He caught Lord Damion's eyes on him and immediately asked him what he thought the chances of grouse hunting would be later in the week.

Sir Aubrey's sharp eyes caught the expression of impotent fury on the Giddings woman's face. His eyelids drooped and he smiled thinly. "That's the way of it, then?" he murmured. To Victoria, he said,

"I understand that Charles was quite a decent scribbler. He came by the talent naturally, you know, for a number of his forebearers fancied themselves artistic."

"Quite true," said Lady Hortense, nodding. "My own grandmother painted. Indeed, there is a rather good portrait that she did of Robert and me as children that is hanging in the long gallery. You must see it one day, Lady Victoria."

"I should like to very much," said Victoria, honestly interested.

"I offered yesterday to show you the portrait gallery and I perceive that my instincts were correct. You are naturally curious about Charles and his family background." Lord Damion smiled down the table at Victoria.

Margaret lightly touched his arm to regain his attention. "I, too, am fond of portraits, my lord. I would be delighted if you would condescend to treat me to a personal tour."

"Of course, ma'am. I shall give the grand tour to you and Lady Victoria after luncheon," Lord Damion said.

Margaret turned her shoulder on him, irritated. She had a sudden inspiration. "Evelyn, why do you not join us? We will make a party of it." She congratulated herself on her quick wit. Once in the gallery it would be a simple matter to palm off Lady Victoria on Evelyn so that she could have Lord Damion to herself.

Dorothea saw that Evelyn was about to refuse. "You know that you do not care for sitting about, Eve, and that is all I shall do today. Pray don't refuse on my account, for Aunt Hortense and I shall be quite cozy with our sewing. She is helping me with a christening dress, you know."

"All right, then," Evelyn said.

After luncheon the four made their way through a couple of halls into the oldest part of the manor. The long gallery was a drafty room with tall slanting windows on the outside wall. Rows of portraits hung opposite the windows. The visitors' footsteps and voices echoed.

"I can remember as a boy when the gallery was used for formal balls," said Lord Damion. "The musicians played at the far end and the dancers filled the room from end to end. Once the press was so great that several of the windows were opened to let in cooler air."

"How magnificent it must have been! Would it not be glorious to see the gallery that way again, my lord?" asked Margaret, looking with laughing eyes up into Lord Damion's face. He returned her smile. She sensed the moment that his gaze dropped to the low front of her gown and breathed deeply, accentuating the swell of her creamy breasts.

"How would you know about the windows being opened, St. Claire?" asked Evelyn with a grin.

Margaret felt a flash of impatience when Lord Damion's eyes traveled past her to his cousin. "I was in the garden at the time, hiding in a tree where I could watch the party. Imagine my dismay when Lord Robert came out for a breath of air and chose to stop under my tree," Lord Damion reminisced. "I was naturally petrified and prayed earnestly for the opportunity to regain the safety of my room without discovery." Evelyn and Victoria burst into laughter.

"How provoking, to be sure," said Margaret. She slid her hand around Lord Damion's elbow. "Pray do show me that large portrait, Lord Damion. The gentleman is so fearsomely handsome!" Lord Damion obligingly escorted her toward the portrait indicated, leaving Victoria and Evelyn to follow.

Evelyn grimaced and said softly, "Margaret is truly a wonder to observe. I had heard she is called the Fatal Beauty in London and I now understand why. But I would lay a monkey that St. Claire is too wily to be taken in by her tricks. He has been on the town for years."

"Mrs. Giddings is certainly beautiful, but why is she called the Fatal Beauty?" asked Victoria.

"The Honorable Peter Giddings was known never

to have been ill a day in his life, and yet within a year of marriage to the Beauty he died of apoplexy," said Evelyn, and with a wicked grin added, "one night while at home with his loving wife. That was when Margaret became known as the Fatal Beauty."

Victoria's brown eyes danced. "I see. Her sobriquet must be something of a trial to Mrs. Giddings."

Evelyn shrugged. "I imagine rather that she takes pride in it. After all, it gains her the attention she craves. I pitied Peter, you know. I doubt if he felt a moment's security about his wife's loyalty once his old bachelor uncle married."

"Whatever do you mean?" asked Victoria curiously despite herself.

"Only that Peter's worth as a husband dropped tenfold in Margaret's eyes. He had been heir to the old man's title and wealth. That all ended when the old gentleman suddenly married a woman years younger than himself and begat a son," said Evelyn.

"Surely you are not serious!" exclaimed Victoria. "Marrying for convenience is common, of course, but to be so cold-blooded . . ."

Evelyn laughed. "Cousin Victoria, my sister-in-law was definitely among that number. From her point of view it was a very convenient match. Peter was young, handsome, and well off in his own right. And one day he was certain to inherit a title. But she did not count on fate intervening in her happiness so thoroughly. Margaret has been out of widow's weeds for three years now. I suspect she has taken the time not only to lick her wounds but to choose her next husband more carefully." His eyes held a speculative gleam as he gazed at the couple moving ahead of them past the various portraits. "St. Claire embodies everything that Margaret desires, except for his well-earned reputation. But now he is to be the next Earl of March. I wonder if the one counterbalances the other?"

Victoria had listened to Evelyn in horrified fascination. "Evelyn, I cannot believe that you speak this way of your own sister-in-law, and to a comparative stranger at that!"

"You're one of the family now, cousin, and I know full well that Margaret dislikes you intensely because St. Claire has shown a healthy interest in you," said Evelyn. The blood rushed to Victoria's face and he grinned. "I suspect that you are not unaware of the situation."

"Sometimes, Evelyn, you are uncannily like your father," said Victoria shortly. He was startled, but not displeased by the comparison.

Lord Damion looked back at them. "Lady Victoria, this next portrait should be of particular interest to you. It is of Charles as a boy."

Victoria quickly joined him and Margaret before a tall canvas. She looked up at the merry young face and tousled fair hair. She felt shock like a physical blow.

Lord Damion was astonished when Victoria's face turned chalk white. He saw her sway and swiftly caught her arm. "Lady Victoria! Are you all right?"

Dazed, Victoria looked up at him. Her eyes focused on the hard line of his mouth and she shivered. "Of course, my lord," she said faintly. "Of course I am."

Lord Damion stared keenly at her. He had felt her shudder and knew that she operated under some strong emotion that he could not define. "I think that you should sit down."

Despite Victoria's feeble protest he took her across the narrow room to seat her on a settee. Evelyn and Margaret trailed along after them. The latter was furious about her rival's unexpected performance. "I quite admire your sensibility, dear Lady Victoria. It speaks volumes when one is overcome by a childhood portrait of one's husband," she said.

Evelyn took his sister-in-law's arm and firmly led her away. "Come along, Margaret. I'll show you one of Lord Robert's great-great-grandmothers who was burned as a witch. Odd, she looked amazingly like you."

"You are a cad, Evelyn," said Margaret crossly.

"Thank God," sighed Victoria. She leaned her head back against the settee and closed her eyes. She felt the cushions give as Lord Damion sat down beside her. He drew her hand into his and she allowed it to rest there.

After a moment or two Victoria straightened and started to pull her hand away. His fingers tightened and she looked up into his piercing eyes. "Pray let me go, my lord," she said breathlessly.

He did not appear to hear her request. "Why did Charles's portrait affect you so, my lady?"

Her eyes seemed to look beyond him. "Charles's hair was dark when I met him. I did not know that he was blond as a child. But his eyes, that expression!" She glanced at him and snapped back to reality. "Forgive me, my lord. I can hardly convey to you how disconcerting it was. I have never seen a portrait of Charles, except in a locket that he gave me."

"I can understand, I think. The portrait is very well done. You probably felt as though you were seeing a ghost of him," said Lord Damion. She did not answer. He rose and drew her to her feet. "I believe we have toured enough of the gallery for one afternoon."

Victoria quickly put a hand on his sleeve. "Oh no! I should very much like to continue."

He looked at her searchingly. "Are you certain, my lady? You have sustained quite a shock."

"I am quite recovered, I assure you. I shall not embarrass you again, my lord."

"I am not so easily embarrassed." Lord Damion smiled and drew her hand over his elbow. "Very well, madame. I shall treat you to a scandalizing commentary on each and every ancestor who has the misfortune to fall under my stern gaze."

Victoria laughed. Her eyes dancing, she said, "I know that I shall find it most edifying, Lord Damion."

Several paces away from them, Margaret heard her laughter and turned. She frowned at the sight of Lord Damion escorting Lady Victoria slowly down the gallery in the opposite direction. "Come, Evelyn. It is time to rejoin Lord Damion. Lady Victoria is obviously much recovered." She felt annoyed that she had so greatly underestimated her rival.

Evelyn kept a firm hold on her slim arm. "I think not, Margaret. You've done enough damage with your spiteful tongue for one afternoon. You'll stay with me."

Margaret's eyes sparkled like fiery amethysts. "Who are you to order me about?"

Evelyn laughed at her. "Pray do throw one of your spectacular tantrums, Margaret. I should enjoy St. Claire's expression of disgust."

Margaret was firmly trapped and she knew it. She stamped her foot in vexation. "You are the vilest creature alive!"

"You will forget all about it once we begin looking at the portraits," said Evelyn cheerfully.

"I don't care a rap about some idiotic ancestral portraits!" exclaimed Margaret wrathfully. Evelyn paid her no heed, but led her further away from Lord Damion and Victoria.

Victoria spent the next hour very pleasantly as Lord Damion regaled her with tales of intrigue and roguery. When they had reached the gallery's end, she could only shake her head at his inventiveness. "Charles never once let on that he was descended from such a very wicked family," she said, laughing.

"Ah, even so, we are not entirely without our black sheep, my lady," said Lord Damion with mock seriousness.

"No?" Victoria asked, suspecting him of further nonsense.

He gestured broadly at the small portrait before them. "Study this old gentleman well, my lady. Take note of his noble brow and compassionate gaze, but do not be fooled. He is still the shame of the family after five hundred years."

"But whatever did he do?" Victoria asked, astonished by Lord Damion's perfectly grave words.

"He was called William the Good," Lord Damion

94

said simply. He was rewarded with a sputtering laugh and grinned at her.

"You quite took me in, my lord!" Victoria said.

Lord Damion raised her hand to his lips. His eyes gleamed with a devilish light. "It is surely to my credit, my lady, as I may claim kinship with this wicked family."

Under Lord Damion's compelling gaze, Victoria felt oddly light-headed. She fancied that she was drifting gently into uncharted waters with him and she swiftly sought safe anchorage in the mundane. "I am truly grateful for your understanding, my lord. You have quite chased away any lingering shadows," she said.

Lord Damion was struck again by the rare beauty that lighted her face when she smiled. He now thought it little wonder that Charles March had given her more than a passing glance. "I am happy to have been of service, Lady Victoria. I wish only that I had known my cousin Charles better in recent years. He was obviously a fortunate man in his marriage."

Victoria lowered her eyes in a momentary confusion. Lord Damion had the most disconcerting habit of paying her a compliment when she was least expecting it. It occurred to her that his charm was but a tool of the trade for a successful rake and the whimical thought made her smile. His words had reminded her of Lord Robert's hope of bringing Charles back home through her, and though Victoria could not see her way clear to agree to Sir Aubrey's proposal, there was perhaps another way to fulfill Lord Robert's wishes. "I have Charles's sketch case containing his last drawings with me. Pray let me present it to you and the rest of the family," Victoria said.

Lord Damion's astonishment was plain. "That is generous of you, but we could not take such a keepsake from you, my lady!"

Victoria shook her head. "My lord, I have many other drawings that Charles did." She touched his sleeve and met his grave look with an earnest air. "It would give me great satisfaction, my lord. Pray allow me to give at least that much of Charles back to his family."

Lord Damion carried her hand to his lips. "Your generosity does you credit, Lady Victoria. I accept your gift in humble gratitude and I know that we shall all want to study Charles's sketches closely."

"What's that you say, St. Claire? Has Cousin Victoria actually brought some of Charles's sketches with her?" Evelyn asked.

Lord Damion and Victoria turned at Evelyn's query to find him and Margaret approaching. Lord Damion unhurriedly stepped back a pace from Victoria. "Yes, Evelyn. Lady Victoria has generously offered to present Charles's sketch case with his last drawings to the family."

"Oh I say! That's famous!" exclaimed Evelyn. His eyes were alight when he turned to Victoria. "When can we view them, cousin?"

An expression of annoyance crossed Margaret's face at this fresh bid for attention from Lady Victoria. The woman was really quite clever and was becoming something of an irritant, she thought.

Victoria laughed at Evelyn's boyish enthusiasm. "I shall ask Mary to unpack the sketch case and while we are at dinner bring it down to the sitting room afterwards."

Lord Damion drew out his pocket watch and commented that it was already time to change for dinner. Margaret at once claimed his arm. "For I swear that I should be positively lost without someone to guide me back to the main hall, my lord," she said with a little laugh.

Lord Damion was willing to act the part of guide and together they exited the gallery, leaving Victoria and Evelyn to trail behind once more. Leaning close to Victoria's ear, Evelyn said, "I almost wish that I were Margaret's escort. I could have shown her such a roundabout way that she would never have forgotten it." Victoria only shook her head at him, amused.

Thirteen

Over dinner, Evelyn announced the treat that was in store for them. Lady Hortense turned to Victoria, who was startled to see tears in her faded blue eyes. "My dear, that is so very generous of you."

"So it is. I believe that we are all discovering that our new cousin is an unusual woman," said Lord Damion, a certain warmth in his gaze as he smiled across the table at Victoria.

Seated beside him, Margaret fiddled irritably with the silver bracelet on her wrist. Her sojourn at the Crossing was not going altogether as she had planned. She had hoped to bring Lord Damion to the point of marriage by this time, but instead she had been consistently upstaged by this stranger from Portugal. She critically studied Lady Victoria and wondered, not for the first time, how someone so unremarkable in appearance could prove so skillful a rival. For she hoped she was not such a fool as to believe that Lady Victoria did not cherish hopes of Lord Damion for herself. Lady Victoria had succeeded in stealing the limelight too often for it to have been coincidental. Margaret even had to admit she held grudging respect for the woman. Lady Victoria's pretense of fainting at the sight of her husband's childhood portrait had been a masterful stroke. And now there was this business of the sketch case.

Margaret glanced at the handsome profile of the man beside her. No, Lady Victoria undoubtedly saw opportunity when it was before her eyes. Margaret's soft lips tightened. But however clever Lady Victoria thought herself to be, she would not walk away with the prize. Margaret intended to see to that. She had taken great pains with her attire for that evening. She was wearing a gown of watered silk that perfectly matched the violet of her eyes and that clung enticingly to her exquisite figure. Margaret, not trusting the maid given her, had herself dressed her hair in a cascade of gleaming black curls that brushed over one bare shoulder. She was satisfied that no sketch case could possibly draw attention away from her.

Margaret touched Lord Damion's sleeve to gain his attention. On the pretense of directing an amusing tale to his ear alone, she leaned slightly forward so that he could not fail to notice her cleavage.

As he listened, Lord Damion's eyes strayed occasionally from Margaret's animated face to the revealing cut of her gown. Under her gaze her smooth rounded bosom rose and fell slowly, stirring him. It was not the first time since coming to the Crossing that Lord Damion admitted to himself that Margaret Giddings attracted him. He had known almost from the first that she would not spurn his advances if he cared to approach her. But for some reason he could not explain, he had held back. Perhaps it was because the excitement of the chase was missing.

Down the table Sir Aubrey could not fail to note the lengthy animated conversation between his nephew and Margaret Giddings. He did not bother to hide his irritation. "Damn the woman!" he uttered softly as his sharp eyes saw the direction of Lord Damion's glance. He thought he could guess what was on his nephew's mind.

Sir Aubrey turned glittering eyes on Lady Victoria. Surely she could see what was happening. If she didn't pay attention, the Giddings woman was going to outplay her. He saw Victoria glance at the couple across the table. Then she must have felt his gaze because she looked straight at him. Sir Aubrey was astonished by the amusement in her dark eyes. Lady Victoria turned to address a remark to Lord Damion and Margaret Giddings, effectively joining in their conversation. Observing it, Sir Aubrey could not help the faint upward turn of his mouth. He thought he had just witnessed one of the smoothest maneuvers of his wide experience.

After dinner the gentlemen did not spend long over their wine, but instead joined the ladies in the drawing room. Anticipation was high as Victoria handed a worn leather sketch case to Lady Hortense. "He spoke of you with affection, ma'am. I think you should be the first to open it," she said.

"Oh, my dear," said Lady Hortense with a speaking look. She opened the sketch case and brought out a handful of loose drawings. She handed them to Dorothea, who sat beside her on the sofa, while Evelyn leaned over the back. "There is a sketch pad as well," said Lady Hortense. She began to leaf through the pages.

"Do but look, Evelyn! One can even see the trim on the ladies' hats," exclaimed Dorothea, entranced.

Hardly hearing her, Evelyn was staring at another drawing. He whistled slowly. "Charles certainly knew his trade. This cavalry charge looks damnably real. St. Claire, you will be certain to recognize this business."

The drawings were quickly distributed around, and even Margaret felt herself drawn by curiosity. Finally the sketch pad made the rounds. Victoria was besieged for explanations and hardly had a spare moment to look at the drawings in her own hands. The drawings were a random collection of scenes drawn from military life and Lisbon society with a few portraits thrown in. As she described the scenes and named the people, Victoria found her mind flooded with memories.

Lord Damion held up a swiftly done portrait of almost rough vibrancy. "Who is this rugged gentleman?" he asked curiously. The man's dark eyes stared boldly from a face of strong lines and only a faint touch of humor softened the harshness of his expression.

Victoria smiled in recognition. "That is Carlos Silva y Montoya." Her voice held respect and even pride.

"I remember that you mentioned the name before. I believe you said that he helped your father in his horse breeding. He was obviously a very old and valued friend."

"Yes," said Victoria. Her attention was then claimed by a brusque demand from Sir Aubrey for information on a sketch.

Margaret remained beside Lord Damion throughout the entire evening and thought she had done fairly well in holding his interest despite the novelty of the sketches. But as he studied each drawing, he seemed to grow ever more distant to her and did not respond as readily to her witticisms. She became increasingly frustrated as the moment passed.

Lord Damion's memories of his own participation in the Peninsular War were rekindled by many of the sketches of the familiar Portuguese scenes. But it was the portrait of Carlos Silva y Montoya that most captured his interest. He studied the portrait once more, feeling for some odd reason that the man was somehow familiar to him.

Eventually the novelty of the drawings wore off and Lady Hortense gathered them together. "Thank you, dear Lady Victoria. This has been a very special evening," she said softly.

"I am only happy that I was able to make it so," said Victoria warmly.

Evelyn challenged his cousin to a game of billiards and Lord Damion good-naturedly accepted. Margaret was chagrined to find herself truly abandoned. Sir Aubrey demanded that the card table be set up and at his insistence a card party was got up. When he called on Victoria for a partner, she firmly declined and suggested Dorothea in her place. Dorothea accepted with clarity and Sir Aubrey was forced to accept her, though he did so with ill grace. Lady Hortense and Margaret made up the rest of the party.

Left to herself, Victoria took the drawings back

out of the case so she could look at them at her leisure and without interruption. As she lingered over several, a smile sometimes flitted over her features. She was unaware that Lord Damion glanced her way often.

It was after eleven when the card game broke up, Sir Aubrey and Dorothea emerging the winners. He was in a cheerful mood and even went so far as to compliment Dorothea on her shrewd play. "You've some card sense in that pretty little head. I've always liked women who could hold their own in a friendly game with the pasteboards," he said gruffly.

Dorothea looked up at him in great amusement. "I am happy that I have met with your approval, sir." She excused herself and joined Evelyn with the remark that it was very late. He immediately took the gentle hint and offered to escort her upstairs. Their exit became the signal for the evening to end and the rest of the company soon found their own beds.

Fourteen

The maid was pulling back the curtains to reveal a leaden sky when Victoria woke early the following morning.

"Good morning, m'lady," said Mary cheerfully. "I 'ave taken the liberty of ordering a bath for your ladyship. I hope I did right."

Victoria stretched under the bedclothes. "Oh yes, Mary! A bath will be marvelous."

Delighted that she had correctly anticipated her new mistress's needs, Mary said eagerly, "I 'ave towels and a robe ready, m'lady, and if your ladyship should care for it, I shall order up a cup of chocolate."

Victoria laughed and shook her head as she got out of bed. "Coffee would suit me better, Mary. I fear I am unfashionable in that I dislike anything sweet when I rise." As she spoke, Victoria crossed the room to the fireplace. She stepped behind the screen that had been placed around it to capture the heat from the fire and ward off any drafts. A brass hip bath filled with warm water stood in front of the fire.

Victoria dropped her chemise to the carpet and stepped naked into the hip bath. She slid down into the warm scented water until it lapped under her chin. "I cannot begin to tell you how marvelous this is, Mary. You are truly a jewel."

The maid flushed at her praise and picked up the discarded chemise. "Thank you, m'lady. Is there aught else your ladyship will be needing at the moment?"

Victoria smiled up at the eager young face. "You have amply cared for me, Mary. Thank you."

The maid bobbed a curtsy and left her mistress alone. Victoria found the washcloth and soap and sudsed herself thoroughly. She could very easily become used to such service, she admitted to herself. She had always had at least one servant, but never a lady's maid. When she returned to Portugal she would engage the services of a personal dresser. She could afford it. The breeding stables that her dear father established had prospered under her and Charles, especially since the British army so desperately needed mounts that could survive the Portuguese climate.

As she washed her hair Victoria wondered if Mary would consider accompanying her when she returned to Lisbon. She voiced her thoughts a little while later when the maid returned to pour rinse water over her head. "What do you think, Mary? Would you like to return to Portugal with me? I promise you all the comforts of home," said Victoria, accepting the towel that Mary handed her.

"Oh m'lady, I couldn't say. I've family here and all," stammered Mary. She said hurriedly, "But I am that honored your ladyship thought enough of me, I'm sure."

"I shan't be returning home for some little time, so you shall have awhile to think about it," said Victoria. "I won't press you for an answer now."

"Thank you, m'lady," said Mary gratefully. She heard a knock on the door. "That'll be your ladyship's coffee." Bobbing a quick curtsy, she hurried out from behind the screen.

Victoria slipped into her thin undergarments and stockings. Mary had thoughtfully laid the dressing gown over the back of a chair where it could be warmed by the fire's heat and Victoria put it on, belting the robe loosely around her trim waist.

As she came from around the screen she heard Mary exclaim, "Ye cannot, m'lord. M'lord!"

Startled, Victoria found herself looking directly into Lord Damion's gray eyes. Mary hovered behind him, making distressed noises and wringing her hands. Unconsciously Victoria clutched tight the front of her dressing gown.

"Perish the thought, Lady Victoria." Lord Damion's glance raked over her slim figure and he suddenly grimed. A wicked light dancing in his eyes, he said, "But I must admit that as a rake I find the temptation hard to withstand."

Victoria flushed bright scarlet. Her stomach tightened with half-pleasant suspense. With all the dignity she could muster, she said strongly, "What the devil are you doing in my room, Lord Damion?"

Lord Damion allowed his gaze to linger a moment longer on her body before he met the molten gold sparks in her eyes. "It is as you predicted. Starfire is foaling early."

Victoria nodded affably. "Of course. Your presence is now made perfectly clear. You did not think a polite message given through my maid to be sufficiently dramatic. So you decided to deliver it personally."

Lord Damion blinked at her, then flushed under his tan. "My apologies, Lady Victoria. I shall await you more correctly in the hall." He sketched a bow and turned on his heel to leave the room.

Mary closed the door behind him with a decided snap. "Well! Ye certainly taught him, m'lady. To think he came in bold as brass with your ladyship but half dressed. I'll never fathom the gentlemen, I'm sure."

Trembling in reaction, Victoria laughed. The little knot of tension eased in her stomach. She could not remember the last time a man had affected her so. "I don't believe any of us ever understand them, Mary. But help me now quickly. My lord was right; I do want to see Starfire."

Mary ran to the wardrobe to fulfill her mistress's requirements. Ten minutes later Victoria was attired in a serviceable riding habit and sturdy boots. She threw a cloak over her arm and went into the hall to join Lord Damion.

As he took her arm to escort her, Lord Damion spared her a brief glance and was surprised by her composure. She meet his eyes with no hint of any discomfort over his visit to her room. Only her still-damp curls betrayed the haste with which she had dressed. Again Lady Victoria had proven to be disturbingly unpredictable. Unused as he was to such rejection, her setdown had caught him totally off guard.

Without a word Lord Damion ushered her swiftly through the halls. Victoria found that she was forced to lengthen her stride to keep up with him and thought of pointing it out to him. But a swift upward glance at his frowning expression kept her silent. She was hardly one to beg for a man's indulgence. She had fought for and won an independence in her life that few women ever attained.

They exited the manor from the small side door that they had used on their last visit to the stables and crossed the uneven ground of the yard. Lord Damion opened the stable door. Victoria slipped inside and pasued to allow her eyes to adjust to the gloom while Lord Damion let the door fall closed. He stepped past her, calling out for the stable master.

John Dickens's head appeared over the top of a large stall and he waved. "Over here, m'lord."

Lord Damion and Victoria went swiftly to the stall. The stable master touched his forehead in deference to her ladyship and promptly launched into his report. Victoria listened with half an ear, her eyes on the mare's heaving sides. A stableboy was in attendance, holding the mare's head.

In a corner of the stall was a tiny dark form, and even as John mentioned the foal and its slim chances of survival, Victoria had already realized what it was. Before the men knew what she was about, Victoria was on her knees beside the foal.

" 'Ere now!" exclaimed John, dismayed to see a lady of quality sitting in the straw.

Victoria disregarded him, her attention focused on the foal. She felt its trembling weakness. "This one needs nourishment immediately." She shot an eagle look at the gaping stableboy. "You there! Bring a bucket of milk, diluted with water, and a handful of sugar. And you will need a clean cloth. Now go!"

The stableboy hesitated, casting a look for guidance to the stable master, who motioned for him to do as the lady required. "I know what ye would do, m'lady, but the fact is the colt be too weak to nurse," said John.

"We shall see," said Victoria.

He shook his head over her stubborn tone and exchanged a look with Lord Damion that spoke volumes.

"Let her try, John," Lord Damion said quietly.

When the stableboy returned, Victoria instructed him quickly and concisely on how to feed the colt. While the stableboy made his preparations, she stroked the foal, then joined Lord Damion and John Dickens with Starfire.

The mare's condition had worsened; and she was still laboring to no avail. Victoria ran her hands over the mares sides with swift assurance. "The second one is turned some way. I can feel a hoof here," she said. "We shall have to turn it before it can be born. You and my lord shall have to do it, Dickens. It requires strength."

The stable master eyed her in growing respect. "Aye, m'lady." He waited a few moments until he realized that she had no intention of leaving. He threw an entreating look at Lord Damion. "M'lord, it isn't seemly!"

Lord Damion, who had removed his coat and rolled up his sleeves, gently touched Victoria on the shoulder. "Perhaps it would be best if you waited outside, Lady Victoria. This is no place for a lady."

Victoria shook off his hand. "Pray do not be ridiculous," she said impatiently. "I have witnessed hundreds of foalings. I shall hold her head and you help Dickens." As he began to remonstrate, she looked up with a challenge in her steady eyes. "Wrangling over my presence shall profit us nothing, my lord, and will most certainly reduce Starfire's chances of survival."

Lord Damion nodded, recognizing her determination. "However, I shall not pick you up should you faint, my lady," he said grimly. He took his position beside the stable master with the mare.

For the next half hour the gentleman and the stable master labored together. At the end, another living foal lay in the straw and the tired mare was resting peacefully. Victoria rose stiffly to shake the straw from her skirt. "Well, John Dickens, I know now why my lord places such implicit trust in your judgment."

"Thank you, m'lady," said the stable master with quiet respect.

"M'lady!" Victoria turned. The stableboy's face was split in a wide grin. "See, he is sucking." The colt had its head in the bucket, sucking vigorously from the stableboy's cloth-wrapped fingers that were held submerged in the sweetened milk.

"Come, Lady Victoria. I think it time that we left John and his men to do their work," said Lord

Damion. He had washed off his hands and arms in a bucket of clean water and now donned his coat.

"I will come willingly, sir," said Victoria.

Lord Damion escorted her from the stable. Victoria put back her head to breathe deeply of the clean air. "Isn't it a glorious morning!" she exclaimed.

Lord Damion concurred, hardly able to take his eyes from her vibrant eyes and the smooth curve of her cheek. He had never known a woman who could be at once so frank and so intriguing. He reached up to pluck a stray straw out of her hair and grinned. "Straw becomes you, madame, but I fear that others would not regard it lightly when you have been in my company all the morning."

Victoria felt herself reddening and to cover her sudden confusion said flippantly, "Innocence is forever suspect in the eyes of others. I perceive that a rake's lot is a hard one, my lord!" She was busily brushing off her skirt once more and did not see her companion's startled face.

Lord Damion schooled his expression and when Victoria looked up again she saw only his amusement. "You are an extraordinary woman, Lady Victoria," he said, and left it at that as he escorted her back into the manor. He spoke only of Starfire and her foals on the short trip through the side passage to the main hall.

Evelyn hailed them from the open door of the sitting room where he was engaged in a solitary game of billiards. "Cousin Victoria, St. Claire! I heard that Starfire was foaling this morning. Have you seen the colt?"

"I shall be with you in a moment, Evelyn," said Lord Damion. He turned to Victoria, who had started up the stairs. Raising her hand to his lips, he said, "Allow me to thank you for your capable assistance this morning, my lady."

"I would not have missed it, my lord," said Victoria with a mischievous light in her eyes.

Lord Damion contemplated her a moment, then said abruptly, "You were magnificent." Victoria stared at him, startled. He stepped back to bow to her and then crossed the hall to join Evelyn.

Victoria turned to resume her ascent of the stairs and her eyes met Margaret's frozen face. The woman had obviously heard the exchange between her and Lord Damion. Victoria could not help being glad, for she thought the woman's arrogance intolerable, but offered a civil greeting and immediately forgot Margaret as her thoughts settled happily on Starfire and her foals. When she reached her door, she discovered that Margaret had followed her.

"You have created a niche for yourself very quickly, Lady Victoria," Margaret said. "I must certainly congratulate you on your superior tactics."

Victoria's brows rose. "I beg your pardon?"

Margaret laughed spitefully. "Come now, Lady Victoria. You have been here but a few days and already you have two staunch allies. It was a stroke of genius to make yourself friendly to poor Doro, for Evelyn will defend the basest creature on the road if Doro feels kindly toward it. And Sir Aubrey has let his partiality for Charles March blind him to your duplicity. He is truly a senile fool."

"Mrs. Giddings, you are speaking of our host," said Victoria levelly. She did not much care for Sir Aubrey herself, but it was beyond good *ton* at once to accept his hospitality and to tear him down behind his back.

Margaret snapped her fingers. "I give that for Sir Aubrey. He is nothing to me." Her eyes narrowed. "However, Lord Damion is a different matter. These pretty tales you have spun about Charles March and his sketches were clever. Even Sir Aubrey stayed awake long enough to listen. But you will need more than imagined nonsense about a dead cousin to hold Lord Damion's interest for long, my lady!"

Victoria put her hand on her doorknob. "I perceive that we are about to cover the same ground that we did during your nocturnal visit, so I shan't detain you. Good day, Mrs. Giddings."

She opened the door and started through, but

108

Margaret pulled her around by the arm. "You and your fine airs!" she hissed. "I'll not be outdone by a common army baggage. You may have fooled the others for now, but inevitably you shall make a fatal error, my fine lady, and then I shall enjoy watching your speedy departure."

Victoria looked at her coolly. "How extremely vulgar you are, Mrs. Giddings. I'm not at all surprised that my presence arouses such jealousy in you, for Lord Damion strikes me as a man who would prefer a lady to a shrew."

Margaret stared at her, amazed, then suddenly threw back her head in a peal of laughter. When she looked again at Victoria, her violet eyes were contemptuous. "I? Jealous of a drab creature like you! You poor fool, what have you to offer the Demon? I can speak from experience, my lady. Lord Damion prefers a sophisticated woman who is prepared to satisfy his every whim. Believe me, my dear, you hardly qualify."

Victoria felt a surge of anger impossible to contain. She said hastily, "And certainly your own vast experience qualifies you to satisfy a rakehell. Or any other man, for that matter!"

Margaret gasped. "How dare you—" She slapped Victoria hard across the cheek. "Leave this house at once!"

Victoria immediately slapped her back, hard enough to rock her on her heels. Margaret stared at her with shocked eyes, one hand shielding her stinging cheek.

Victoria's eyes blazed, yet she spoke softly. "Do not ever again presume to deal me such treatment, madame. I will not tolerate it. Furthermore, I shall interact with whomever I choose in this house. And pray spare yourself further humiliation and recall in the future that I am a member of this household while you are the guest!" She turned on her heel and slammed the bedroom door in the woman's face.

Her face was flushed and her breast rose swift with her anger as she met her maid's half-frightened eyes. Victoria forced a laugh. "I do apologize, Mary.

You must have heard every word. You must believe me a perfect savage."

"Oh no!" exclaimed Mary. "Your ladyship was wonderful. Ye have set madame in her place proper."

Victoria accepted the little maid's help in unbuttoning her dress. "I take it that you do not care for Mrs. Giddings, Mary?"

"Oh, nobbut does, m'lady," said Mary earnestly. "She is always wanting this or the other done and never satisfied. Not at all like your ladyship, to be sure. It was a good day when madame's own dresser finally came. We had all come to fear that she had run off, belike!"

Victoria burst out laughing. "Oh Mary, you do have the knack of restoring my good humor."

"Aye, m'lady," said Mary agreeably, though unsure what she had said that had restored her ladyship's spirits. After Victoria had bathed in the basin, Mary efficiently helped her to change into a soft lavender gown with pearl buttons. Victoria slipped her slender feet into soft kid slippers and sat down at the vanity so Mary could brush her hair. The maid was giving a last pat to Victoria's short curly hair when the luncheon bell rang.

Victoria rose from her seat and gave Mary a quiet dismissal. Her expression was composed and her appearance impeccable. No one could have guessed that under the surface her anger still smoldered. The more Victoria had thought about her confrontation with Mrs. Giddings, the more she realized that she was not so much bothered by the woman's spite as by her contempt.

Victoria felt sorely tempted to show the woman up. She knew she could capture Lord Damion's interest if she wished, for she thought she understood that gentleman very well. *And I can feel you urging me to it, dear Charles. You always were one for a challenge,* thought Victoria dryly. But Lord Damion was not a man to be idly trifled with. Victoria had once been recipient of his wrath and she did not want to be so again. She would need to tread warily with that gentleman if she was not to arouse the demon sleeping within him.

Fifteen

On Sunday morning the family went to their first public chapel service since Lord Robert's death. Their appearance caused a stir in the congregation.

Sir Aubrey haughtily ignored the curious glances that followed him as he escorted Lady Hortense to the March family pew. Lord Damion followed with Victoria and there were whispers as several individuals recognized him. "But whoever is that with him? Surely he has not married?" asked one lady of another. Her neighbor intimated that perhaps Lord Damion's companion was one of those Cyprians that they had heard about. The first lady drew her breath in sharply and frankly stared at Victoria.

Evelyn and Margaret brought up the rear. Dorothea had felt unwell that morning and Evelyn, resigned to his fate, escorted his sister-in-law. He would have vastly preferred his new cousin's company, but Lady Victoria March took social precedence over Margaret and so she was accompanied by Lord Damion.

Margaret liked such distinctions as little as Evelyn, but was somewhat consoled to find herself seated in the pew beside Lord Damion. Well pleased, she glanced down at her heavenly blue pelisse trimmed with black velvet ribbons. The family members all wore mourning and Lady Victoria a half-mourning gown of pale lavender velvet. Surrounded by her companions' more somber hues, Margaret stood out like a bright jewel. She knew that the contrast had excited interest in the congregation and she smilingly acknowledged the admiring glances of the gentlemen with a complete disregard for their wives' outrage.

After the service ended, several neighbors came up to offer their condolences. Lady Hortense received them gracefully.

Sir Aubrey maintained a haughty air that put off all but the stoutest characters, but even he was kind in his remarks when Squire Terrell and his lady stopped to offer their sympathy. "I appreciate your sentiments," Sir Aubrey said. "His lordship was not only my brother-in-law but my dear friend as well." His nephew and Lady Victoria were making their way past at that moment and Sir Aubrey took the opportunity to introduce Lady Victoria to the bluff squire and his wife.

The squire's heavy brows moved up and down with extraordinary rapidity as he regarded Victoria. "Charles March, heh? He was always in one scrape or another, that one. I thought it a pity when the earl cut him off without a farthing. Understandable, of course. Young March drove his lordship to fury with his wild ways. Then the boy took it into his head to join the army! His lordship could never abide the military, as young March well knew." He shook his head in remembrance. "They were forever carping at one another. It was the disgrace of the county."

Mrs. Terrell plucked at her husband's sleeve. "Now his lordship did harbor a certain affection for the young man, dear. I am sure I never saw a prouder man than his lordship when Charles March was mentioned in the dispatches."

The squire patted his wife's plump, beringed hand. "True, my dear. I had forgotten. It was an odd relationship, to be sure. His lordship was not the same man after young March was reported killed."

Just then Victoria was claimed by Lord Damion

and with relief she turned away from the squire and his lady. Lord Damion glanced down at her pensive expression and said in a low voice, "You are distressed, my lady. It was but an idle tongue, after all."

Victoria looked up into his gaze. "But how much of it was truth, my lord?" She read the answer in his eyes and sighed. "I feared as much. Charles never conveyed to me that he was as much to blame as his father's character for the breach between them."

Lord Damion paused before the open carriage door to raise her gloved hand to his lips. He held her eyes with a steady glance. "The tragedy lies in the past, my lady."

"Yes." Victoria was warmed by his lordship's sensitivity. She smiled up at him and pressed his fingers briefly. "Thank you, my lord." She turned and mounted the step into the carriage.

Lady Hortense stood close by in company with the reverend's wife. Mrs. Pherson watched with interest the quiet exchange between Lord Damion and Lady Victoria, and in particular the seeming intimacy in their clasped hands. She hoped that she was as respectful of her betters as the next person, but she had heard of Lord Damion's reputation and now felt she had proof of its truth. Mrs. Pherson had heard the gossip about how Lady Victoria March had arrived, without a female companion and in Lord Damion's company. And as for the finely tricked-out creature on Evelyn St. Claire's arm, Mrs. Pherson knew exactly what to make of her. *She* had not missed the coquettish glances that Mrs. Giddings so liberally dispensed. The woman was a born seductress, thought Mrs. Pherson with outrage.

Lord Damion turned to receive his mother. He bowed courteously to Mrs. Pherson. She nodded to him and said in freezing accents, "Good day, my lord." After saying a brief farewell to Lady Hortense, Mrs. Pherson withdrew to greet a neighbor and drop a word in her ear about what she had observed.

Lord Damion's brows rose in surprise at the woman's stiff manner. As he assisted Lady Hortense into the carriage, he asked, "What have I done to affront the good reverend's wife?"

Lady Hortense shrugged. "Oh, Adelia Pherson takes her odd humors now and then. Pray do not heed it, my dear."

"I hope I am not such a poor creature to do so, dear ma'am," retorted Lord Damion. He handed in Margaret and shut the carriage door.

Lady Hortense remarked to Victoria and Margaret as they returned home to the Crossing that they could expect the usual condolence calls to begin in a week.

"A high treat, to be sure," said Margaret, smothering a yawn.

Lady Hortense's prediction was borne out, for exactly one week later two carriages drove up to the Crossing within ten minutes of one another. The first carriage expelled Mrs. Pherson. Within five minutes, both Victoria and Margaret thoroughly detested her.

Mrs. Pherson commented disparagingly on the cost of London dresses, all the while eyeing Margaret's exquisite merino and lace gown. "For I am sure our own dressmakers are as nimble with their needles but they know better than to charge more than the gown is worth," she said. Upon being introduced to Victoria, Mrs. Pherson opined that the women who followed their husbands to war were certainly the oddest creatures. "They would do far better at home teaching their maids proper Christian thrift and humility." Even Dorothea, good-natured as she was, preferred to address her sewing rather than converse with the woman and Lady Hortense found herself upholding the other end of a laborious conversation almost single-handedly.

The second visitor was like a breath of fresh air after Mrs. Pherson. The lady was attired in a fashionably cut velvet pelisse trimmed in dark gray ribbons that won even Margaret's jaded attention. Her blue eyes sparkled with goodwill and innate merriment.

Lady Hortense greeted her with warm friendliness

and a hint of relief. "Miranda, how very nice to see you! Of course you know Mrs. Pherson." Mrs. Pherson acknowledged her with a stiff bow. "Lady Belingham, I should like you to meet my niece Dorothea St. Claire and her sister, Mrs. Margaret Giddings. And this is Lady Victoria March, who has just come to us from Portugal. She was Charles's wife, you know."

Lady Belingham nodded to Dorothea and Margaret, but she held out her hand to Victoria. "My dear! I am happy to meet you at last. Harry wrote me so many times about you and Charles. But why ever did you not let me know that you decided to visit first with Charles's family. I have been expecting you for days." Mute with astonishment, Victoria mechanically shook her hand. Lady Belingham read her expression and lowered her voice. "Is there anything wrong, Lady Victoria?"

"Oh no, ma'am." Victoria smiled, recovering from her shock. "I was but surprised for a moment, for I did not know that you had returned home."

"Whatever do you mean, my dear? I have not been away from home these past several months," said Lady Belingham, puzzled.

"I see," said Victoria. She thought she did indeed understand. Sir Aubrey had manipulated her and made a complete fool of her.

Lady Belingham, observing the gathering storm in Victoria's expressive eyes, drew her apart from the others. "Pray be seated beside me, Lady Victoria. Now explain to me why you should have thought I was away from the neighborhood."

Victoria examined her face. She saw only a kind light in Lady Belingham's eyes and was persuaded to confide in her. "A storm caused me to change my plans and stop here at the Crossing. When I informed Sir Aubrey that I was expected at Belingham Manor, he gave me to understand that you had taken your daughter to Bath. He said the trip was made to remove your daughter from an ineligible suitor and he did not know when you would return.

I consequently accepted his offer of hospitality until such time as you were again at home."

"How extraordinary! But why should he concoct such a fanciful tale?" asked Lady Belingham. She saw Victoria color and thought there was more to the story than had been divulged. She placed her hand over Victoria's fingers and squeezed them gently. "Never mind, my dear. If you should not wish to tell me, then I shall understand. Sir Aubrey is known to me only casually, but I am aware that he has odd humors."

Her soft voice held only sympathy. Victoria shook her head, tears suddenly gleaming in her eyes. "Dear Lady Belingham! I see now where Harry gets his extraordinary kindness. How could I not confide in you?" She took a deep breath and plunged into a thorough summary of her experiences since she had met Lord Damion St. Claire, including Sir Aubrey's scheme.

When she was finished, Lady Belingham blinked and could only say, "Well, well." After a few seconds of thought, she patted Victoria's hand. "You have been placed in a very awkward position indeed. Sir Aubrey is an odd creature to believe that he may force Cupid's work in such a manner. You are naturally welcome to remove to Belingham Manor whenever you wish. I will gladly send the carriage for you at a moment's notice." She directed a glance at Lady Hortense and Mrs. Pherson, who listened to her ladyship with an acid smile. "However, I do believe that to do so now would excite unwelcome talk in certain quarters that would distress dear Lady Hortense very much."

"You are right, of course, I am now caught fast. If I had removed to Belingham before the family began to receive calls, it would not have mattered," said Victoria. "But how I wish I had known before of your presence, dear ma'am! I would long since have come to you."

"You shall come to tea soon and meet Erica. Then

you may see for yourself if she is as flighty as she has been painted," said Lady Belingham.

Victoria laughed. "But it is Harry's own descriptions that led me to so readily believe Sir Aubrey, my lady."

"Then I shall have a great deal to scold him for when he comes home," said Lady Belingham, her eyes twinkling.

Dorothea caught her last words. "Oh, does your son come home soon, Lady Belingham?"

"He has written to me that he is to receive a leave of absence shortly. I shall be very glad to see him," said Lady Belingham.

"And I also. He is my very dearest friend," said Victoria.

Mrs. Pherson glanced sharply at her but remained silent as Lady Hortense began to tell Lady Belingham of the sketches that Victoria had brought to them.

Lady Belingham soon rose to take her leave and the reverend's wife reluctantly followed her example. Mrs. Pherson's small eyes avidly inspected every object and person within sight as Lady Hortense showed both ladies to the door.

"Salvation at last!" exclaimed Margaret dramatically, bringing a spontaneous laugh from Victoria and Dorothea.

On the front steps Mrs. Pherson waited until Lady Belingham had driven away before she unexpectedly clasped Lady Hortense's arm. "My dear Lady Hortense, I felt compelled to have a private word with you before I left," she said.

"Of course, Adelia," said Lady Hortense.

"Our understanding is such that I may surely unburden my heart to you without reproach," said Mrs. Pherson.

Lady Hortense regarded her with astonishment. "But of course you may."

Mrs. Pherson nodded. "Indeed, it is my duty to speak to you. I have long approved of your goodliness, but I believe your amiable nature has led you astray in this instance."

Lady Hortense was at once bewildered and amused. "Forgive me, Adelia, but I do not follow you."

"I have been reliably informed that Lady Victoria was brought to the Crossing by Lord Damion himself. I must tell you that I was shocked beyond measure," said Mrs. Pherson.

Lady Hortense thought she understood and laughed. "My dear Adelia, I assure you that whatever you may have heard was greatly distorted. While it is true that Lady Victoria did not have a maid with her—"

With a pitying smile, Mrs. Pherson interrupted her. "Dear Lady Hortense, my heart bleeds for you. It must be difficult for you, indeed. Lord Damion proves himself an utterly selfish son to introduce his paramour into your presence."

Lady Hortense gasped. "Mrs. Pherson, I assure you—"

"And that fallen woman! The instant I clapped eyes on Mrs. Giddings I knew that she was not here for the comfort of her wretched sister. She dares to parade herself in such dress that makes one blush. And such fine London airs!" Mrs. Pherson's thin mouth twisted in distaste. "I shudder to imagine the loose conversation that must grace your drawing room each evening, my lady. It is particularly repugnant that poor Mrs. St. Claire is subject to such debauchery in her blessed condition. For her sake alone, those two creatures should be routed from this house."

Lady Hortense's voice shook with anger. "Enough madame. It is all utter, despicable fiction. I shall not listen to another word. Indeed, you have outstayed your welcome, Mrs. Pherson."

"My lady, your son—" began Mrs. Pherson.

"My son is not subject to your judgment, Mrs. Pherson," said Lady Hortense coldly.

Mrs. Pherson drew herself up, affronted. "Well! I see that I have misjudged your breath of understanding, my lady." She flounced around and entered her waiting carriage. As the carriage began to draw away, she put her head out the window. "You choose to turn a blind eye, my lady, but I must warn you that others shall not!"

When Lady Hortense returned to the sitting room, she found Margaret parodying the reverand's wife with a wicked skill that delighted her companions. She observed Margaret's performance silently for a few moments, then said with finality, "I dislike to speak ill of anyone, but Adelia Pherson is an odious woman." Two bright spots of color stained her cheeks and her mild eyes had become rather hard. Margaret suspended her charade and turned to stare at her, as did Dorothea and Victoria.

Victoria went to her and guided her to a sofa. "My dear ma'am, what could possibly have occurred?"

"The reverend is a very good man. How he could have allied himself with that viper's tongue I am sure I do not know," said Lady Hortense, still seething.

"Aunt Hortense!" exclaimed Dorothea.

Even Margaret was alarmed by her ladyship's unusual temper. She sat down beside her and took her hand. "Lady Hortense, pray calm yourself. What has the good lady done to affront you so?"

"Mrs. Pherson has had the audacity to lecture me on the company I choose to keep. She hinted that both you and dear Victoria are Damion's mistresses. Can you imagine?" exclaimed Lady Hortense wrathfully.

"Oh no!" said Dorothea in distress.

"Yes, and she told me that I should turn both out, for you, Dorothea, are in danger of corruption from these two fallen women."

There was a short silence, broken when Margaret said, "I am disappointed in Mrs. Pherson. A 'fallen woman' sounds so common, don't you think? She could have at least called me a Jezebel."

Victoria gave a peal of laughter. Lady Hortense said indignantly, "Margaret, how can you joke about it? That woman will spread it over the countryside that it is just as she supposed—the both of you are living in Damion's pocket. Drat that boy's reputation!"

"But does Mrs. Pherson honestly think that you

would ever countenance such an outlandish arrangement, ma'am?" demanded Victoria.

"Such households are not unknown in certain sets in London, Lady Victoria," said Margaret.

"And our family's reputation for eccentric behavior is well established, my dear, though we have never had anything along this line," said Lady Hortense bitterly. "Mrs. Pherson but needed to establish that you were a soldier's daughter and that dear Margaret was well known in London circles before she became convinced of her idiotic fancies."

"I hardly consider that the intelligence of a Christian lady," said Dorothea quietly.

"No indeed, but there are those in the neighborhood who enjoy nothing more than a bit of choice gossip. And they will not be behind in carrying the tale even as far as London," said Lady Hortense angrily.

"I do not believe that I should care for that," said Margaret musingly.

"Then, dear ma'am, we must prove her a fool," said Victoria. "You shall give a party at which Margaret and I shall appear as thoroughly respectable as one could wish. And Lord Damion shall treat us as strangers."

"We are in black gloves, Victoria. We cannot possibly have a party," said Lady Hortense.

"But the twelve days of Christmas are approaching and even those in mourning celebrate the season by bringing together friends and family." Victoria's eyes danced. "It need not be an open house, of course. Just a small respectable gathering which naturally would include Reverend Pherson and his good wife."

"Oh marvelous! And I shall be the most respectable of chaperones for you and Margaret at the gathering," said Dorothea, patting her rounded stomach.

"To be sure, a small intimate gathering would be eminently suitable," said Lady Hortense, a smile tugging at her lips.

"You have a positively fiendish streak, Lady Victoria, which I must admire." Margaret laughed.

Victoria acknowledged the compliment with a laugh of her own. Then the ladies put their heads together to begin planning for the Christmas gathering.

Late that afternoon Victoria, who had hidden herself away in the library for some solitary reading, was surprised when a footman came in to inform her that a messenger had asked for her. "Are you certain that he did not ask for Lady Hortense?" she asked, rising from the wingback chair.

"Positive, m'lady," said the footman.

"Very well. Please show the man in," said Victoria, setting aside the novel that she had been reading. When the messenger entered the room, she clutched the tall back of the chair, her heart jumping. She immediately recognized the man's livery and could scarcely contain her impatience until the door was again closed.

Victoria held out her hand. "Pray give it to me at once," she said. The messenger bowed as he handed her a slim envelope. Turning away from him, Victoria ripped it open and unfolded the single sheet.

As she expected, the letter was from her former companion, Miss Rebecca Webster. She was relieved to read that the solictor had visited her daughter and that all was well.

Victoria sat down at the cherrywood desk to pen a short note and sealed it in an envelope. She took out of the desk several of the pound notes that Lord Damion had put there for her use, and gave the notes and her letter to the messenger. "Pray do not tarry here, but return directly to Miss Webster. The notes are for your board at the inn tonight. Keep a close watch on the innkeeper, for he shall try to overcharge you," said Victoria. "And whatever there is left over the tab you may keep for yourself."

The messenger bowed. "Rest assured that I shall do as you wish, m'lady," he said with a quick grin. He was gone a second later.

Victoria tucked the note from Rebecca into her

pocket and attempted to return to her reading. But she quickly discovered that she was too restless to concentrate. Finally she put aside the novel and wandered from the library with no particular destination in mind.

Some time later Lord Damion found her in the sitting room at the pianoforte. He listened a few moments and quickly realized that she was playing at random. He went forward to bring himself to her notice. "Allow me to turn the pages for you, Lady Victoria," he said quietly.

Victoria thanked him quietly and began to play the selection he had chosen. It was several minutes before she warmed to the music and Lord Damion took that to be his cue.

"I have looked through Charles's sketches again this afternoon," said Lord Damion, his eyes on her profile. "He was quite good."

Victoria flashed a pleased smile at him. "You are gracious, my lord. But truly, his ability constantly astounded me. Charles was able to capture with a very few pen strokes the essence of whatever he was looking at."

"He certainly did that in the sketch of you, my lady," said Lord Damion.

Victoria glanced at him in surprise. "Was there a sketch of me? How odd that I did not see it the other evening. Actually, I was not even aware that he had done one."

"I discovered a slit inside the sketch case lining and inside it a drawing that I had not seen before. The drawing was much creased, as though Charles often gazed at it." Lord Damion watched her face closely. "He apparently thought often of you. And of the child." Victoria's fingers faltered on the pianoforte keys. She smoothly regained control. Lord Damion said quietly, "Where is Charles's child, Victoria?"

Sixteen

Victoria's heart pounded. "What should I know of any child, my lord?"

Lord Damion said softly, "He must have loved you and the babe very much," and caught the sheen of tears in her eyes. He leaned over to take her hands away from the pianoforte keys so that she was forced to turn her attention to him. He said carefully, "My dear lady, you have nothing to fear from me or anyone in this house. I swear to you that I only wish to assure myself that Charles's child is alive and well."

Victoria stared into his sincere eyes. She freed her hands to dash away tears that threatened to overflow. "Jessica is safe and is with friends, my lord," she said in a low voice.

Some of Lord Damion's tension eased. She had at least admitted to the child's existence. But he still needed to understand why she had kept Charles's daughter a secret. "Why did you never tell any of us that you and Charles had a daughter?"

Victoria looked away from him, shaking her head. "I did not know if Charles's family would accept me or our daughter. For myself I did not particularly care. I have established my own life. But I feared for Jessica. I feared that she would be branded a bastard. I could not have borne that. I *would* not have stood for it."

"I assure you, my lady, that would not have happened," said Lord Damion.

She faced him squarely, her dark eyes flashing molten gold sparks. "You forced me to come with you here from spite, my lord. And because I was in your company I was subjected to insult by nearly every member of this family. Believe me, I was soon utterly convinced that Jessica did not need her father's family. And so I said nothing about her."

Lord Damion stared at her, white-faced. He was appalled by the consequences of his own hasty actions. "I can only beg your forgiveness, my lady. I had no right to treat you as I did, nor to question your motives for coming to England."

Victoria gazed at him steadily. Her smile was cool. "But you were right, my lord, and so was Sir Aubrey in his way even though his opinion of my character was baser than yours. For I am at the very least a mercenary woman. I came to claim what rightfully belongs to my daughter."

Lord Damion regarded her in silence. Finally he said, "When Sir Aubrey made public the contents of the solicitor's letter, you did not seem in the least distressed. I thought then that it was odd you were so unmoved when even Margaret, who stands to gain nothing, expressed surprise. You must have realized almost instantly that the solicitor was referring to your daughter."

At her nod, Lord Damion said, "Then I must assume that you contacted the solicitor immediately upon setting foot in England. It was a wonder that he gave you a hearing at all."

Victoria smiled again. "On the contrary, my lord, Mr. Bernard was already aware of my existence and of Jessica's."

Lord Damion raised his brows. "You surprise me profoundly, madame."

"Sir Aubrey was not as privy to Lord Robert's business as he believes," said Victoria. "His lordship wrote to me that Charles had sent a sketch of myself and a notarized copy of both our marriage license and Jessica's birth papers to the family solicitor. Upon being informed of the documents by Mr. Bernard, Lord Robert instructed him to make provisions in his will for Jessica. In his letter to me, his lordship made it clear that Jessica's inheritance would not be affected if I chose not to accept his invitation to come to England."

Victoria was silent a moment, remembering her mixed feelings about the letter. She looked up to meet Lord Damion's intent gaze. "Lord Robert sounded like a very lonely man. In the end, I decided that perhaps he could be allowed the opportunity to meet his granddaughter."

"But you did not altogether trust him," said Lord Damion.

Victoria laughed. "My lord, Charles spoke so rarely of his family and hardly any good. I did not know what to expect, but I was determined to protect my daughter," she said frankly.

"And what is your opinion of us now, Lady Victoria? Are we to be trusted with Charles's child?" asked Lord Damion quietly.

Victoria studied the arrogant cast of his features, recalling that moment of weakness in front of Charles's portrait. She had felt fear when she had looked up to recognize the hard planes of Lord Damion's face. She had feared the ruthless streak that she knew existed in him. But the fear had been an exaggeration. She did not now believe that he would harm herself or her daughter. "I have sent a message this afternoon for Jessica's nurse to bring her to the Crossing," she said quietly.

Lord Damion sighed. As the silence lengthened, he had begun to fear her answer. He raised her finger to his lips. "I am grateful to you, Lady Victoria. It will mean more than I can say to us all."

"And now you are fully informed, my lord. I have no more secrets," said Victoria briskly.

"I wonder if that is so," murmured Lord Damion, his quick memory already casting back over their conversation. "What did you mean about Sir Aubrey's opinion of your character being baser even than mine?" She flushed, further arousing his curiosity.

Two ladies entered the drawing room. "Oh! How awkward of us, to be sure. We seem to have interrupted a tête-à-tête, Doro," said Margaret. The glittering expression in her eyes belied the smile fixed to her lips.

Lord Damion's lips tightened as he drew slightly away from Victoria. He had been on friendly terms with Margaret Giddings for several London Seasons and had always found her to be amusing company. But lately Margaret's presence had become progressively more irritating to him. He disliked her arch airs and the possessive attitude she tended to display toward him. Lord Damion decided that the woman was in need of a sharp setdown.

Victoria saw the hardening of his expression and forestalled his retort. "Here is Margaret now, my lord, prepared to practice the duet with you for the Christmas celebration," she said smoothly. She diplomatically overlooked the stunned expression in Lord Damion's eyes. "We were but this moment discussing a suitable selection, Margaret, and I think we have settled on a traditional carol. If you will join his lordship, Doro may be the judge of our performance."

In the face of Margaret's swiftly departing surprise and growing satisfaction, Victoria presented a sheet of music to Lord Damion and remarked it would be necessary for the couple to share it.

Dorothea seated herself in anticipation. "You slyboots, Margaret. You never even let on," she said. "I think it is a delightful idea."

"Indeed it is," murmured Margaret. She smiled up at Lord Damion as she joined him at the pianoforte. Carefully avoiding Lord Damion's eyes, Victoria advised the duo of their cue before she turned to the pianoforte and began to play.

Surprisingly, Margaret possessed a fine, clear voice that soared above Lord Damion's rich baritone. Lord Damion glanced down at her, astonished by her obvious enjoyment of the old song. She was in her element and reveled in it. When the piece was finished, he said, "I was not aware that you could sing, Margaret. You have a truly lovely voice." Margaret blushed rosily, unused to such sincerity from a man.

"She does indeed. And so do you, Damion. I had quite forgotten," said Lady Hortense from the doorway.

Doro turned in her chair as the older woman came toward them. "Oh ma'am, Margaret and Lord Damion mean to sing for the company at our Christmas gathering. Is it not splendid?"

"To be sure, we are all in for a decided treat. I shall look forward to it, for I enjoy good music above all things," said Lady Hortense.

Recognizing that he was firmly caught, Lord Damion glanced down into Victoria's laughing eyes. With an answering glint of humor in his expression, he said dryly, "We must thank Lady Victoria for this inspiration. Without her to guide us, I doubt that Margaret and I would ever have come together over a sheet of music." Victoria busied herself with the music sheets, biting her lip to keep from laughing.

Margaret had no such inhibition and she laughed delightedly. With more warmth than she usually showed, she said, "Indeed, I for one approve your excellent suggestion, Lady Victoria!" The two women exchanged smiles, each tacitly acknowledging a temporary peace between them.

Lord Damion stood up from his place at the pianoforte. "Mama, I believe that Lady Victoria has an announcement that she wishes to make."

Victoria looked up at him quickly. She met the sudden implacable expression in his eyes and realized that he meant to be certain that she would announce her daughter's existence without delay.

Lady Hortense and Dorothea regarded her with friendly curiosity, waiting for her to speak. Margaret supposed that Lady Victoria had unearthed more sketches and glanced down at the sheet of music in her hands.

Victoria was angered that Lord Damion had not allowed her to choose her own time or to lead up to the subject in her own way. Very well, she thought as she drew a breath. Lord Damion would receive exactly what he demanded. Therefore, without preamble, she said, "The letter which Sir Aubrey received from the family solicitor made reference to another heir. That person is Charles's and my daughter, Lady Jessica Marie Silva y Montoya March."

An astonished silence greeted her abrupt announcement. Then her audience burst out in surprised exclamations. Margaret sat down abruptly on a sofa, stunned. She stared in wonderment at Victoria. Once more the woman had managed to snatch the limelight.

"Somehow I did not expect such a bald statement," said Lord Damion, both surprised and displeased. Victoria spared him a cool glance and he found that he was beginning to recognize the dangerous light in her eyes.

"Pray recall that I am quite capable of choosing my own course, Lord Damion, and I am unused to interference," said Victoria in a low tone for his ears alone. Lord Damion stared at her, speechless. He had never before encountered such censure from a female.

"But why did you never tell us of Charles's daughter?" asked Lady Hortense, bewildered.

Lord Damion inclined his head in apology to Victoria before he replied to his mother's query. "Lady Victoria felt that she needed to meet Charles's family before she would trust us with the knowledge of his daughter's existence."

"Oh my dear," murmured Lady Hortense sorrowfully. For the first time Victoria felt a stab of guilt over her duplicity.

"Or perhaps it has taken this long for Lady Victoria to discover a suitable child to pass off as Charles's daughter," said Sir Aubrey harshly from the doorway. In the shocked silence he advanced into the room until he stood over Victoria. His smile was thin. "So you have taken my advice, young woman. I thought you might once you had learned the terms of his lordship's will."

Lord Damion shot a startled glance at Victoria's set expression. He realized that he had misinterpreted his uncle's discussion with her on the morning after her arrival. He now understood Victoria's reference to Sir Aubrey's opinion of her.

"I have taken no advice of yours, Sir Aubrey," said Victoria quietly.

"Of course you have not. It is all simple coincidence, my dear," said Sir Aubrey affably. "But why not produce a son for Charles? You would have had much more to gain with an heir to the title. Or is your solicitude for this unknown girl because she is your own bastard?"

"Aubrey! That is quite enough!" exclaimed Lady Hortense wrathfully.

Victoria was white-faced as she rose to her feet, so hastily that the pianoforte stool was sent tumbling. "This is precisely the sort of insult that I feared and the very reason that I did not bring Jessica forward from the first. I shall not have my daughter treated to slander and cruelty." Her eyes blazing, Victoria started past Sir Aubrey. Lord Damion caught her arm in an unyielding grip. She said furiously, "Unhand me at once, my lord! I shall not remain a moment longer in the same house with that odious man."

"Then you would not hear Sir Aubrey's apology, my lady," said Lord Damion. He looked grimly at his uncle as he drew out a folded sheet and extended it to the older man. "This drawing was put away in a slit inside Charles's sketch case. I discovered it this afternoon and immediately took the liberty of asking Lady Victoria about it, for which I owe her an apology. You will undoubtedly recognize the young woman holding the child."

Sir Aubrey stared at the sketch for several seconds. Lady Hortense grew impatient. "We should like to see it as well, Aubrey." Without a word he passed the sketch over to his sister-in-law. Lady Hortense snatched at it and she, Dorothea, and Margaret soon had their heads together over it.

"Why, it is Cousin Victoria with a baby!" exclaimed Dorothea. "How very clever Charles was. One can see that motherhood positively suits you, cousin."

She realized what she had said and a look of astonishment passed over her face.

Margaret's feelings were vastly different from those of anyone else in the room. She looked over at Victoria with an almost friendly expression. Lord Damion could never seriously be interested in a woman who had a child. Margaret thought that her own chances of becoming the next Countess of March were suddenly much improved with Lady Victoria's newest revelation.

Sir Aubrey barked a laugh and eyed Victoria in sardonic amusement. "I have underestimated you once more, my lady. My apologies are indeed in order."

At that moment Evelyn entered the sitting room. He immediately recognized that something of import had occurred. "What has happened? What have I missed?"

Dorothea urgently held out her hand to him. "Eve, do but come look. Charles did a sketch of Cousin Victoria and their baby."

"The devil you say!" exclaimed Evelyn, dumbfounded. He peered intently at the drawing, then straightened to grin at Victoria. "Well, cousin, no one can accuse you of adding a dull element to our lives."

"That is surely an understatement, Evelyn," said Lord Damion dryly. He caught Victoria's glance and bowed to her. She flushed slightly.

"But where is Charles's daughter now, Lady Victoria?" asked Lady Hortense.

"I left Jessica in the care of her nurse, Miss Rebecca Webster, at her brother's home in Leicestershire," said Victoria. She saw a look of astonishment cross Lady Hortense's face. "Are you perhaps acquainted with the bishop, my lady?"

"But of course I am. I have known Horace Webster half a lifetime and before he ever dreamed of becoming a bishop," exclaimed Lady Hortense. "He always spoke highly of his younger sister Rebecca, whom I never met. I understood that she had resided for years with a rather well-connected Portuguese family."

"Rebecca has indeed been a valued member of my family for some time," said Victoria, smiling faintly. Her dark eyes were steady as she glanced around at their faces, which were beginning to register expressions of astonishment. Lord Damion alone seemed unaffected by her statement, though as he recalled her fluent Portuguese he wondered that he had not guessed the truth sooner.

"A properly bred young lady in Lisbon is accompanied always by her chaperon. And because my father wished that I should be familiar with English manners as well as those of my mother's country, Miss Webster was retained as my companion," said Victoria. "I was fortunate that I found a friend as well."

"But I thought you were English," said Evelyn, then reddened as he realized how his statement had sounded.

"My father was Colonel Arthur Reginald, an Englishman to his fingertips. He married Maria Teresa Silva y Montoya," said Victoria quietly. She inclined her head to Lord Damion. "The portrait that you inquired about was of my uncle, Carlos Silva y Montoya. He was at once my father's brother-in-law and trusted friend."

"And he was also the gentlemen you mentioned in connection with your father's horse breeding," said Lord Damion. Victoria nodded. He knew now why the man's face in the protrait had been so familiar to him. Lady Victoria's eyes were of much of the same shape.

"What is this about horse breeding?" asked Sir Aubrey sharply.

"It seems that Lady Victoria's father, and later she and Charles, have built a successful breeding enterprise. Our own army is likely a prime customer. For that reason I suspect that Lady Victoria has very little use for whatever provisions Lord Robert may have made for her in his will," said Lord Damion.

"Indeed, my lord. I have ample income and to spare," said Victoria with a smile.

Sir Aubrey had difficulty grasping the meaning of what had been said. He could not believe that Lady Victoria was not a supplicant to the March family wealth. "Pray do not exaggerate your independence, my lady. I daresay your income is at best paltry. You'll still dance for your desserts!" he said contemptuously.

"I hardly think six thousand a year is to be counted as paltry, Sir Aubrey," said Victoria deliberately. She had the satisfaction of watching his mouth drop open. While astonishment held them all in thrall, she dropped a curtsy in general to the company. "Pray excuse me. It is nearly time to dress for dinner." She swept out of the sitting room. Her exit snapped the others from their mesmerized state.

"Six thousand! Cousin Victoria is nearly an heiress," exclaimed Evelyn.

"Impossible!" snapped Sir Aubrey. "She would have hinted at it long since if it were true."

"Can you be so certain, Aubrey? Lady Victoria has proven so often to be completely unpredictable," said Lady Hortense.

"I for one have never heard a truer word spoken," said Margaret, recalling several irritating incidents in the past. But she was smiling, for she no longer considered Lady Victoria to be a rival. The lady was hopelessly handicapped by the existence of her own child. Lord Damion was not likely to consider allying himself to a woman who already had a family.

"Do you know, we never even asked Cousin Victoria what her daughter is like," said Dorothea, astonished at her own lack of curiosity.

Lord Damion quietly left the others to their discussion and stepped into the hall. He made a brief inquiry of a footman and then made his way to the breakfast room. He opened one of the french doors and let himself out on the terrace. The breeze was unseasonably warm for November and ruffled his hair.

Victoria turned when she heard his step on the stones. In the dusk he saw that she had been crying. He said gently, "My pardon, Lady Victoria. But I could not let you go off without conveying my deepest apologies for the conduct of myself and my relations. We are a mannerless lot."

Victoria laughed shortly. "It is hardly necessary to point out the obvious, my lord. From the moment that you abducted me, I have wondered how I had the misfortune to become entangled with this family."

Lord Damion joined her at the stone balustrade. "I believe that you can best answer that question, my lady."

Victoria smiled waveringly. "True, my lord. Charles March was the first tie and now I am caught fast through my little Jessica. But for her, I would have rejected Lord Robert's invitation."

"And we would never have come to know the best about Charles's life," said Lord Damion simply.

Victoria glanced at him quickly. Surely he could not be dallying with her at such a time. But his face was perfectly grave and she was surprised into a warm blush. "That is a very pretty compliment, my lord," she said in a low voice. He could not know how her heart warmed to his kindness.

"When shall your daughter arrive, Lady Victoria?" asked Lord Damion.

"On Thursday two days hence," said Victoria. She quickly looked up into his face and discovered relief in his expression. "My lord, you were not certain that I would still have her brought to the Crossing!"

"I am beginning to know your determination and independence well, my lady. I thought it a possibility," said Lord Damion.

"I hope I am not also petty, my lord," said Victoria. He bowed in acknowledgment.

They stood in silence a few moments, each once more at ease with the other. Lord Damion presently directed her attention to the splendor of the sun setting through the trees. He stared at her rapt profile. It was a paradox to him that a woman could be so full of fire and yet still so comfortable a companion.

Seventeen

With the exception of Sir Aubrey, whose gout had flared up, the entire household assembled for dinner. By tacit agreement the conversation skirted the subject of Lady Victoria's daughter and her financial worth, although nearly every breast was filled with curiosity about them.

Victoria realized that she would have to break the polite barrier herself. She turned to Lady Hortense and said pleasantly, "I hope that having Jessica and Miss Webster here will not put the household out."

"My dear! No such thing," said Lady Hortense, happy that Victoria had broached the subject, "My only concern was that you would think me too pushing if I suggested opening up the old nursery."

"On the contrary, my lady. I am willing to be guided by you in every respect," said Victoria.

Lady Hortense beamed. "Thank you, my dear. I have thought also of Miss Webster. There is a sitting room adjacent to the nursery with a bedroom connected that I thought she might like. And the arrangement is all very near to your own room."

"It sounds ideal, ma'am," said Victoria.

"Good! I shall make the arrangements immediately. And Doro, you may assist me if you would care to." Lady Hortense turned an inquiring glance on her niece.

"Oh, I should like it above all else," said Dorothea quickly.

The three ladies began to discuss the preparations. Under cover of their conversation, Margaret seized the opportunity to address Lord Damion. "I find domestic discussions to be rather tedious, I am afraid. I infinitely prefer the give and take between a man and a woman. Do not you, my lord?" She smiled at Lord Damion over the rim of her wineglass.

Lord Damion met her warm gaze. "You are a wicked temptress, Margaret. Do I dare to voice what your lovely violet eyes seem to signal?" he asked softly.

Margaret lowered her lashes and slanted a glance up at him. "Why, as to that, my lord, you must rely on your own judgment."

Lord Damion was about to reply when Evelyn, who had become bored with domestic planning, interrupted. "St. Claire, do you mean to do some grouse hunting tomorrow? I should like to accompany you, if I may."

"Of course, Eve. But I hope you are not planning to bring that outmoded flintlock of yours," said Lord Damion.

Evelyn quickly defended his firearm. The gentlemen fell into a sporting debate that allowed little opportunity for dalliance, but Margaret remained serene. She rather thought that she and Lord Damion understood one another very well.

The next two days saw a clearing of the skies and were spent industriously by the various members of the household. The nursery and the rooms for Miss Webster were opened up and prepared at Lady Hortense's direction with Dorothea acting as her able lieutenant. Victoria was consulted and the cook was given a list of Jessica's favorite dishes. When every imaginable comfort was provided for, Lady Hortense and Dorothea turned their attention once more to their sewing. Margaret joined them in the sitting room to read aloud from the ladies' magazines.

Victoria chose to spend much of the second day at the stables. She and John Dickens were soon fast friends and he began to view her frequent visits with an indulgent eye. When Victoria was asked at dinner how the mare and the foals were coming, she was able to report favorably. She did not voice the homesickness that suddenly welled up within her while she watched the horses. Victoria understood herself well enough to know that anticipation over her daughter's arrival made those feelings all the more keen.

Lord Damion and Evelyn took advantage of the fine November weather. They tramped across the fields and woods from dawn to dusk, returning with full game bags. Lady Hortense promised to teach the cook how to prepare her own recipe for stuffed grouse.

Sir Aubrey was not pleased to observe a deeper intimacy between Margaret Giddings and his nephew. When the company retired after dinner to the sitting room, Lord Damion and Margaret drew a little apart and were obviously enjoying one another's company. Sir Aubrey was furious with Victoria, but she appeared content with playing the pianoforte as a gentle backdrop to the others' quiet conversation. Dorothea, who was blossoming in her pregnancy, eventually remarked that she should soon find her bed. The two hunters confessed to unusual weariness and the evening ended early.

When Thursday dawned, Victoria was up early. She did not know what time to expect her daughter and Miss Webster. Though logic told her that they would certainly not arrive before noon, she could not help feeling restless. All morning her ears were tuned for any unusual sounds in the hall. Dorothea took pity on Victoria's unemployment and quietly bullied her into sewing on the christening robes for the coming infant.

At last Victoria's vigilance was rewarded. In the main hall she heard the sounds of arrival, closely followed by an imperious voice that she instantly recognized. She was on her feet in an instant.

"Victoria? What is it?" asked Dorothea.

"I imagine that Victoria's daughter has arrived, Doro," said Lady Hortense, putting aside her sewing.

"Oh!" Dorothea got clumsily to her feet. "Do wait for us, Victoria!"

Victoria did not heed Dorothea's plea. She ran out of the sitting room into the hall where a tall angular woman was conversing with a footman. She was holding a small child in her arms.

"My dearest Rebecca!" Victoria exclaimed.

Miss Rebecca Webster turned. Her pale blue eyes warmed as she smiled. "Well, Lady Victoria! It is good to see you." She bent to stand the little girl on her tiny feet and give her a gentle push. "Go, child," The little girl held back, wide-eyed and awed by her strange surroundings.

Victoria went down on one knee and held out her arms. "Oh my little Jessica. I missed you so, *menina*!"

"Mama! My mama!" The child flew across the space separating them. Her hood fell back and her white-blond hair streamed free. Victoria scooped her daughter up and held her close, murmuring softly to her in Portuguese.

The sounds of arrival had brought Lord Damion from the library and he joined Lady Hortense and Dorothea in time to witness the reunion. "It appears a happy meeting," he said with a half smile as he turned to Lady Hortense. He discovered her to be abnormally pale. Alarmed, he asked, "Dear ma'am, what is it?"

Lady Hortense glanced up at him before staring again at Victoria's daughter. "The child. She could be twin to Charles when he was a boy."

Lord Damion's brows rose. He looked at Lady Victoria and her daughter, at once fully comprehending why she had been so startled by Charles's portrait.

With Jessica held fast on one hip, Victoria put out her free hand to Miss Webster and clasped her fingers. "Thank you, Rebecca," she said quietly.

"And is everything as it should be, Lady Victoria?" asked Miss Webster meaningfully.

Victoria flashed her a mischievous smile. "It is regarding Jessica. I shall divulge all later when I visit with you in your room. But first I wish you to meet a very dear lady." Victoria beckoned to Dorothea, who shyly joined them. "Rebecca, this is my cousin, Mrs. Dorothea St. Claire. Dorothea, allow me to present Miss Rebecca Webster, my longtime companion and now Jessica's nurse. Between us, we shall be able to offer all sorts of good advice on caring for your own wonderful little monster, for we have had plenty of practice with our Jessica."

"Oh, how can you say so? She is beautiful," said Dorothea.

Victoria smiled tenderly as she stroked her daughter's soft hair. "Yes, she is. My *menina belleza*."

Lady Hortense and Lord Damion now came up and Victoria made the introductions. Miss Webster and Lady Hortense soon engaged in an animated exchange on the doings of mutual acquaintances as they went into the sitting room.

Victoria smiled at Dorothea. "I am about to take Jessica upstairs to show her the nursery. Should you like to accompany us, Doro?"

Dorothea shook her head with a small smile. "It is kind of you, but I can see that you would rather be private with Jessica. I shall visit later." Victoria nodded. She excused herself to Lord Damion and Dorothea and started upstairs with her daughter nestled securely in her arms.

Lord Damion quietly asked a footman to take up the baggage that had been brought in from Miss Webster's carriage. He turned to find Dorothea staring after Victoria with a wistful expression. "Never mind, Doro. You will not have to wait much longer," he said gently, drawing her arm through his.

She blushed furiously and cast a hesitant glance up at him. "Am I then so transparent, my lord?"

Lord Damion smiled. "Yes, child. But come into the sitting room for now. I have the most lowering feeling that Miss Webster shall be very happy to volunteer endless advice on the joys of raising a child." Dorothea gave him a grateful smile as he escorted her into the sitting room. Under his breath he murmured, "Courage, Damion."

When Miss Webster entered the nursery two hours later, she found Victoria gently laying a sleeping Jessica into bed. Victoria smiled at her friend but remained gazing down at her daughter's rosy-cheeked face for several moments before she followed Miss Webster into the small sitting room.

Miss Webster glanced around as she drew off her kid gloves. "Very pretty, 'pon my word. I assume that door there leads to the bedroom?"

"Yes. And I am but a few doors down the hall," said Victoria. With a sigh she seated herself in an elegant chair beside a small table. Victoria gestured at the pot of tea and tea cakes on the table. "The housekeeeper, Mrs. Lummington, sent up tea when she heard of your and Jessica's arrival. Jessica and I have already made inroads, as you can see."

"Most obliging of Mrs. Lummington. Lady Hortense, however, has already done the pretty and I am awash with tea," said Miss Webster as she took the other chair. She glanced keenly at Victoria's pensive face. "You seem preoccupied, my lady. Is it Jessica?"

Victoria smiled at her affectionately. "You could always read my heart, Rebecca. It is Jessica, and more. I missed her so. And I am homesick for my life as it was before I received Lord Robert's invitation."

Miss Webster nodded in understanding. "They seem a friendly enough lot. But one could not be altogether comfortable among them, I suppose."

"I am better situated than in the beginning. At least I am no longer suspected to be Lord Damion's mistress," said Victoria humorously.

Miss Webster stared at her. "Perhaps you should begin at the beginning, Vicky. I perceive it is a highly edifying tale."

Victoria obliged by swiftly outlining her meeting with Lord Damion and her subsequent introduction to the Crossing and its inhabitants. "Needless to say I have never before come in the way of such astonishing behavior. And my own conduct is becoming as bad, for I actually contemplated the idea of pretending to fall in with Sir Aubrey's scheme so that later I may show them up for fools," confessed Victoria.

"Madness indeed. Perhaps you should accept it instead in all sincerity," said Miss Webster.

"Rebecca!"

Miss Webster ignored Victoria's astonished tone. "Wealth cannot buy you the warmth of companionship, Vicky. Lord Damion looks a decent man despite his rakehell reputation."

Victoria was silent a moment. "I do not love him, Rebecca."

"You married once for love. It is not likely to come again in such full measure," said Miss Webster. "So marry with an eye to simple companionship and gradual respect for one another."

"Rebecca, I can hardly believe my ears. You have never before advised me in such a fashion," said Victoria, bemused.

"I have lately given the matter much thought," said Miss Webster, fiddling uncharacteristically with her gloves.

Victoria's mouth dropped open. "My dearest Rebecca, do not tell me that Carlos has at last posed the question!" Miss Webster's embarrassed expression told her that her guess was correct. Victoria jumped out of her chair and flew around the table to catch her friend in a quick hug. "Dearest Rebecca, I am so glad for you. I know that you shall make me a splendid aunt," she said warmly, laughing.

Miss Webster returned her quick embrace. "Thank you, my dear. I am most happy."

"But this must have happened before we ever left Lisbon and you never said a word," said Victoria, almost accusingly.

"I did not know quite how to tell you, for you needed me for Jessica's sake. I spoke to Carlos and he agreed that my duty lay with you at this particular time," said Miss Webster.

"You are so caring, Rebecca," said Victoria softly. "I hope that Carlos realizes what a jewel he is getting."

Miss Webster's cheeks held a soft bloom of color. "Thank you, Vicky. You know that my home shall always be open to you and little Jessica."

"Yes." Victoria suddenly laughed. "I feel so like a matron with her first daughter to be married. What does the bishop think about it all?"

"Horace is the most unflappable creature in nature. He says that he has been expecting something of the sort for years," said Miss Webster. Victoria chortled and her companion found it impossible to keep her countenance. The bishop was renowned for his lack of proper anxieties.

"But surely Carlos will not want you to remian indefinitely with Jessica and me," said Victoria when she had sobered.

"True, Vicky. I must return to Lisbon in a very few weeks," said Miss Webster with something of an anxious air.

Victoria squeezed her hand. "My dearest Rebecca, you are not to spare a thought on my account. My business here will be complete then. I only hope that I may return to Lisbon in time for your wedding."

"You have greatly relieved me." Miss Webster smothered a yawn. "Forgive me, my lady. I find that I am fatigued of a sudden."

"Then I shall leave you for now, Rebecca, and allow you to rest before dinner. And I shall take dinner in the nursery with Jessica so you may sit down with Charles's family. I shall enjoy hearing all your impressions," said Victoria.

"I infer from your tone that I am in for a high treat," said Miss Webster. Victoria only laughed as she left the room.

Victoria did not return to the drawing room but stayed in the nursery to watch her daughter sleep. Miss Webster had given her a great deal to think about, for she had assumed that Rebecca would always be with her. Also, she admitted candidly to herself that she had been unusually encouraging to Lord Damion. It was almost as though she had already made an unconscious decision to further Sir Aubrey's scheme.

When dinner was served downstairs, no one thought it particularly remarkable that Victoria had chosen to take the meal with her daughter. "After all, she has not seen the child for days," said Lady Hortense. "I hope, however, that Lady Victoria means to bring Jessica down to meet us tomorrow."

"I am certain that she will, my lady," said Miss Webster, and casually directed the conversation into other channels. She proved herself an agreeable dinner companion, offering news of the war and describing the society of Lisbon. However, any inquiry regarding Lady Victoria or her daughter was adroitly turned aside with a small witticism.

When the ladies rose from the table and left the gentlemen to their wine, Sir Aubrey remarked, "There goes the most closemouthed female of my experience."

"Indeed, Miss Webster is remarkably skillful in fending off the curious," said Lord Damion. "One understands why Lady Victoria felt safe in entrusting Jessica to her."

"I'm rather awed by her," said Evelyn. He tossed back the last of his wine and set down the glass. "I am for joining the ladies directly. Cousin Victoria must surely mean to make an appearance." Evelyn's companions agreed to his suggestion and the gentlemen repaired to the sitting room. But nothing was seen of Victoria that evening.

Victoria did not feel apologetic for spending the evening alone with Jessica. Since her daughter's arrival she had been poignantly aware of how much she had missed her. She could not feast her eyes enough on Jessica's little face or hold her too long. Her heart pained her when Jessica clung to her for reassurance. "I stay with you now, Mama?" Jessica asked, her eyes somber.

"Yes, my sweet girl," said Victoria, hugging her close. When Jessica finally nodded off and Victoria laid her in bed, she promised herself that she would never again leave her.

Eighteen

Victoria woke early the following morning. She dressed quickly and immediately went to the nursery, for she had promised to be with Jessica when she awakened. Jessica was just stirring as she approached the bed. Victoria bent to kiss her. "Good morning, Miss Slugabed," she said softly.

"Mama!" Jessica threw herself into Victoria's arms and clutched her tightly around the neck.

Victoria laughed at her, protesting that she could not breathe. Jessica began chattering excitedly and Victoria cautioned her to quiet. "Or someone will hear and come just when we are telling our best stories."

"I tell them to go away," Jessica said, nodding emphatically.

"And I shall let you," Victoria said. They spent a very happy two hours alone together before Miss Webster put in an appearance. Victoria turned a flushed, happy countenance to her. "Do but look, Rebecca. We are building a tower and have a place for each tin soldier," she said.

"Very pretty indeed." Miss Webster suitably admired their efforts and then seated herself to one side, loath to interrupt their play. There was a knock on the door and a maid entered with a breakfast tray. Miss Webster asked her to set the dishes on the table in the sitting room.

Victoria reluctantly got to her feet. "I suppose this is my signal that breakfast is being served downstairs. I wish that I had thought to have a portion sent up for myself."

Jessica sensed immediately that her mother was leaving again and she ran to Victoria to bury her head in her skirts. "No, no! Mama stay here."

Victoria sank down on her knees and put her arms around the small girl. "Pray listen to me, *menina*. I am not leaving you again. I shall come back later to play, I promise you." Jessica was still uncertain. But Victoria repeated her promise and the little girl was able to watch her mother leave the nursery without tears.

When Victoria entered the breakfast room, she found only the ladies at the table. She returned the various greetings with a smile as she took her seat and inquired about the gentlemen. Margaret informed her that Lord Damion and Evelyn had once more left the manor at dawn with their firearms and game bags.

"I know that you must have already been to the nursery. Pray, how is little Jessica this morning?" asked Dorothea.

"She is very well, Doro. Should you care to visit with her later this morning? I know that Rebecca shall not mind company while Jessica plays."

"Thank you, cousin," said Dorothea, her eyes bright.

"I am all admiration for you, Lady Victoria, for I see that you are the best of mothers," said Margaret. Victoria was startled by the friendly note in her husky voice and stared at her, but she detected only sincerity in Margaret's expression. Victoria wondered what had brought such a change in the woman's manner.

Lady Hortense, whose appearance at breakfast was most unusual, announced that she wished to return the morning calls of Lady Belingham and Mrs. Pherson. "I know that you do not care for such things, Margaret, and so I shall understand perfectly if you prefer to remain here with Doro," she said. "Victoria, I know, will accompany me."

"But I would not miss it for the world," murmured Margaret.

Lady Hortense observed the hard violet brightness

of her eyes, then shrugged. "Very well, Margaret."
She instructed a footman to have a carriage brought
around to the front steps after breakfast.

During the past week, true winter had at last descended over the rugged Derbyshire countryside.
When the ladies stepped up into the carriage their
breath frosted in the cold, clear atmosphere. Victoria
was grateful for the rugs tucked over their knees.
She put her face up and sniffed of the icy air appreciatively. She had always loved the cold. "Is it not
truly wonderful weather?" she exclaimed.

Margaret looked at her as though she were mad.
"I am wrapped as tight as a sausage, but I swear the
chill penetrates still. Believe me, my misery does
not allow for admiration of the season."

"Never mind, my dear. We shall soon be at the
parsonage and there we may find a warm welcome."
said Lady Hortense comfortably.

"From whom, ma'am?" retorted Margaret tartly,
raising a laugh from her companions.

The reverend's cottage was a charming dwelling
set back from the road among a few trees. A white
picket fence framed the yard. When the carriage
stopped at the gate, Reverend Pherson and his wife
came to meet them. The reverend greeted the ladies
respectfully, and invited them in out of the wind.
"And I may promise you refreshment after your
cold drive, for Mrs. Pherson has just finished baking
a plum cake." Mrs. Pherson echoed her husband's
civilities to Lady Hortense, but as her eyes shifted to
Victoria and Margaret her lips thinned.

Lady Hortensee graciously accepted the reverend's
invitation and was escorted inside by him and his
wife. Margaret and Victoria brought up the rear.
"She would as lief have us freeze as allow us to sully
her home," Margaret murmured softly in Victoria's
ear. Victoria agreed with a laugh. Mrs. Pherson looked
back and raked them with an unfriendly glance.

The reverend showed the callers into the parlor
and made them comfortable in chairs before the
fire. Lady Hortense declined his invitation to remove

their outer garments, saying that they could only stay a moment. "For my coachman shall not want the horses idle for long in this cold," she said with a smile. Reverend Pherson agreed and several minutes were passed in the exchange of pleasantries while the ladies accepted tea and a slice of Mrs. Pherson's excellent plum cake.

Lady Hortense thought it time to bring up the point of their visit. "Now, Reverend, I must tell you that I have a request and I hope that you will not deny me," she said with a smile.

"If it is at all in my power to grant, I shall do so," he answered gallantly.

Lady Hortense embarked on an explanation of the Christmas gathering. "Naturally it will be a private gathering only for our family and friends out of deference to Lord Robert's passing. We are in black gloves, of course, but I felt it appropriate to recognize the season of our Lord's birth in whatever small way we may. Do you not agree, Reverend?"

"Of course, dear ma'am," said the reverend promptly. "I am touched by your gentle devotion. And how may I be of service?" Victoria glanced at Mrs. Pherson and noted the look of stiff disapproval on the lady's thin face.

"I should like you, and Mrs. Pherson, to join us that evening, dear Reverend, for you must know that I count you very much my good friend and pastor," said Lady Hortense.

The reverend, moved by her kindness, cleared his throat. "I am overwhelmed, my lady."

"Your presence could only lend distinction and . . . respectability, sir," Margaret said sweetly, looking straight at Mrs. Pherson. The dame's expression sharpened and she turned red with anger.

Lady Hortense hastily intervened. "We thought, too, of my nephew Charles's little daughter. She is but three years old and, having been born in Lisbon, the child has never seen an English Christmas. I feel it would be a great pity to deny her that treat, for Christmas season is for the children."

The reverend nodded. "Indeed it is. My dear Lady Hortense, I appreciate your consideration towards myself and Mrs. Pherson. We shall be delighted to attend your Christmas gathering."

Lady Hortense thanked him with a smile. "I shall be counting on you, Reverend." As she rose to take her leave, she so lavishly complimented her hostess on her plum cake that Mrs. Pherson was promising to send her the recipe even as the visitors settled once more into their carriage. Lady Hortense signaled to the driver and gave a final wave.

"You are the most complete hand, my lady," said Victoria appreciatively.

"I could hardly leave the woman time to think of an objection, could I?" Lady Hortense said chuckling. She turned to Margaret with a twinkle. "Really, Margaret, it was a great deal too bad of you to goad her."

Margaret bowed to her from the waist. "But what can one expect from a thoroughly unrespectable creature such as myself?" she asked mildly.

The ladies made merry the short distance to Belingham Manor. Upon their arrival, they found Lady Belingham and her daughter at home and were ushered into the drawing room. Lady Belingham received them with delight. "Pray make yourselves comfortable," she said, waving the ladies to be seated. A beautiful young woman pleasantly greeted them. She was very slim and possessed a head of glorious red hair. "Lady Hortense, you will remember my daughter Erica, of course."

"Indeed I do, but you have become a young lady since I last saw you, my dear," said Lady Hortense, smiling.

Erica laughed, shaking her head. Her green eyes gleamed with mischief. "I left the hoyden behind only yesterday, ma'am, I assure you."

"And these are the ladies I have been telling you about, Erica," said Lady Belingham. "Mrs. Giddings has come down to be with her sister who is increasing and this is dear Harry's friend, Lady Victoria."

Erica nodded civilly to Margaret before addressing Victoria. "I am happy to meet you at last, Lady Victoria. Harry has written about you so often that I feel I know you almost like a sister," she said.

Victoria laughed with her. "And I also, for dear Harry was forever doting on you."

"Was he truly? He was careful not to spoil me, then," said Erica wryly. She turned to Margaret. "Have you had occasion to meet my brother, Mrs. Giddings?"

"I have not had that pleasrue," said Margaret politely. The sight of Miss Erica Belingham's beauty had startled her and her first impression had only been reinforced as they spoke. She had never met anyone who could seriously rival her for beauty and it was a distinctly unusual feeling.

As the ladies exchanged greetings, Lady Belingham beckoned a footman aside and gave him quiet instructions. Now she turned once more to her guests and urged them to remove their gloves and bonnets. "For I do wish you all to stay for a good long visit. Erica and I have been going over the latest fashion plates this past hour and we cannot seem to make up our minds which ensembles are the most appropriate for a Christmas assembly."

"Mrs. Giddings, I know that you may guide us, for I understand that you have just come down from London. And one may see from the cut of your pelisse that you must patronize a superb modiste," Erica said enthusiastically.

"I am flattered," Margaret said, and though she laughed, she did feel a glow of satisfaction that her own dress excited such admiration.

The young ladies soon put their heads together over the fashion plates and Lady Belingham drew Lady Hortense a little apart. "Now, dear ma'am, I may speak a few moments for your ears alone. I must tell you that this past week I have heard distressing rumors in the neighborhood concerning Lady Victoria and Mrs. Giddings."

Lady Hortense smiled faintly. "You do not need

to say anything more, Miranda, for I am fully aware of Adelia Pherson's poisonous speculations. She had the audacity to inform me of them herself, if you please."

Lady Belingham looked at her with concern. "But what shall you do? Mrs. Pherson's word carries weight in certain quarters and I fear for our young ladies' reputations."

"I intend to prove Mrs. Pherson a fool," said Lady Hortense. "We are giving a party, Miranda." She had to laugh at her friend's polite and bewildered expression. Quickly she explained.

"How splendid, Hortense," exclaimed Lady Belingham. "Of course we shall come, the three of us."

Lady Hortense was about to ask who the third individual was when a tall young man dressed in a military uniform entered the drawing room. "I believe you sent for me, Mama?" he asked in a pleasant voice.

Victoria looked up, disbelieving. "Harry!" she cried, springing up.

"Victoria!" He disregarded her outstretched hands and caught her up in his arms. He swung her around laughing.

When he had set her once more on her feet, Victoria demanded, "Whatever are you doing in England? I quite thought your next leave wasn't until the Christmas holiday."

"I arranged a few days more on my furlough. I but arrived last night," said Harry easily. He examined her face closely. "How are you getting along, Vicky?"

Victoria flashed a warm smile at him. She knew that his concern went much deeper than the conventional words revealed. "I'm fine, Harry, and especially since Jessica and Rebecca are now with me. Oh, it is good to see you again! But do come greet the ladies. I am certain Lady Hortense must remember you."

"Indeed I do remember you, Sir Harry," said Lady Hortense as he bowed smartly over her hand. "But you have long since turned out as a well-set young man. Alas, there is nothing left of the small rascal who used to raid my father's favorite peach trees."

Sir Harry laughed. "I am covered in shame, ma'am."

"I was never more shocked, Harry. You have led me to believe you were a paragon of virtue," Erica said teasingly.

"Pray rescue me, Victoria," pleaded Sir Harry. She laughingly obeyed, drawing him over to introduce him to Margaret Giddings.

Margaret had been stunned by Sir Harry Belingham's appearance. His laughing face and tall form were magnificent. She thought he was quite the most virile man that she had ever beheld. She recovered quickly, however, and was prepared to be at her most charming when Victoria introduced him to her. She offered her hand to him, saying softly, "I have long had an admiration for the military men. There is something so exciting about a uniform."

Sir Harry's blue eyes kindled and a very few moments saw him seated beside Mrs. Giddings. He was not long is discovering that the lady was a widow, and by the time the ladies rose to take their leave, Sir Harry had made certain that he had a standing invitation to call at the Crossing. He escorted the ladies to their carriage, and as he handed Victoria up into it, she murmured, "You're shameless, Harry."

"You know that I always set up a flirtation with the most beautiful woman I can find," said Sir Harry in a low voice.

"I think Margaret shall be a match for you," said Victoria. He only laughed and waved them off.

That evening at dinner Lady Hortense dismissed the servants so that she could announce the family's Christmas gathering. "And I have set it for a fortnight from now," she said.

"Whatever are you thinking of, Hortense?" asked Sir Aubrey. "We cannot possibly have a party."

"Of course we can. I have already had acceptances," said Lady Hortense.

" 'Pon my soul, madame! Have you forgotten that

we are in mourning?" demanded Sir Aubrey, glaring at his sister-in-law across the table.

"Of course I have not forgotten. But I believe that the reputations of the living are more important than the deceased and I know dear Robert would have agreed, for he was very conscious of the family's honor," Lady Hortense said spiritedly.

"Come, Mama. What are you talking about?" asked Lord Damion.

"Only that there is scandalous talk in the neighborhood regarding certain members of our family and I mean to squelch it," said Lady Hortense.

Sir Aubrey snorted in disgust. "They have talked about us for years, and especially Damion. There is nothing new in that!"

"Aubrey, be so kind as to be quiet." Lady Hortense glared at him and he raised his brows in offended surprise. She was satisfied and continued. "The gossip concerns Lady Victoria and Margaret. Certain persons do not consider them to be respectable women. And that, coupled with Damion's presence, has led to open speculation that our family is engaged in wicked liaisons and even orgies."

"What rot!" exclaimed Evelyn.

Lord Damion threw back his head and laughed. "My dear ma'am, you cannot be serious."

"But I am, Damion," said Lady Hortense quickly. "And I fear that if unchecked, the rumors will prove irreparably harmful. I do not intend to allow such malicious lies to be spread."

"But who could bear us such ill will, Aunt?" asked Evelyn. "Do we know the guilty party? For I promise you that I shall thrash him to within an inch of his life."

Dorothea touched his sleeve. "Eve, I fear that it began with the good reverend's wife, Mrs. Pherson. When she came to pay her condolences, she advised our aunt that Margaret and Cousin Victoria were not suitable companions for me. She accused them of being Lord Damion's mistresses."

There was a short silence. Sir Aubrey leaned back

in his chair, his eyes half-hooded and glittering. Victoria and Margaret exchanged glances as the hush lengthened. Finally Lord Damion reached over the table to take his mother's hand. "Forgive me, dear ma'am. I see now that it is not a laughing matter. Mrs. Pherson is a respectable woman and her word must carry weight."

"It is the fault of your damned rakehell reputation, St. Claire," Evelyn said bitterly.

His wife once more placed a gentle hand on his arm. "Eve, I believe that you speak unjustly," she said quietly.

He turned red. "I apologize, cousin. Dorothea is correct, I had no right to cut up at you."

"But you were quite right, Evelyn," said Lord Damion. His eyes were like agate. "As the Demon, I must excite such speculation for I am sunk quite beyond reproach."

"Nonsense, Damion. I am sure I have never known you to be other than a gentleman," said Lady Hortense stolidly. Lord Damion bowed to her but was silent.

"So you mean to show us off as respectable with this Christmas celebration, Hortense?" asked Sir Aubrey.

She turned to him eagerly. "I envision a small gathering with a select few whose opinions are respected. We shall observe the holiday with proper reverence, nothing more, and our guests may see for themselves that there is nothing untoward in our manner. That ought to do much toward putting to rest the preposterous gossip."

"Outflank the enemy and roll them up, is that it, Mama?" asked Lord Damion with a faint grin.

Lady Hortense laughed at him. "Exactly, my dear. I have even Reverend Pherson's blessing and his assurances that he and Mrs. Pherson shall attend. Let that but get about and his good wife's speculations will come to naught."

"Bravo, Aunt Hortense," said Evelyn, grinning. "The sainted reverend himself will grace us with respectability."

Reminded of Margaret's remark to Reverend Pherson, Victoria glanced swiftly at her. Margaret shaded her eyes. Victoria could not help laughing, and said, "How utterly priceless!"

"What is the joke, pray?" Evelyn asked, puzzled.

Lady Hortense rose from the table. "I believe it is time for the ladies to leave the gentlemen to their wine. Come, Doro. I shall impart the source of our campanions' amusement, but you are on no account to tell Evelyn later. We must occasionally have our own little jokes, you know."

Dorothea laughed at her husband's indignant expression. "Oh, I should never do so, ma'am." She knew Evelyn would badger her unmercifully at the first opportunity and she was as ready as Lady Hortense to tease him.

Nineteen

The following days fell into a quiet pattern as the weather grew colder. Each day Victoria spent the two hours before breakfast with Jessica and often returned to the nursery in the afternoons after Jessica had finished her nap. She asked Mrs. Lummington's advice in finding a nursemaid and the housekeeper recommended her own neice, Eliza, who was a buxom young woman of eighteen. Victoria felt an instant liking for the good-natured girl and engaged her services on the spot.

Miss Webster quietly observed how Eliza got along with Jessica and was able to comment a few days later that the new nursemaid would do very well. "When I leave, I shall rest easier knowing that little Jessica is safe in Eliza's capable hands," she said.

"I shall miss you, you know," Victoria said soberly.

Miss Webster reached out to squeeze her hand. "I am not gone yet, my lady."

When Dorothea paid her first visit to the nursery, she was all trepidation about her reception. But her genuine interest and willingness to participate in Jessica's play quickly established her as a favorite with the little girl. One morning Dorothea introduced the two spaniels to Jessica and from then on it became a special treat for her to be allowed to play with the little dogs.

Lady Hortense was not behind in her own attentions to her new great-niece. But none of the gentlemen met Jessica until Victoria brought her down for tea one afternoon.

The novelty of being allowed downstairs made Jessica quieter than usual, but when Victoria led her into the drawing room, the sight of the three strangers silenced her completely. Jessica clung to her mother's hand and stared at the gentlemen, who had risen upon their entrance.

Miss Webster had come down with Victoria and her charge and now looked on with an eagle eye. She was very curious to see the gentlemen's reaction to this new little heiress.

"Here they are now," said Lady Hortense. She smiled at Jessica. "Do not be afraid, dear Jessica. See, here is Doro beside me and you have met Margaret once, I know."

"Indeed. Doro was particularly insistent that I should," said Margaret with a laugh. Privately she thought the importance placed on the little girl's introduction at the tea was ridiculous, but she took care not to allow her boredom to be too evident. She had been astonished when even Lord Damion, who as a man of the world could be expected to share her impatience, had actually expressed eagerness to meet the child.

Lord Damion silently studied Jessica and decided that she was an exceptionally attractive child. Her fair hair was threaded with a blue riband that matched her large eyes and she wore a darker blue merino frock. He glanced at Lady Victoria's face to satisfy himself that the child's delicate features did indeed echo the mother's fine bone structure. Charles March may have bequeathed his once-fair coloring to his daughter, but Lord Damion rather thought that as Jessica grew older she would resemble the mother more.

Miss Webster detached herself quietly to take a chair on the far side of Lady Hortense where she could be close to the fire. Victoria drew her daughter nearer the group. "Jessica, this is Sir Aubrey, who is your papa's uncle. He remembers Papa as a boy just your age," said Victoria.

Jessica's eyes rounded. Her shyness was forgotten as she stared intently at Sir Aubrey. "You knew my papa?"

"To be sure I did," Sir Aubrey said, nodding. "And a fine rascal he was."

Victoria drew her daughter's attention to the other two gentlemen. "This is Lord Damion and the gentleman standing by the mantle is Evelyn. They are your papa's cousins. They are your cousins, too," said Victoria.

"Hullo, Cousin Jessica," Evelyn said with awkward friendliness. He wasn't certain what he should say next to the three-year-old girl and stared at her.

Sensitive to Evelyn's silence, Jessica drew a little closer to her mother, again feeling self-conscious. She knew she was the object of all eyes and she was uncertain of what was expected of her.

"Lady Victoria, pray allow me to serve you and our cousin Jessica a slice of cake," Lord Damion said, gesturing to the tea board that had been set up a few minutes before by the butler and a footman. He glanced at Jessica. "I assure you, it is a very good cake."

Lively interest showed in Jessica's eyes and she stood on tiptoe to see the top of the table. Victoria almost laughed at her. "Thank you, my lord. We would be delighted."

In very short order Victoria and Jessica were seated on the sofa opposite Doro and Lady Hortense. Jessica finished her cake with great satisfaction and she looked curiously around at the adults. Miss Webster was telling an anecdote to Lady Hortense and Sir Aubrey, while Margaret listened with a half smile. Dorothea and Victoria were laughing at Evelyn's nonsense. Jessica discovered that only Lord Damion was watching her. She stared uncertainly at him.

Lord Damion smiled. "It was a good cake, don't you think?" he asked quietly.

Jessica continued to stare at him. Suddenly she smiled. She slid off the sofa and went over to lean against his knee. "Mama says you are Papa's cousin," she said.

Lord Damion nodded. "I am also your cousin, Jessica."

"I have many cousins," she declared solemnly. She stared thoughtfully at him. "Do you have a little girl?"

"No, Jessica. But if I ever do I should like her to be as pretty as you are," said Lord Damion. He held out his hand and without hesitation she put her tiny fingers in his.

Jessica swung their clasped hands to and fro. "Do you like horses?" she inquired.

"Very much," said Lord Damion. She nodded, satisfied.

Evelyn had observed their meeting and directed Victoria's attention. "St. Claire's charm wins over even the babes," he said humorously.

Victoria was astonished to see that her shy daughter had climbed up beside Lord Damion in his chair. Lord Damion chanced to meet her gaze and he grinned. "Pray do not look so surprised, my lady. Jessica and I have discovered a mutual passion for horses. I have just been telling her about Starfire and the foals," he said. "With your permission, I am engaged to take her to visit them this afternoon."

"Jessica will enjoy such a treat. We will be most happy to accompany you, my lord," said Victoria.

She was amazed not only by his efforts to please a little girl he had never seen before, but that he should apparently have a knack with her. Somehow Victoria had not expected a man of his reputation to care overmuch for children.

"I shall go along with you, St. Claire. I've not seen them yet," said Evelyn.

Margaret laughed, thinking it ironic that she should now lose Lord Damion's attention to a child. "To be sure, it will be quite the family outing," she said.

Lord Damion glanced at her, suspecting that he heard a forlorn note in her voice. He thought that the entertainment offered thus far at the Crossing must be tedious to someone like Margaret, who regularly attended every social function in London. Perhaps as host he should show her a little more consideration. He set Jessica on her feet and rose from his chair.

The little girl dashed over to Victoria, her eyes alight. In a high clear voice, she said, "I am to see the horses, Mama!"

"So you are, *menina*," said Victoria, laughing. She saw that Miss Webster was rising from her place on the settee near the fire. "Pray do not stir, Rebecca. I shall take her out, for I well know how you detest the cold."

Miss Webster nodded to her as she settled back in comfort beside Lady Hortense. "Indeed, my lady. And my present company is too pleasant to leave willingly." Her glance included both Lady Hortense and Sir Aubrey, who made a short bow to her from his chair.

Lord Damion approached Margaret. "You are naturally welcome to join the party, Margaret."

She shook her head, giving him a demure glance. "Pray do excuse me from this particular outing, my lord. I shall be more in my element if I remain here with Doro."

He lowered his voice. "As a favor to me, Margaret."

Margaret looked up at him. There was a warmth in his eyes that she thought she understood. Her heart beat a little faster. "I must certainly honor your wishes, my lord," she said huskily. He bowed and held out his hand to her and Margaret allowed herself to be drawn from her chair.

Doro sighed as they left. She would never say so, but she wished that she could participate so easily in whatever was proposed. However, she put on a cheerful face, not wanting to spoil anyone's enjoyment or to make Evelyn anxious on her account.

The small party was quickly bundled in warm cloaks and on its way to the stables. The stable master was taken aback by the number of visitors but he watched calmly enough while the little girl was introduced to the foals and their dam. He wondered a bit at the beautiful woman who clung to his lordship's arm. Her expression was polite but she did not seem particularly interested in the horses. He nodded, unsurprised when she stepped back hastily as one of the foals came too close to her skirt. She was obviously one of those females who had no business invading a man's stable.

Margaret would not have argued with the stable master's opinion. She was bored within five minutes of entering the stable and wondered that Lord Damion appeared to enjoy himself so thoroughly. She herself saw nothing entertaining in the spectacle of Lady Victoria, Evelyn, and the child squatting in the straw to pet the smelly animals. Margaret was relieved when they decided to return to the manor a half hour later.

The party used the small door into the manor once more and entered into the narrow passageway. Victoria and Evelyn walked ahead with Jessica, who kept up a steady stream of questions and exclamations about the foals. Evelyn was delighted to discover that sometime during the visit to the stables he had been elevated to the level of friend and Jessica turned to him with questions.

Lord Damion and Margaret brought up the rear. She deliberately kept their pace slow as she talked animatedly of London. When Margaret saw that Victoria and Evelyn had turned a corner and were no longer in sight, she pretended to stumble. "Oh!"

Lord Damion quickly put his arm about her. "Are you all right, Margaret?"

Margaret leaned against him, ostensibly to reach for her ankle. "I but turned my ankle, my lord. It will be better in a moment." She looked up at him with a brave smile.

Lord Damion felt her soft curves against him. It was not an unpleasant sensation, and though he suspected that her turned ankle was a pretense, he was not unwilling to prolong the moment. He smiled down at her. "Margaret, I understand you too well for your own good."

"Do you, my lord?" Margaret straightened and slipped her arms around his neck.

Lord Damion put his hands about her waist, preparing to push her away gently. "Margaret, this is not—" He was silenced when she reached up to press her lips urgently against his.

When Jessica had addressed a question to Lord Damion and did not receive an answer, she looked back curiously to find that the other couple had disappeared. "But where is he?" asked Jessica. Evelyn glanced at Victoria, his brow raised.

"Lord Damion and Mrs. Giddings will come along in their own time, Jessica," said Victoria.

"But I wish to talk to him," said Jessica. She pulled her hand loose and ran back the way they had come.

"Jessica!" Victoria hurried after her but did not catch up with her daughter until she turned the corner. Jessica stood stock-still in the middle of the hall, staring. Victoria looked up to see what had so captured Jessica's interest. Margaret's arms were wound tightly around Lord Damion's neck and they were exchanging a passionate kiss. Victoria felt an irrational stab of fury.

Lord Damion sensed eyes on him and lifted his head. He met Victoria's outraged eyes. At once he loosened Margaret's arms and stepped back from her. "My lady—"

Victoria picked Jessica up and whisked back around the corner. She almost collided with Evelyn, who took one look at her face and fell into step with her silently.

"Mama, what are they doing?" Jessica asked innocently.

Victoria felt heat rise in her face. "Hush, Jessica!"

Evelyn tousled Jessica's fair hair. He said easily, "His lordship and Mrs. Giddings were flirting, Jessica. That is a game for grown-up men and women."

"Oh," said Jessica, thinking about it. "When I am grown, I shall not play flirting. It doesn't look fun at all," she said finally.

Evelyn laughed and after a moment Victoria joined him. She gave her daughter a hard hug. "You are a darling, *menina!*"

They returned to the drawing room without further incident and a few moments later Lord Damion and Margaret appeared. Margaret's expression was complacent. She had not meant to have a witness to the interlude with Lord Damion, but nothing could have been more fortuitous than to have Lady Victoria chance upon them. She rather thought she had at last put Lady Victoria in her place.

Victoria had been sensitive before to the increased intimacy between Lord Damion and Margaret and her feelings had been curiously mixed. Lord Damion's reputation and Margaret's professed interest in him had made a liaison between them seem almost inevitable. But now that it appeared a fact, Victoria was furious. She did not examine her anger too closely, and knew only that she could hardly bear to be in the same room with them.

When Miss Webster remarked that it was past time for Jessica's nap, it was taken by the others as a signal that tea was over. Victoria kissed her daughter and bade her go with Miss Webster. Jessica did not demur, being already half asleep. Doro decided that she would also lie down for an hour and Evelyn escorted her upstairs. Lady Hortense asked Margaret if she would help her to match some yarns. "For I know that I may rely perfectly on your color sense," she said.

"You flatter me, Lady Hortense," Margaret said, but she was happy to prove that her ladyship did not misplace her trust. The two ladies soon had their heads together over Lady Hortense's sewing basket and were sorting the various yarns.

Victoria seized the opportunity to escape from Lord Damion's scrutiny. She rose, saying, "I have yet to finish a novel that I started. Pray excuse me." She left the room, fully aware that Lord Damion's eyes were on her.

Sir Aubrey, about to request a rubber of whist from his nephew, saw the direction of his frowning gaze. He decided to await further events and was not disappointed. Lord Damion left the drawing room.

Lord Damion found Victoria reading in the library. She had hardly settled herself before the fire when he entered. Victoria stiffened. "I hope that you do not mind my company, ma'am," he said with a faint smile.

Victoria looked at him coolly. "Indeed, my lord, I would prefer to be alone just now." She turned her gaze to the pages of her novel.

He ignored her snub and seated himself in the opposite wingchair. "My lady, I feel compelled to break etiquette with you and offer you an explanation. I realize that you were disgusted by the display you witnessed. I can only say that it was not all it seemed—"

"Pray do not go further, my lord. I do not ask for an explanation," said Victoria. "Indeed, your private affairs are no concern of mine."

Lord Damion raised a brow at the hard note in her voice. "Lady Victoria, I'm not making a confession. As you say, my private affairs are of my own concern. However—"

"Then pray leave off this topic, sir! I have no desire to discuss your alliance with Margaret Giddings," exclaimed Victoria. She felt compelled to add, "Though to *flaunt* your relationship—"

"I have not made Margaret my mistress!" Lord Damion said furiously.

"And I have not asked, my lord," Victoria said coldly. "But I shall say that I do not care for my daughter to witness such particular attentions as those you favor Mrs. Giddings with."

"What do you accuse me of, my lady?" Lord Damion asked softly, a hard look about his mouth.

Fine color rose in Victoria's face. She did not stop to analyze her hurt anger. "You are a rakehell, sir, entirely without shame or conscience!"

Lord Damion laughed at her. Mockery lighted his eyes. "And I believe you are jealous, my lady."

Victoria leaped to her feet. The novel tumbled to the carpet. "You are insufferable, Lord Damion!" She ran out of the library, leaving him with an astonished expression on his face.

Victoria sought refuge without thinking. Miss Webster looked up in surprise when her sitting-room door flew open. She saw Victoria's face and her voice was filled with quick concern. "My dear Vicky, what is it?"

"Oh Rebecca!" Victoria threw herself down at her old friend's knee and burst into tears. Between sobs she attempted a tangled explanation of the scene between her and Lord Damion.

Miss Webster was able to piece enough together from Victoria's incoherent words to make sense of what had happened. Gently she raised Victoria's face from her lap. "My dear, do you not see? It was not that Jessica was exposed to her first flirtation that has upset you."

Victoria wiped her eyes. Her heart thumped painfully. "What are you saying, Rebecca?"

"I believe you know," Miss Webster said quietly.

Victoria bent her head. "I have made a fool of myself, haven't I?"

Miss Webster laughed and touched her hair. "My dear, love makes fools of us all."

"Oh, pray do not call it that!" exclaimed Victoria, raising her hands to her burning cheeks. "I cannot bear to think of him in that fashion."

"Then do not. However, one day you will be compelled to put a name to your feelings, Lady Victoria," said Miss Webster. "And I hope that you will be honest with yourself." She hesitated, looking down at Victoria's somber profile. "My dear, I received a letter from Carlos in the post."

Victoria looked up quickly, all thought of her own confused state forgotten. "You are leaving us, then?"

"In only a few days. I am sorry, Vicky," said Miss Webster unhappily. "I feel that I have failed you."

Victoria rose from her knees to give her a quick hug. "Nonsense, Rebecca. I can deal with whatever happens. And I shall have our splendid Eliza to assist me. Oh, I am so glad for you! How I wish that Jessica and I were returning also, but we shall follow as soon as the will is read. And then we shall all be merry, I promise you."

Miss Webster agreed to it, but she was concerned as she looked at Victoria's determinedly cheerful expression. She knew that stubborn unconcern of old and hoped that her former charge would do nothing foolish. However, she kept her reservations to herself and hoped that she was not making a terrible mistake in leaving the Crossing just at this time.

Twenty

It began snowing the morning that Miss Webster left. Victoria stood at the front of the small group that had gathered on the steps to see off her former companion. She held Jessica in her arms.

"Wave now, *menina*, Rebecca is going," she said quietly. The little girl did as she was told and Miss Webster returned her wave from the carriage window.

The carriage pulled away and Miss Webster continued to wave from the open window until the carriage made the curve in the lane. Victoria felt a lowering of her spirits and stared after the carriage while fine snow peppered her dark hair.

Lady Hortense glanced at Victoria's somber face and patted her arm. "We shall all miss Rebecca, I am sure. But she has her own obligations and we could not keep her with us forever," she said. Victoria agreed rather forlornly.

Dorothea exchanged a glance with Lady Hortense. "Do come out of the cold, Victoria. Eliza is waiting to take Jessica up to the nursery for her tea time and I need your support," said Dorothea.

"Of course," said Victoria. She reentered the hall with the other ladies and gave her daughter over to the nursemaid. Then she accompanied Dorothea to the picture gallery, the younger woman leaning lightly on Victoria's arm.

Dorthea and Victoria took their daily exercise in the long gallery. As they walked slowly up and down the gallery they wrapped their shawls close to ward off the drafts. Doro's black and white spaniels ran with exuberant energy, but the ladies' pace was always leisurely because Dorothea had become clumsier as her pregnancy advanced.

Victoria and Dorothea were much closer since the younger woman had discovered that Victoria was a mother. Dorothea had since learned her friend's moods and she was sensitive to Victoria's distance after losing Miss Webster's companionship. She therefore attempted to keep the conversation light, but they soon entered on one of their more far-reaching discussions.

"Of course I want a son. Evelyn does not admit to it, but he very much wants our first child to be a boy. And for his sake, I hope that it is," said Dorothea.

"Do you always put Evelyn's desires first?" Victoria asked.

Dorothea laughed at her. "Oh Victoria, what an odd question! I love Evelyn and naturally his desires are mine. Yet I do have ambitions of my own, which Evelyn will do all in his power to satisfy because he returns my love tenfold." She looked curiously at her taller companion. "Was it not that way between you and Charles?"

"I hardly know how to reply. Charles and I had such contrasting natures," said Victoria. "Yet we were happy. And particularly when Jessica was born."

"That is all that mattered, is it not?" asked Dorothea gently.

A voice hailed them and they turned to discover that Lord Damion had entered the gallery. "I hope that I may join you ladies, for I am in dire need of exercise and fresh company. I have just escaped my mother and Sir Aubrey, who are hotly debating a point of honor in cards," said Lord Damion ruefully.

Victoria and Dorothea laughed at his expression. Then Doro said, "I fear you must excuse me from any further walking, my lord. I have finished mine for the day and now I desire only a comfortable chair. But I am certain that Victoria shall oblige you, for she is always full of energy."

Before Victoria well knew what Dorothea was about, she had called to her spaniels and left the gallery. Victoria found herself alone with Lord Damion for the first time in days. Since their quarrel she had taken pains to avoid his company.

Now Victoria walked arm in arm with that same gentleman. She did not know what to say or where to look. She could only wonder if Lord Damion recalled that she had fled upon being accused of jealousy.

After several failed attempts at conversation, Lord Damion finally stopped her. "My lady, I behaved shamefully with you," he said quietly. "If there were any way I could make amends, I would, for I have lost a friend."

Victoria flushed, then paled. She met his gaze steadily. 'I cannot mistake your meaning, my lord. But indeed, the fault lies with me. I should not have provoked you—" She stopped, her lashes falling to mask her eyes.

Lord Damion gently tilted up her chin with one finger. "My darling Victoria, you are very dear to me," he said softly. At once he was amazed by his own words. It had not been what he meant to say. But the look of wonder in Victoria's eyes surprised him more. The blood pumped faster in his veins. Slowly Lord Damion lowered his head to take her half-parted lips in a long, seeking kiss.

When Lord Damion raised his head, he felt as though he had wakened from a languorous sleep. He stared deep into Victoria's softly glowing eyes and carefully drew her toward him, uncertain if she would bolt. But she came willingly into his arms and her kiss was welcoming.

"Victoria! Victoria?" Evelyn entered the gallery and abruptly stopped short at sight of the embracing couple.

Immediately Lord Damion released Victoria and took a step forward to shield her from Evelyn's amazed scrutiny. "Yes, Evelyn?"

Evelyn took note of Victoria's furious blush before he settled his gaze on Lord Damion. "Doro told me that I might find you both here. The solicitor has arrived and is ready to begin with the reading," he said shortly.

"We will come immediately," said Lord Damion, half turning to offer his arm to Victoria. But she had already made for the door and did not see his gesture. She could think only of escaping her feelings for him.

Lord Damion fell into step with Evelyn as they followed her. "I shall be glad to have this business done. Did the solicitor say why he has taken so long to come to us?" he asked casually, his eyes on Victoria's retreating back.

"He said he took time to have some documents

pertaining to Jessica's inheritance notarized." Evelyn saw the peculiar light in his cousin's gaze and was startled. Suddenly uneasy, he put out a hand and caught his cousin's sleeve. "St. Claire—" Lord Damion turned his head, raising a thin brow. Evelyn looked into the taller man's arrogant face and his own jaw firmed. "We will talk later, cousin."

"As you wish, Evelyn," said Lord Damion, mildly surprised by Evelyn's unusually grim tone. But he dismissed it quickly as they joined the rest of the family in the library where the solicitor had chosen to hold the reading of the will.

The will occasioned few surprises. Lord Damion ascended to the title and became the Sixth Earl of March. Various objets d'art were left to Sir Aubrey and Lady Hortense, while Evelyn was given a handsome income. The most noteworthy item was Lord Robert's surprising generosity to the daughter-in-law and granddaughter he had never met. "Of course, the funds are tied up in trust for Miss Jessica until she reaches her majority," said the solicitor, looking over his steel-rimmed eyeglasses at Victoria. She nodded her understanding. He glanced down once more at the parchment in his hands and cleared his throat. "There is also a rather unusual codicil pertaining to you, Lady Victoria, which provides for a possible future increase of your income."

Victoria felt heat rise in her face. Her fingers were clasped tightly together, but otherwise she showed no other outward signs of her distress. It was monstrous that the entire family was to know of Lord Robert's manipulations, but especially that Lord Damion would learn firsthand the particulars only moments after the kiss in the gallery.

"It will not be necessary to make public the codicil at this time," said Sir Aubrey brusquely. "I was in the earl's confidence and took it upon myself to inform Lady Victoria beforehand of the codicil's import. If she wishes, she may request a private explanation from you, sir."

"I believe that an excellent suggestion," said the

solicitor, much relieved. He turned to Victoria. "I hope that meets with your approval, my lady."

"Oh yes," Victoria said quietly.

The solicitor nodded and began shuffling together the papers before him. "Then I believe we have concluded the business for which we have gathered."

Lady Hortense rose immediately. "My dear Mr. Beckworth, you have not yet taken time for luncheon, I know. Do pray join us before you set out once more." He bowed and thanked her.

As the family members dispersed, Evelyn held Lord Damion back. "A private word with you, my lord." Lord Damion raised his brows at his hard tone.

Sir Aubrey, who had paused to congratulate Lord Damion on his ascendancy, glanced sharply from one to the other. "What is this about, Evelyn?"

"Pray go on, sir. We shall join you and the ladies momentarily," said Lord Damion. Sir Aubrey hesitated, then finally nodded and left.

Lord Damion seated himself and unstoppered a decanter of wine. "I assume that this has to do with your earlier request for an audience." He poured a glass of wine and looked over at Evelyn. "Will you join me?" Evelyn shook his head, his jaw tight. Lord Damion took note of the hardness of his expression and sat back to await events. From all signs his cousin was operating under some distress.

Evelyn took hold of a chair back, his knuckles tight on the wood. It was more difficult to begin than he had imagined. Though he had always gone to pains to conceal it, he stood in awe of his elder cousin. He said abruptly, "I wish to discuss Cousin Victoria with you."

Lord Damion's brows shot up. Of all topics this was the least expected and he curiously waited for Evelyn to continue.

"When I first met Lady Victoria and learned that she had arrived in your company, I mistakenly assumed that you had brought your mistress to the Crossing," said Evelyn.

"That was gross misjudgment on your part, Evelyn," said Lord Damion quietly.

Evelyn reddened. "I know it, St. Claire. I quickly discovered how much in error I was. Cousin Victoria is a lady of quality and I have come to respect and admire her."

"Where is this leading us, Evelyn?" asked Lord Damion. "For I must assume that you have a point."

Evelyn stared down at him. "Only this, my lord. I wish to know in what light you regard our fair cousin. For I tell you straightly that I shall not stand idly by if you mean to give her a slip on the shoulder."

Surprise and anger crossed Lord Damion's face. "You forget yourself, Evelyn," he said evenly, his eyes hard.

"I think not, my lord," Evelyn said doggedly. He had always before been intimidated by his elder cousin's icy hauteur, but on this occasion he was determined not to back down. "I witnessed what passed between you and Lady Victoria in the long gallery and—"

"What has passed between Lady Victoria and me does not concern you," said Lord Damion bitingly.

"It does, by Jove!" Quick anger flared in Evelyn's blue eyes. "I care for Victoria as though she were my own sister and I shall protect her if I can. I am all too familiar with your damnable reputation, my lord. In London you are called the Demon for your amorous activities."

Lord Damion's voice was flinty. "You may rest easy, cousin. Though I fully earned my reputation, it was not done by ravishing unwilling females."

Evelyn slammed his palm against the back of the chair. "Damn you, St. Claire. Do you take me for a fool? I saw how Victoria responded to your lovemaking. You have her half on the road to ruin now. No, my lord, only your word of honor that you will stay away from Victoria will satisfy me."

"And that you shall not have, Evelyn," said Lord Damion, keeping his annoyance in check.

Evelyn heard the note of finality in his hard voice.

He stared down at Lord Damion silently for a moment, then said quietly, "I once envied your position in life, St. Claire. I envied your noble birth, your wealth, and, yes, even your reputation. But I find that I regard honor more, and in that I believe I am the better man."

Lord Damion was stunned. The contempt reflected in Evelyn's eyes penetrated and wrath kindled within him. He half rose, knocking back his chair. But before he could deliver the blistering snub that formed on his lips, his cousin had turned on his heel and strode out of the library.

Lord Damion stared at the closed door, breathing heavily. His clenched fists slowly relaxed and he dropped back into his chair. Evelyn had undoubtedly gone to join the others for luncheon. He was himself not in the mood for polite company. Lord Damion refilled his wineglass. He had not realized before how he had taken Evelyn's respect for granted and it galled him that he should smart now under his young cousin's new found contempt.

As for Evelyn's accusations, Lord Damion assured himself that he had no intention of offering Lady Victoria a slip on the shoulder. But she attracted him more than had any other woman in several months. A nagging doubt that Evelyn was right in thinking that he was taking advantage of Lady Victoria formed in his mind. But he squelched the thought firmly. Lady Victoria was a woman of the world. She would understand the consequences of a flirtation between them. He was not acting dishonorably in any way. Lord Damion felt a resurgence of anger toward Evelyn for causing him to doubt himself. He tossed back the wine and reached again for the decanter.

Lord Damion realized well enough that he would do better to wait until his displeasure cooled before he rejoined the family. At the moment he felt entirely capable of taking Evelyn to task regardless of who was listening. And Lord Damion preferred to keep the subject of their disagreement private.

* * *

At luncheon Dorothea found that she could hardly force herself to swallow a mouthful. She had not felt well for several days and had managed to ignore her discomfort fairly well. But even the smell of the barley soup now turned her stomach. When Evelyn entered the dining room and sat down beside her, he immediately noticed that she had merely picked at her plate. "Doro, you need to eat," he said shortly, still upset by his interview with Lord Damion.

Dorothea interpreted his anger as being directed at her and she flared up defensively. "Pray attend to your own plate, sir, and leave me in peace. I am not a child that must be urged to clear her plate."

Evelyn stared at her in surprise. "Doro, I merely—"

"Oh, do be quiet! I am wearied to death by your bullying," said Dorothea. She burst into tears.

"Now see what you have done, sirruh! I'll thank you to treat that girl with proper respect," said Sir Aubrey angrily.

Evelyn reddened. "She is my wife, sir. I shall address her however I wish!"

Lady Hortense rose hastily and went around the table to Dorothea. "Come, my dear. You are merely overwrought because of the baby. Let us go upstairs and lie down to rest for a few minutes." She urged Dorothea up from her chair and supported the weeping young woman from the dining room. Sir Aubrey turned wintery eyes once more on his son.

"Damnation!" exclaimed Evelyn, throwing down his napkin. He flung himself out of his chair and strode out of the room.

The solicitor, who was astonished by the scene, made a distressed noise and rose. "I fear that I must be on my way, Sir Aubrey. If there is anything I may do, you have but to contact me."

"Yes, yes." Sir Aubrey waved his hand irritably, his eyes still on the door through which Evelyn had just disappeared. The solicitor shook his head. He bowed to Victoria and Margaret and went out into the hall to ask that his carriage be brought around to the door.

Victoria and Margaret uncomfortably stared at one another. "Well," said Margaret, and shrugged.

Sir Aubrey turned his gaze on them and snorted in disgust. "Why so grave, ladies? Surely you have heard quarrels before."

Victoria chose not to hear him. She rose from the table, saying, "Margaret, will you not join me in the drawing room? I believe that we may safely leave Sir Aubrey to his wine."

"Indeed, and very willingly," said Margaret, rising in her turn. She followed Victoria out of the dining room.

Over twenty minutes later Lord Damion presented himself in the drawing room. He glanced around. Victoria was at the pianoforte and he hesitated, then approached Margaret instead. She was reading a ladies' magazine but she glanced up with a welcoming smile. Immediately Margaret saw by the look in his lordship's eyes and the hard cast of his features that he was in a foul humor. The look of animosity he exchanged with Evelyn, who had come in sometime earlier to play restlessly at billiards, spoke volumes and Margaret wondered what the gentlemen could possibly have quarreled about.

Frowning, Lord Damion sat down beside her on the sofa. She attempted to make light conversation but found him to be unresponsive. Finally, she laid her hand on his sleeve. "My lord, I see that you are distressed. If you will not confide in me as a friend, at least allow me the benefit of your company for a short hour."

Lord Damion smiled down at her. "What do you have in mind, Margaret?"

"I noticed earlier that the weather has cleared. Perhaps a ride on horseback will refresh you and I would certainly find it invigorating."

"An excellent suggestion, Margaret," said Lord Damion, already rising from his place. "I will order up mounts directly."

Evelyn caught the gist of their conversation. He

threw a challenging look at his cousin. "Do you go riding, then? By Jove, I could use the exercise myself. This place is closing in on me today. Victoria, leave off your playing and go change into your riding habit. We are all going riding."

"What a marvelous idea. It has been too long since I have been on a horse," said Victoria, her eyes brightening.

"You are naturally welcome to join us, my lady," said Lord Damion. He gave a short bow to Evelyn, who understood that his presence would be tolerated.

Margaret could only stand by in astonishment as her intimate outing with Lord Damion became all too public. But in the face of Victoria's swift enthusiasm she could only accept it with grace. "We shall be quite the party, my lord," she said, summoning up a smile.

"So it appears," said Lord Damion. He raised Margaret's hand to his lips. "I shall await you and Lady Victoria at the front steps."

Twenty-one

The four met on the frozen gravel in front of the manor. The wind had swept most of the snow in drifts against the house, creating a pretty effect as the sun touched fire to ice crystals. Grooms held mounts ready for them. Victoria was pleased to discover that she was to ride a high-stepping mare. She looked around at Lord Damion. "My lord, I truly thank you. You could not have chosen a more appropriate mount for me."

He bowed and turned to Margaret, who was pulling her crop through her fingers irritably. "I remembered that you preferred a calmer beast, Margaret."

"Thank you, my lord. You have always been a most attentive host," said Margaret throatily. She stood waiting with an expectant air and Lord Damion lifted her into the saddle. Margaret thanked him with an intimate smile.

Victoria turned away sharply. She allowed a groom to help her mount and gathered the reins. Evelyn and Lord Damion were quickly on horseback and the party moved off.

Margaret noticed Victoria's reaction and mistakenly assumed that she was feeling the smart of wounded pride. She had observed a coolness between his lordship and Lady Victoria in the last several days. She thought that Lord Damion must have made his preferences clear at last and could even find it in her heart to feel compassion for the woman. It was a pity that Lady Victoria had not heeded the warning she had given her so long ago.

Margaret did not dwell long on Victoria's loss of face as she became more aware of the horse beneath her. She sat the animal with uneasy grace, but felt any lack of skill on her part was more than amply balanced by the ravishing picture she presented. Her dark blue velvet habit was cut close to her exquisite figure and her black hair was tucked up under a small silk hat trimmed with several short white egret feathers. She glanced at Lady Victoria, whose own trim figure was shown to advantage in green velvet and gold braid. Margaret decided that her own toilette was the superior.

The thought put her in a sparkling mood and she contrived to keep Lord Damion beside her with a constant stream of witticisms.

Falling behind the couple, Victoria could not help noticing how easily Lord Damion sat his horse. He moved with his mount as though part of the animal. Victoria glanced over at Evelyn. He was also a good rider but he did not have the same instinct for his horse that Lord Damion had. Victoria glanced again at Lord Damion's mount, feeling certain that this was the famous Black Son. The stallion was built for power and speed. He was restive, obviously wanting his head, but Lord Damion held him close to a walk.

Evelyn was also studying riding form and was moved to compliment. "The mare definitely knows who her mistress is, cousin. You have an excellent seat. One can see that you have ridden a great deal."

"I ride a great deal in Portugal, of course. Indeed, Charles and I met while on horseback." Victoria laughed at the memory. "He had the audacity to haul my mount to a stand from a full gallop. I was furious and determined to lash into him, but Charles teased me into laughter within moments."

Lord Damion was apparently listening with half an ear to their conversation. "Our cousin was a remarkable man to have braved a woman's righteous wrath so audaciously," he said over his shoulder. Evelyn laughed, but Margaret was not amused. She came to the unpleasant realization that she had not had Lord Damion's undivided attention after all.

The trees around the manor opened out into clear fields. The open dale, swept clean by the wind of all but a powdering of snow, tempted Victoria unbearably. "This glorious day demands a gallop!" she exclaimed. She slapped spurs to the mare's side and the beast leaped forward in a run across the hard ground. Almost immediately a fence rose up before them and Victoria took it without hesitation.

"Oh, well done! She is a bruising rider," exclaimed Evelyn admiringly.

Black Son could not stand to see the mare running free ahead of him and pulled testily at the bit in his mouth. "All right, boy," said Lord Damion. He gave the stallion his head, glad for the excuse for a vigorous gallop. He left Margaret and Evelyn in a thunder of hoofbeats. The black stallion lifted and soared gracefully over the fence to land at full tilt on the far side.

Evelyn whooped and slapped spurs to his mount, preparing to follow.

"Evelyn, do not dare leave me alone!" commanded Margaret, shrilly. She was furious that Lord Damion had left her side, but it particularly enraged her that her own riding skills would never allow her to follow Lady Victoria's outrageous example.

Evelyn heard her as he took the first fence. Reluctantly he reined in, his head turned to watch Lord Damion and Victoria disappear into the distance. He envied them the freedom of their ride.

"Evelyn, I demand that you act the gentleman and open the gates for me," Margaret said imperiously.

Reluctantly Evelyn turned back toward the fence. "Damn good breeding," he muttered.

Victoria urged her mount on. She could hear the pounding of hooves grow louder behind her. Then the horse was racing beside her and out of the corner of her eye she saw Lord Damion leaning close over his mount's withers. She laughed aloud for sheer joy.

Neck and neck the riders raced for a copse of trees. The trunks flashed past on either side, thin at first but swiftly growing denser. Victoria drew rein at last when the low branches became threatening. She turned in the saddle, breathless with laughter. Her eyes glowed and the cold wind had whipped high color into her cheeks. "That was wonderful, my lord!" she exclaimed.

Lord Damion dismounted and tied the blowing stallion to a tree. As he approached her, he was struck by her beauty. Without thinking, he reached up to clasp her around the waist and lift her down from the saddle. Slowly he let her slide close against him to the snow-powdered ground. Victoria was no longer laughing, but stared at him with huge somber eyes.

"Victoria," he breathed softly. Lord Damion drew her to him and his kiss was at once warm and sensuous. Victoria's senses reeled with long-denied ardor. His hand slid up to cup her full breast and her body arched against him. He began to undo the buttons on the front of her habit.

Instinctively Victoria put up a shielding hand, but his hand brushed past her fingers to slip inside to caress her naked breast. He raised his head a moment to stare at her with desire in his eyes. His warm breath was ragged on her face.

Victoria pulled down his head and hungrily sought his lips. Lord Damion broke away once more to find the throbbing pulse in her neck. Her head fell back and his mouth once more crushed hers. Victoria wound her arms around his neck, giving him back equal passion.

In the distance a shrill voice cut through Lord Damion's consciousness. Slowly, reluctantly, he released Victoria. She protested incoherently, then she too heard Margaret's voice and Evelyn's impatient answer. She stumbled back from him quickly and Lord Damion left her to retrieve their horses.

Swiftly Victoria buttoned her habit and smoothed her hair, her hands shaking. Before she turned to face Lord Damion, she closed her eyes tightly and took a deep breath.

Lord Damion gave her a moment to collect herself before he took the mare over to her. Wordlessly Victoria accepted his help in mounting and then pressed the mare forward. Lord Damion vaulted into his saddle and pulled the stallion around to follow her. They rode silently through the trees until they met up with Evelyn and Margaret at the edge of the copse.

Evelyn looked harassed. Restlessly he shifted in the saddle, hardly acknowledging the two riders' return. A nagging unease had settled on him some minutes past and he had the increasing conviction that something was wrong with Dorothea.

Margaret was swift to notice Victoria's downcast eyes and subdued air. She glanced sharply at Lord Damion to discover that he was thoughtfully observing Victoria's profile. Margaret was no fool. She knew that something of moment had passed between the two. Furious, she yanked on her mount's reins and the placid mare tossed her head in surprise. "I should like to return to the Crossing, if you please, my Lord! I have been bored to tears and Evelyn has given me the headache," she said.

Evelyn jerked upright, his temper flaring "I have been at great pains to open each gate and show you goodwill, Margaret. But I'll be damned if I'll sit here and listen to your abuse!" He slapped spurs to his mount and raced off toward the Crossing.

"I shall go after him," said Victoria, seizing on Evelyn's upset to escape Lord Damion's eyes. She put the mare into swift motion. Her thoughts whirled. Their passionate interlude in the copse had shocked her to the depth of her being. She had been willing to surrender herself to him without thought for the consequences. Victoria believed that she could be but a passing fancy to him, but she had hoped that she was mistress enough of her own feelings to protect herself. Instead she had allowed him to glimpse the passionate fire in her heart, and in such a manner that stripped her of all pride.

"Well!" Margaret was astounded to find herself so suddenly alone with Lord Damion. She turned to him with an arch look. "It appears that we have been abandoned, my lord."

"I will be most happy to escort you back to the manor, ma'am," said Lord Damion formally.

It was not the reaction that Margaret had wished for, but she thought, given a little time, she would see an improvement and deliberately held her mount to a slow pace. Glancing toward Lord Damion, she smiled brightly. "It is a gorgeous day, is it not, my lord? I had thought it quite chilly before, but it has warmed most gratifyingly."

"Indeed, madame," Lord Damion said with distant courtesy. His thoughts were far away. He could not forget the feel of Victoria in his arms or how she had responded to him. Nor could he ignore the echo in his thoughts of Evelyn's accusation that he was using Victoria for his own ends. For the first time Lord Damion questioned his own motives.

Lord Damion and Margaret traveled a good distance toward the Crossing and his unfailing yet impersonal urbanity discouraged even her determined vivacity. Margaret was silent for the remainder of the ride and her headache had become very real.

When Victoria returned to the manor and entered the hall, she found the household in an uproar. Servants stood idle in the entryway, wearing anxious expressions. Upon her inquiry, a footman quickly informed her that Mrs. St. Claire was having her baby.

Victoria stripped off her riding gloves, asking swiftly, "Has Dr. Chatworth been sent for?"

"Aye, m'lady, an hour ago," said the footman.

A furious voice came clearly down the stairs. "Damn you, she is my wife!"

Victoria looked at the footman, raising her brows. The man shook his head. "Master Evelyn is that wild," he said simply.

"I see." Victoria thought quickly. "Where is Sir Aubrey?"

"I believe he went to his rooms, m'lady," said the footman.

"Send for him immediately. Inform him that I need him in Mrs. St. Claire's chambers," Victoria said, starting swiftly up the stairs. She reached Dorothea's room and paused in the door, glancing around the scene.

At the head of the four-poster bed Mrs. Lummington stoically sponged Dorthea's brow as the girl lay on her pillow. Evelyn and Lady Hortense stood beside the bed. Lady Hortense had a hand on her nephew's forearm. "Evelyn, you cannot stay. Surely you must see that."

"I have told you, Aunt, I'm staying," Evelyn said with stubborn insistence.

"Then you are a selfish fool," Victoria said coolly. They turned as she advanced. In pithy terms she made Evelyn understand that his presence was harmful for Doro's peace of mind.

"Very well, if it is better for Doro," he said, subdued. He accepted his banishment and accompanied

Victoria to the door, where he paused. His expression was fierce. "But if anything should—"

"I shall send for you immediately," said Victoria. "But the baby will take its own time, Evelyn, remember."

Sir Aubrey appeared outside the door. Evelyn threw a challenging look at Victoria, who said promptly, "Yes, I was going to ask Sir Aubrey to throw you out if you refused to leave peacefully."

Evelyn grinned reluctantly. "I go peacefully, cousin." As he turned away with the older man, Sir Aubrey glanced sardonically at Victoria. With relief Victoria closed the door.

"Well done, Victoria. I was never so glad of anything in my life. I thought we should never pry him loose," said Lady Hortense.

"Neither did I," said Victoria. She sat down on the side of the bed and took up Dorothea's fragile hand.

Dorothea smiled at her gratefully. "Thank you for sending Eve away. He is so easily upset, you know."

"So I have learned," Victoria said dryly.

"Victoria, had Damion or Margaret returned when you came up?" asked Lady Hortense.

Victoria felt a pain in her heart. She shook her head. "I left them behind when I followed Evelyn in."

"How odd. Damion is not usually a laggard. Perhaps I should go down and be available when Margaret returns. She will naturally be concerned for Doro. I shall be back, never fear." Lady Hortense left the bedroom.

There was a short silence. "Dear Mrs. Lummington, could you leave Lady Victoria and me alone for a few moments?" asked Dorothea.

"Of course, ma'am. I shall just go and see about the doctor," said Mrs. Lummington.

When they were alone, Dorothea turned to Victoria with a somber expression on her flushed face. "You have become a good friend to me, Victoria. I hope I may confide in you now."

"Certainly you may, Doro." She gave the girl's slim fingers a reassuring squeeze.

"Victoria, I fear—I am afraid I may lose the child," said Dorothea quietly.

"And I think not." Victoria gently brushed the soft hair back from Doro's brow. "Dear Doro. You have as much heart as Starfire and she brought two babes into the world."

Dorothea laughed, the shadows in her eyes receding. "You say the oddest things!" Her eyes suddenly widened. "Oh! It is beginning again. And I feel most vilely ill!"

Downstairs in the drawing room Sir Aubrey had managed to bully Evelyn into a hand of whist. His waspish insults stirred Evelyn's pride and forced him to focus on the cards.

Sir Aubrey noted how often his son's eyes strayed to the door. "Never mind about that girl, Evelyn. She will come through her confinement with flying colors," he said gently.

Evelyn quickly turned his head to stare at him, struck by the moderate tone of his voice. "Sir?"

" 'Pon my word, boy! Have you never looked at your young wife? She is pluck to the backbone for all her docile ways. In the past two months I have been pleasantly surprised by her," said Sir Aubrey gruffly. He fell silent, and his eyes took on a faraway expression. Almost under his breath he said, "At times she reminds me most strongly of my dear Amanda." There was a wealth of regret and sorrow in his voice.

Evelyn looked at his father and perhaps for the first time in his life he understood him a little. He said diffidently, "If it is a girl, we wished to christen her Amanda after my mother."

Sir Aubrey looked at his son. His heavy-lidded eyes lit with a true smile. "She would have liked that very much. Thank you, Evelyn."

Twenty-two

When Lord Damion and Margaret entered the hall, they met Lady Hortense who quickly informed them of the situation. She turned to Margaret, who stood snapping her crop between her gloved fingers. "I know that you shall wish to see her, Margaret. But truly, it would be best if you waited," she said.

Margaret stared at her in amazement for a bare second, then said hastily, "To be sure, Lady Hortense." She was appalled by the very idea of entering Dorothea's room at such a time. It would never have occurred to her to express her sisterly concern in such a fashion. "I shall go up to change, however. I do not care to be sitting about in my habit all the afternoon." She turned her glance to Lord Damion. "I know that you will excuse me, my lord."

Lord Damion bowed but it was Lady Hortense who replied. "Of course, my dear. And I shall go up with you to fetch the christening robe which Doro and I have been embroidering. You may help me to finish the sewing, for it will be needed in a very few days now," she said, linking her arm with the younger woman's. Margaret accepted her suggestion with good grace. She was mindful that Lady Hortense was beloved by her son and must be accorded every courtesy. Lord Damion appeared entirely self-contained, but Margaret had long since come to the conclusion that his mother's opinion mattered greatly to him. Margaret therefore intended that nothing should give that lady a prejudice against her.

Lord Damion went into the drawing room and

settled down to observe the cardplayers. He was not long in concluding that Evelyn's concentration had gone begging.

Lady Hortense and Margaret returned within minutes. Lady Hortense carried her sewing basket and was remarking, "Is it not odd that the dear creatures always know when something is afoot?"

Margaret agreed, glancing down with mixed feelings at the two small dogs gamboling about her feet. When she had paused briefly at Dorothea's room to inquire about her, the spaniels had attached themselves to her in joyful recognition. Margaret seated herself beside Lady Hortense on the sofa and threaded a needle. She actually did not mind embroidery, but she did not often ply a needle because such activity did not fit her image of the idle society beauty.

Lord Damion gestured at the spaniels. "I did not know you were such a favorite," he said humorously.

Margaret threw him a laughing glance. "And neither did I, my lord. They are silly creatures. I had thought them entirely loyal to Doro." She sternly admonished the spaniels to behave. They obediently sat down, panting happily, and looked up at her with expectant eyes. "Oh very well," said Margaret, unable to withstand their eager gaze. She found a scrap of fabric in Lady Hortense's basket and tossed it to the spaniels. The small dogs attacked it in a mock-ferocious tug-of-war. Margaret laughed and Lord Damion joined in her amusement. Lady Hortense regarded the two with a benevolent smile.

It was upon this scene that the butler announced visitors. Sir Harry and Miss Erica Belingham entered the drawing room.

"Oh, what precious spaniels!" exclaimed Erica, bending to stroke one as it dashed into range. "Do they belong to you, Mrs. Giddings?"

Margaret shook her head, affecting unawareness of Sir Harry's glance as he bowed civilly over Lady Hortense's hand. "Lucinda and Smudge are my sister's charges, thank goodness. They have simply attached themselves to me this afternoon since they have not been allowed into her room." She patted one of the affectionate spaniels when it placed a feathery paw on her knee, then she brushed its paw gently down.

Quick concern crossed Sir Harry's face. "Dr. Chatworth came in with us and I wondered—I hope that Mrs. St. Claire is not ill?"

"I think you have only to observe Evelyn's agitation to guess the cause of dear Doro's affliction," Lady Hortense said humorously.

Comprehension came swift to the Belinghams. Sir Harry and Erica exchanged a glance and Erica said, "Then you must certainly wish us gone, ma'am. We shall pay our social call at a later time when Mrs. St. Claire is out of her confinement."

"Oh, do not go!" exclaimed Margaret, dismayed. She had been thinking that the Belinghams' arrival was the most pleasant interlude of the afternoon. Sir Harry glanced her way and Margaret summoned up her most winning smile. "Pray do not allow them to leave, Lady Hortense. Fresh company is just what we all need to occupy us."

"Of course Sir Harry and Miss Belingham shall not leave. I will not hear of it. It is too long a drive to return immediately to Belingham in this cold," Lady Hortense said firmly. She tugged on the bell rope hanging beside the sofa. "I shall order tea immediately. Sir Harry and Miss Belingham, I urge you to make yourselves comfortable."

The Belinghams gave in to Lady Hortense's overtures and soon settled themselves near the fire. Lord Damion and Sir Harry exchanged pleasantries, each taking the other's measure and liking what they saw. Erica leaned close to see the christening dress that Lady Hortense and Margaret were sewing, commenting that it was a very pretty gown.

Sir Aubrey and Evelyn gave scant attention to the newcomers. Sir Aubrey was using all his wiles to keep his son attentive to the card game and he spared them only a bare nod.

The butler and a footman brought in the tea board,

and urn and cakes were soon brought. Lady Hortense, concerned about Evelyn's paleness, pressed him to take some refreshment. Evelyn refused vehemently.

Sir Aubrey threw a comprehensive glance at his son's greenish gills. "Leave the boy alone, Hortense. I wish him to concentrate on the card play and he cannot be swilling tea, too!" he said testily.

"Very well, Aubrey," said Lady Hortense, affronted. She returned to her place on the sofa and began to exert herself in amusing her guests. She was ably assisted by Margaret, who liked nothing better than to have more than one handsome gentleman in her vicinity. To her credit, Margaret made a point of including Erica. The ladies gradually drifted into a discussion of laces and velvets and the gentlemen were left to fend for themselves.

Lord Damion turned to Sir Harry. "We seem to be forgotten, Sir Harry. Allow me to propose a game of billiards." He lowered his voice, not wanting Lady Hortense to hear. "I should like to hear privately anything you may tell me about the war. We hear so damnably little these days."

"Of course, my lord," said Sir Harry, bowing. He had been awaiting just such an opportunity to converse privately with Lord Damion so that he could get a better understanding of the man. Victoria had said very little about the earl, but Sir Harry was sensitive enough to the nuances of her voice to know that she had fairly strong feelings toward Lord Damion. The gentlemen rose from their chairs and went to the billiards table.

Erica expressed her interest in Margaret's description of a blue velvet pelisse trimmed in gold frogging and ribands that was the latest rage in London. "How I envy you the chance to observe firsthand the fashions," she said, sighing. "Dear Mama has promised me a Season next year but it seems very hard to wait before one may refurbish one's wardrobe."

"I had the pelisse packed when I came down with Doro, not knowing if an opportunity to wear it would not occur," said Margaret, sparing a glance in Lord

Damion's direction. "Should you care to see it? Indeed, we are almost the same size. I believe it might fit you, if you would care to try it on."

"To be sure, how very generous of you!" exclaimed Erica. "I should very much like to gather ideas for my own seamstress to copy." Margaret, wondering at her own unusual generosity, led the younger woman out of the drawing room and upstairs. The two spaniels followed them, racing dizzily around their feet.

Lord Damion noticed when Miss Belingham and Margaret left the drawing room. He glanced over at his mother. "I perceive that you are quite deserted, ma'am," he said with a smile.

"And to my great satisfaction," said Lady Hortense, aware that he meant to interrupt his billiards game if she allowed him. "I shall accomplish much more without holding up my end of a conversation. Pray do not trouble yourself, my dear." She began to turn the hem on the white muslin and lace christening dress. Lord Damion was satisfied that she was truly content and turned his attention once more to the billiards table.

Victoria suddenly entered the drawing room. Evelyn's face drained of color when he saw her. She smiled at him and her eyes danced. "You have a lusty son, Evelyn. And Dorothea is already asking for you," she said, laughing.

Evelyn whooped for joy. He leaped to his feet and caught Victoria in a spin that left her breathless. An instant later he released her and dashed upstairs.

"Well, it seems as good a time as any to make my way upstairs. I want very much to congratulate the new parents. And I know that Margaret will wish to be informed," said Lady Hortense, putting away her sewing. She rose and followed Evelyn.

Sir Aubrey sat back in his chair. His eyes snapped and a faint smile tugged at his thin lips. He looked up as Lord Damion approached him. "The pair of them have made me a grandfather, damn them," he said gruffly.

Lord Damion smiled and squeezed his shoulder.

He knew how pleased the old gentleman was though he attempted to hide it. "They will allow us to see him in a few moments. Would you like to go up now, sir?"

Sir Aubrey nodded. "Aye. I'll want to know what those two name my grandson. Lend me your arm, Damion. I've mislaid my cane." Lord Damion helped him to his feet and walked with him out of the room. Sir Aubrey leaned heavily on his nephew and for the first time Victoria was struck by Sir Aubrey's age.

"Vicky."

She turned as Sir Harry stepped around the billiards table. Without a thought Victoria went straight into his arms. "Dearest Harry. You are so comfortable." She sighed against his shoulder.

Laughter rippled in his voice. "My dear girl, what if someone should enter? I doubt that our reputations could stand the scandal."

"Oh, let them all talk. Jessica and I shall soon be beyond the reach of Lord Damion or anyone else," said Victoria.

Sir Harry frowned over her head. It was very unlike Victoria to be so flippant and the fact that she mentioned the Earl of March was revealing. He thought he knew her better than any other living being and he was disturbed. "Victoria, has Lord Damion done anything to upset you? When I received your letter in Portugal, I was franky alarmed for I had heard of his reputation. That is why I applied for an early leave," he said.

Victoria shook her head. "Harry, how nonsensical you are. Whatever could he have done?"

Sir Harry's sensitive ear caught a strange inflection in her voice. He held her away from him by the shoulders. There was a hard look about his mouth. "You cannot gammon me, my girl. Come, do not be afraid to tell me, Victoria. Has he hurt you?"

Victoria's face flamed and she put up her hands to hide it. "Oh on, no! Not in the way you think, but— oh Harry, I am so confused!"

Sir Harry suspected that she was distressed over

more than Lord Damion's actions. He took hold of her wrists and gently forced down her hands. "Look at me, Vicky." Reluctantly Victoria raised tearful eyes and Sir Harry whistled in astonishment. "Dear girl, you have fallen hard for him! No, it's no use denying it, love. Remember how well I know you. I haven't seen you this upset since word came that Charles was dead. His lordship has evidently struck a very deep chord."

"Oh Harry!" Victoria flung herself against his chest, her tears flowing over. He folded his arms about her and gently rocked her, crooning comfortingly. After several minutes Victoria straightened up. He offered his handkerchief to her and she thanked him quietly, drying her eyes.

He strolled over to the window. He noticed that it was beginning to snow again. "Well, love, what is to be done?"

Victoria joined him by the velvet drapes. With her composure once more intact, she said, "I shall return to Lisbon after Christmas and forget Lord Damion."

"You are jesting. Surely you would not leave England before you discovered whether he returned your regard," said Sir Harry in disbelief.

"Harry, you have forgotten Sir Aubrey's scheme," said Victoria quietly.

"What the devil does that have to do with anything?" asked Sir Harry impatiently.

"It has a great deal to do with it. You see, the scheme did not originate with Sir Aubrey. He was merely attempting to carry out Lord Robert's wishes, which are stated in his will. Lord Robert provided that I should be rewarded handsomely if I should marry Lord Damion." Victoria clasped her arms about herself against a draft coming through the leaded window panes.

"Good Lord," said Sir Harry blankly. "Is Lord Damion aware of this provision?"

"I do not think he knows the actual contents of the codicil. At least, I believe he does not. But you must see now, Harry. How can I ever hope for any better ending when my motives will be suspect if I should dare to approach his lordship?" asked Victoria.

Sir Harry opened his lips to reply, but she held up her hand to stop him. "Not a word more, Harry, I pray you. My mind is made up and I shan't be bothered further," she said.

"I bow in respect to your wishes, madame," said Sir Harry. He did not care for it, but he was shrewd enough to realize that she needed time to sort out her own way. He made a flourishing leg and Victoria laughed, grateful to him for his tact and sensitivity.

She heard activity in the hall. "Erica must be awaiting you. I doubt if Margaret kept her long once the news of the baby found her." They turned toward the drawing-room door and Victoria tucked her hand inside his elbow as they crossed the carpet. "I shall miss you when I return to Lisbon, Harry. You have been quite the best friend I have ever had, barring Rebecca."

Sir Harry turned and caught her in a brotherly hug, then looked down at her with a grin. "I think you are a fool, you know." Victoria nodded, returning his smile somewhat waveringly.

The door opened and Lord Damion stood on the threshold. At sight of Victoria in Sir Harry's arms, a sudden frown gathered between his eyes. Sir Harry released Victoria, raising his brows at the flash of jealousy he saw in the other man's eyes. Lord Damion addressed him shortly. "Miss Belingham awaits you in the hall."

Sir Harry nodded. He and Victoria together moved through the doorway. As Victoria was nearly past him, Lord Damion stepped forward. Victoria was amazed when he pulled her back into the room. "I know that you will excuse us, Belingham," Lord Damion said somewhat grimly, his fingers tight about Victoria's slender wrist.

Ready laughter sprang to Sir Harry's eyes. He saw that Victoria was to learn what Lord Damion's feelings were toward her whether she willed it or not. He bowed formally. "Of course, my lord. Good-bye, Lady Victoria."

Twenty-three

"Harry!" Victoria stared in astonishment as Sir Harry gently closed the door behind him, leaving her alone with Lord Damion. She rounded on Lord Damion furiously. "Unhand me at once, sir. I shall not be dragged about like an army baggage yet again!"

Lord Damion grasped both her arms and shook her. "God help me, but I should like to strangle you. You dare to flirt with Belingham! I demand to know what he is to you."

"How dare you!" gasped Victoria, shaking herself free. "Harry is my very dearest friend. How dare you suggest that we—that I—oh!" Before she gave thought to her action Victoria slapped him full across the cheek. She stared at him defiantly, expecting him to retaliate in some fashion.

Lord Damion stared down at her becomingly flushed face. He realized that she was truly angry at his insinuation. Suddenly he laughed. "You are the first woman ever to strike the Demon with impunity, my girl," he said humorously.

Victoria was bewildered and suspicious of his friendliness. She eyed him warily.

"Perhaps I could choose a more auspicious beginning, my lady, but I wish to inform you of my sincere affection for you," said Lord Damion. He smiled gently at her. Recalling the passion that she had revealed to him in the copse, he continued with a comfortable assurance. "I know that you are not indifferent to me, Victoria. My dear girl, I am doing it so badly! But I am asking if you will become my wife."

Bright confidence shone in his gray eyes and Victoria dropped her gaze. Her heart thudded painfully against her ribs as she allowed his words to sink in. Despair threatened to overpower her and with a mighty effort of will she forced herself to speak calmly. "I am honored, truly honored, Lord Damion. But I cannot accept your proposal." Her voice quavered and she turned her head away so that he would not see the sudden tears in her eyes.

Lord Damion stared at her in shocked disbelief. "Victoria!" He caught her hands urgently. "My darling Victoria, pray look at me and tell me the truth. Can you say that you care nothing for me?"

Victoria shook her head. "Oh no, no. I do care for you, my lord, more than I should. But there lies so much between us. My scruples will not allow me to accept you."

Lord Damion thought he understood. "You must believe me when I say that not Margaret, nor any other woman can come close to rivaling you in my esteem, my lady. Only you have ever truly held my heart."

Half laughing, Victoria freed one of her hands to lay a cool palm against his hard cheek. Her eyes glittered with unshed tears. "Oh my lord, if it were only so simple. But I am your cousin's widow and have borne his child. Surely that must—"

Lord Damion made an impatient gesture. "I care naught for the past, ma'am. And you must realize by now how securely little Jessica resides in my heart. I shall count it an honor to be her father."

"Oh Damion, pray do not make it so difficult. Pray, pray do not press me," exclaimed Victoria, putting her hands to her cheeks and turning away from him. Her thoughts were agitated. If only Sir Aubrey had not perpetuated that despicable scheme of Lord Robert's. If only he had not told her of the codicil in the will. It would all be so different even if she could but claim ignorance.

Lord Damion caught her tight by the shoulders and whirled her to face him. He stared down into her soft dark eyes. "You care for me, Victoria. I know it," he said with soft grimness. When she tried to look away, he shook her. "Admit it, my lady!"

Victoria clutched his arms for support. "Yes, my lord, I do care! But I shall not marry you."

Lord Damion stared down at her, frustrated almost beyond endurance. He could think of no good reason why his chosen lady should spurn him unless— His eyes narrowed. Victoria gasped as his fingers bit cruelly into her shoulders. "Was I right after all, Victoria? Is it Belingham? Are you already spoken for? Is that why?" he asked softly. She looked up at him with wide, almost uncomprehending eyes. With an oath Lord Damion swept her into his arms and kissed her savagely. His hands played roughly over her body. He tore his lips from hers to seek the pounding pulse in the soft *V* of her neck.

Victoria fought her way free, then slapped him with all her strength. "Is this the Demon's usual method of persuasion?" she asked with loathing. Tears rolled down her flushed cheeks. She wrenched open the door and fled from the drawing room. She was unaware of the staring footmen or departing guests as she ran up the stairs to seek refuge in her room.

While the onlookers stood in amazement, they heard the distant slamming of a door. Almost as one they turned to Lord Damion, who stood stock-still in the drawing-room doorway. His hands were clenched at his sides and a thunderous expression darkened his face. When he became conscious of the various curious and horrified gazes directed at him, he flushed under his tan. Turning on his heel, he strode swiftly away down the hall.

As he disappeared, Erica took hold of Sir Harry's arm and said, "What a truly romantic gentleman, brother! I quite see why Mama disliked my poor soldier last year. He lacked the proper dash. I shall now know what to look for in my next beau."

Sir Harry's eyes happened to be on Margaret's

face and he saw her whiten. His brows rose in surprised understanding. "Oh, do clam up, Erica," said Sir Harry easily. He turned back to Lady Hortense and renewed his leave. Reminded of her manners, Erica warmly seconded his civilities and promised that she would visit again.

"Of course, my dear. You are always welcome," said Lady Hortense, mortified and flustered. She sent the Belinghams on their way with almost indecent haste so that she could go in search of her son.

With Sir Harry's leavetaking, Margaret's composure vanished. She had made a point of being on hand when he left and she now wished that she had remained with Doro, happily ignorant of the quarrel between Lord Damion and Lady Victoria. Margaret went up to her bedroom. She was not in a sociable mood and abruptly dismissed her dresser. It had shocked her to witness what was clearly a lover's quarrel. Once again she felt uncertain of her power over Lord Damion and it was an unsettling sensation. She stared broodingly out of her window at the beautiful cold countryside. This sojourn at the Crossing was decidedly unamusing, she thought.

Lady Hortense made inquiries of her son without success. No one had seen him pass and he had not spoken to anyone of his destination. Finally one of the footmen had the inspiration to send down to the stables and an affirmative message came back. He had taken out the stallion, Black Son. The groom privately confided to the messenger that his lordship had looked as black as thunder and had put Black Son to the fence without any hesitation. As for when his lordship would be back, his lordship had not said.

Lady Hortense was forced to be satisfied with this intelligence. She left orders that when Lord Damion did return he was to present himself in her rooms no matter what the hour. Then she went upstairs to her private sitting room to wait.

Lord Damion returned to the Crossing some hours later. He was cold, wet, and tired. He had run Black

Son almost to the point of exhaustion. The stallion trembled beneath him and he realized that his fury had nearly led him to ruin the splendid animal. His conscience smote him. He turned his mount homeward and let the stallion fall into a comfortable pace that allowed his thoughts to flow uninterrupted.

Lord Damion had been furious with Victoria, not only for refusing him but also for creating the scene in the hall. It had caused him no small mortification. But as he pondered the scene, a calm despondency settled over him. For the first time in his life a woman had denied him and she was the one woman he had ever truly loved.

By the time that Lord Damion returned Black Son to the stables and received his mother's message his anger had burned itself out. As he entered the manor he concluded that he had only himself to blame for Victoria's refusal. He had treated her shabbily from the first. He believed her honest when she admitted to caring for him, but Lord Damion thought his reputation had given Victoria a permanent disgust of him.

It was a subdued man who presented himself in his mother's sitting room. They spoke a few moments of the weather and his hard ride. Lady Hortense did not ask what had occurred between him and Lady Victoria. She knew that he would tell her in his own time.

Lord Damion fell silent for several minutes. Lady Hortense waited patiently, attending to her embroidery by the candlelight. "I have fallen in love at last, Mama," he said finally.

Lady Hortense spared him a brief glance over her embroidery hoop. "Indeed, Damion? I knew that one day it would happen."

He looked quizzingly at her. "You do not appear altogether surprised, ma'am."

"Allow a fond and alert mother her due, Damion. I have had my suspicions these many weeks." Lady Hortense paused in her needlework to look up at him. "I am somewhat surprised, though, that it should be Lady Victoria. She is not in your style at all, my son. But perhaps that is the attraction?"

Lord Damion smiled at her. "I own that I do not know. But have I been so obvious, ma'am?"

"I believe only to me," said Lady Hortense comfortably. "I am most pleased with your choice, Damion. Lady Victoria is a levelheaded attractive young woman of no common sort. I will be most happy to welcome her as my daughter."

Lord Damion bent his head. "She will not have me."

At the underlying desperation in his voice, Lady Hortense dropped her needlework. "My dear!"

He looked up and pain shone in his eyes. "I have bungled it beyond repair, Mama. When she refused me, my only thought was that there had to be another man and I went mad with jealousy. My conduct was totally reprehensible."

"Surely once you apologize—"

Lord Damion leaped up and strode to the mantel. He stared down at the fire. "There is no apology that could possibly excuse me, ma'am!" In his own imagination his bad behavior had assumed devilish proportions. He said hoarsely, "Oh Mama, I am such a fool."

Lady Hortense stared at Lord Damion's bowed head. She could not recall ever seeing her self-possessed son so distraught. "Well. You seem to have gotten yourself into a pretty coil, Damion."

Lord Damion gave a ghost of a laugh and turned. "You have a genius for understatement, my love."

"I do not mean to give you pain, Damion, but does Lady Victoria return your regard?" asked Lady Hortense hesitantly.

His amusement vanished. "I had believed so. Indeed, she admitted— But I was mistaken." His mouth twisted. "Lady Victoria's scruples will not allow her to accept my hand in marriage. I can only suppose that my rakehell reputation has at last totally undone me."

Lady Hortense had pricked up her ears at hearing

of Lady Victoria's reciprocation and she felt a measure of hope for her son. She picked up her needlework once more. "Nonsense. Lady Victoria wouldn't give a thought to your reputation if deciding upon marriage. Women don't, you know. I shall feel her out about it. I'll warrant that her scruples have to do with something far other than your sordid existence."

"Mama!"

Lady Hortense looked up at his astonished expression. She said calmly, "I am well aware of how you have chosen to live, Damion."

He met her eyes for a somber moment of discovery. "I have given you much pain. I most humbly beg your pardon, ma'am."

Lady Hortense's faded blue eyes filled. She stretched out her hand to him. Lord Damion grasped her fingers gently and bowed over her hand, saluting her with a kiss. "My dear son. Of course it wounds me that you squander your youth in frivolous dissipation," said Lady Hortense. "But I am aware that is what society demands of you."

Lord Damion laughed shortly. "My dear ma'am, if I had aught better to do, I would. The truth is that I suffer from lack of employment. I am too well situated in life for my restless nature."

"Then you must marry at once. And if Lady Victoria won't have you, then you must rejoin the army," said Lady Hortense.

Lord Damion was nonplussed. He finally found his voice. "Have you gone quite mad, Mama?"

"Not at all, Damion. I hope I am practical enough to accept what is best for my son. I have known these many months that you are unhappy. I have observed how keen you are about any news from the Peninsula. You did not think that I could overhear your conversation with Sir Harry, but I caught nearly every word. I think perhaps a little excitement or ... or glory will suit you."

"War is hardly that, ma'am!" retorted Lord Damion.

"Oh, I believe it is for many men. Otherwise old men would recollect more than they do," said Lady

Hortense with a sad wisdom. "And though I shall miss you and feel anxious on your account, I shall rest easy knowing that I did not keep you tied to my apron strings."

"You have never attempted to hold on to me, Mama," said Lord Damion.

"Of course I have. Every mother does," Lady Hortense said firmly. "Now as to Lady Victoria, I shall try to discover why she is reluctant to marry my son. Then perhaps we shall have a proper wedding before you return to the army, for I feel certain that you shall do so. I doubt that Victoria will mind following the drum once more, do you?"

"You are incorrigible, Mama," said Lord Damion, laughing at her.

"It is how I keep young. Now do go away, Damion. I have knotted my thread twice in the last hour. Obviously I would do better to retire."

Lord Damion dutifully bent to kiss her. "Thank you, Mama," he said softly. He left the sitting room much cheered. He had somehow to discover a way to overcome his lady's refusal.

After Lord Damion had gone, Lady Hortense sat for a long time before the fire. There was sadness in her eyes that she would never allow to show in public. She knew that she had effectively given her son *carte blanche* about the war. And she feared the consequences.

Twenty-four

Lord Damion did not place any stock in his mother's determination to feel out Lady Victoria's feelings, but he had underestimated her. After dinner the following day and while the gentlemen were still at their wine, Lady Hortense approached Victoria in the drawing room. She asked her to play a favorite tune for her and offered to turn the music. Victoria agreed and as she began to play, Lady Hortense casually began, "I must confess that I find your playing most comforting, Lady Victoria. I wish that after you are done visiting here in the neighborhood, you could visit me at Crestlawn."

Victoria looked at her with surprise. "Thank you, ma'am. But I really must return home to Lisbon after I leave Belingham Manor. I fear that I shall find my household in complete disarray if I absent myself much longer."

"It is a pity," said Lady Hortense with a sigh. "I shall be lonely after Damion returns to the army."

Victoria's fingers faltered momentarily. Margaret glanced their way, surprised by Victoria's mistake, but a moment later she resumed her conversation with Dorothea. "I beg pardon? Surely Lord Damion is not contemplating going to the Peninsula!" said Victoria.

"Oh, but I am certain he will. He is bored to exhaustion by his life here in England so I have urged him to return to the army. I shall be anxious for him, of course. He is my only son, after all. But I thought the excitement might do him good," said

Lady Hortense with a brave smile. She put the corner of a handkerchief to her eyes.

"Oh, my dear ma'am!" Victoria turned to her, holding out her hands.

Lady Hortense gestured hastily as Margaret and Dorothea looked up. "Play, Lady Victoria, do play. I find music to be so sustaining when I am overwrought."

Victoria did as she was bid, her heart touched by Lady Hortense's fortitude. "Surely my lord will not leave you in such distress, ma'am."

"I have told him that he must do what he feels to be his duty. But it would all be so much easier to bear if Damion were married and I had a daughter to support me," said Lady Hortense, glancing sideways at Victoria. "I should wish for a daughter who was much like you, Lady Victoria. And I know that Damion would never do anything foolish if he had someone waiting for him to return. But knowing how careless Damion can be, I cannot help but wonder—" She broke off and patted Victoria's arm. "But never mind. In any event, I wished you to know that I do truly think of you as the daughter that I never had, Lady Victoria."

Victoria went pale. "You compliment me, my lady."

"Oh no, for I admire you greatly, my dear." Lady Hortense gently closed the sheet of music. "Thank you, Lady Victoria. Your music has eased my spirits considerably. I see that the gentlemen have come in. Shall we join them?"

"Of course," said Victoria. She rose from the pianoforte and somehow managed to seat herself beside Dorothea. She listened to the quiet conversation with a semblance of interest, but her thoughts were on Lady Hortense's confidences.

Victoria was stunned to learn that Lord Damion meant to return to the war. After what Lady Hortense had said about his carelessness and his impulsive character, Victoria very much feared that she herself was the cause of his sudden decision.

When Victoria had refused Lord Damion's proposal she had been thinking of herself and her own pride. The thought of what would be said about her if she married Lord Damion and the contents of the codicil became known had been galling to her. That the codicil would eventually become known Victoria had no doubts at all. But she now realized that far more was at stake than her pride. She had known for some time that she was in love with Lord Damion and she had made a conscious decision to bear the loss of her own happiness with fortitude. But leaving him behind in England, safe and whole, was far different from knowing that he would be at war. The thought of losing him completely, as she had lost Charles March, was unendurable.

Sir Aubrey, who had heard of the quarrel between Lord Damion and Victoria, regarded her with antagonism. He suspected that she had killed Lord Damion's interest in her with an overstrong display of temper. His nephew had not addressed her once during the entire dinner and was obviously avoiding her now. Sir Aubrey was seized with bitter disappointment for her stupidity and he made no secret of his displeasure.

Margaret, who more than once glanced at Victoria in escalating frustration as Sir Aubrey exercised his caustic wit, was finally goaded into defending Victoria. Her pointed setdown momentarily silenced Sir Aubrey.

Victoria became aware of the direction of the conversation and was surprised but grateful for Margaret's unexpected championship. Later, as they went upstairs, she thanked Margaret.

Margaret shrugged. "We may not be fast friends, Lady Victoria, but I hate to stand by when someone is torn to pieces by an old reprobate like Sir Aubrey." She glanced curiously at Victoria. "That meekness was not your usual style, my lady. What happened to you this evening?"

Victoria smiled and, unwilling to reveal her true thoughts, said, "I had a headache. But I did not feel that I could make my excuses without appearing as though I were in retreat."

"I shall politely accept that, but I must tell you that

I do not believe it for a moment." Margaret stopped outside her door and smiled at Victoria with more warmth than was her wont. "I know that you go to look in on Jessica now. I shall wish you good night, Lady Victoria."

The ladies parted amicably and Victoria went to enter the nursery. She had thought earlier in the day that Jessica appeared a bit flushed and she now wanted to satisfy herself that her daughter was well before she retired.

The nursemaid's somber expression lightened when she saw Victoria. She rose from her chair. "I am that happy to see you, m'lady. Miss Jessica has been that fretful and asking for you. She has but just dropped off this hour."

Victoria bent over her daughter's quiet form and placed a cool hand against her forehead. She was appalled to feel hot, dry skin. It dawned on her that Jessica's breathing was short and shallow and her small face appeared flushed even in the firelight. Victoria rounded on the nursemaid. "How long has she had this fever? Why was I not sent for?"

Eliza trembled at the blaze of anger in her ladyship's voice. "Fever, m'lady?" she stammered. She put her hand on Jessica's forehead and quickly snatched it away. "Oh, my! M'lady, I did not know. She was but a little warm when I put her down, m'lady, I promise you!"

The nursemaid's genuine alarm penetrated Victoria's anger. She put her hand on the girl's arm. "Forgive me, Eliza. My temper runs away with me. I know that you would not neglect Jessica. Pray ring for Mrs. Lummington immediately. And direct someone to fill the hip bath halfway with lukewarm water, at once."

"Yes, m'lady!" Eliza flew out of the nursery, glad to have services to perform.

Within minutes Victoria had immersed her daughter's hot, lethargic body in the hip bath and knelt beside it to support Jessica's head. At the first touch of the lukewarm water Jessica awakened and howled.

When Victoria crooned soothingly to her, she subsided to tearful moans. Eliza hovered anxiously, standing ready with a towel.

Mrs. Lummington quickly arrived and when she understood the reason for her summons, she called sharply for a candle. Her hapless niece clumsily handed over a taper and Mrs. Lummington leaned over Jessica, shielding the candle with her broad hand to prevent wax drippings. She peered intently at the small child. "Aye, my lady, it looks to be the measles. The spots are ever so faint, but there on her face and breast—"

"Yes, I see them," said Victoria. Jessica stirred in her arms and sighed. Victoria felt the girl's forehead. "Thank God, the fever has gone down at last."

Mrs. Lummington rose with astonishing grace for her girth. "Eliza, help her ladyship and be quick about it!" The nursemaid obeyed with alacrity and wrapped the towel about the child when Victoria took her out of the water. Mrs. Lummington found the warming pan on the hearth and warmed the bed's icy sheets.

When Jessica was once more in her bed, Victoria turned to the housekeeper. "Thank you for coming so promptly. I shall want the doctor, of course. And I shall ask Mary to move some of my things into Miss Webster's former room so that I can be close by while Jessica is ill." She spared a quick smile for the silent nursemaid. "Between us, Eliza and I shall keep a sharp watch on Jessica."

"I understand, my lady," said Mrs. Lummington respectfully. She thought it a rare thing when a lady took the nursing of a sick child upon herself.

Arrangements were soon concluded. Eliza volunteered to sit up with Jessica until the early morning hours when Victoria would spell her. She promised to call Victoria at the first sign of restlessness or fever.

Mrs. Lummington sent a manservant for the doctor. "I have taken the liberty of making up a hot bran poultice, my lady. It will ease the poor child's breathing."

"Thank you, Mrs. Lummington. I truly appreciate your kindness." Victoria unbuttoned her daughter's gown and applied the poultice to Jessica's bare chest.

Mary, who had been sitting up to help her mistress undress, was notified that she was to move part of Victoria's wardrobe into the bedroom recently vacated by Miss Webster. She clucked distractedly as she hurriedly put the gowns away in the new wardrobe. Then she efficiently made up a fire on the empty hearth. Mary's last duty was to turn down the bedclothes and warm the sheets with a warming pan.

Victoria knew that Dr. Chatworth would not arrive for a few hours. She lay down on the bed fully dressed, deciding that she needed to get what rest she could before Eliza came for her. She did not sleep soundly, but tossed and started up at the least noise.

Eliza came in a few hours later to waken her and Victoria rose immediately. The nursemaid followed her back into the child's room. "Miss Jessica has been resting peaceful like, m'lady. The poultice eased her breathing," Eliza said softly as Victoria bent over the child.

"Thank you, Eliza," said Victoria. The nursemaid bobbed a curtsy and left to go tiredly to her bed. Victoria settled into the chair beside Jessica. The night was interminable to Victoria, who dozed fitfully and woke at her daughter's slightest movement.

When Eliza returned in the morning, Victoria got up stiffly from the chair. "I feel as though I were a hundred years old, Eliza," she said, stretching painfully.

"You would feel better for a bit of tea and toast, m'lady. I will keep sharp watch on Miss Jessica, I promise you that."

Victoria knew that the nursemaid was right. "All right, then," she agreed reluctantly, waiting only long enough to see that Eliza was smoothing Jessica's pillows before she went to her room. Victoria splashed water onto her face and smoothed her hair.

When she presented herself in the breakfast room, Dorothea exclaimed in horror at her rumpled appearance and heavy eyes. "Victoria, whatever is wrong?"

Victoria assured her that her own health was unimpaired. "But Jessica is ill. Mrs. Lummington thinks it is the measles," said Victoria.

Lord Damion had risen at Victoria's entrance and held a chair for her. Victoria took her seat with a brief word of thanks. Lord Damion bowed and returned to his own chair. When Victoria made no move to serve herself, he spooned a serving of ham and poached eggs onto her plate. He did not turn his gaze from Victoria until she picked up her fork. Victoria thought she had never smelled such unappealing eggs, but she felt compelled by Lord Damion's interest to make an effort at eating.

"What rotten luck," said Evelyn, quick concern in his eyes.

"Poor little Jessica. I know that she must be miserable. Do you think perhaps I might cheer her if I were to visit?" asked Dorothea.

"On no account are you to go near the nursery, Doro," said Evelyn in swift alarm. He bowed in apology to Victoria. "I am sorry, cousin. But I cannot have Doro exposed."

'Of course not. Evelyn is perfectly right, Doro. You must think of the infant first," Victoria said, easily reading her young friend's stubborn expression. She stretched out her hand to Dorothea across the table. "You are very good, Doro, but I don't wish to be anxious on your account as well, you know."

Dorothea nodded and smiled at her. "Very well, Victoria."

Lord Damion had listened with a grave expression. "I assume that you have already sent for Dr. Chatworth. Pray let me know immediately if there is aught else that I can do on Jessica's behalf, Lady

Victoria. Be assured that I will do all in my power to provide her with the best of care."

Victoria smiled, little knowing how vulnerable she appeared to him. "Thank you, my lord. I have Eliza to assist me and Dr. Chatworth should arrive at any moment." Even as she spoke the door opened and a footman announced that the doctor had arrived. Victoria rose immediately, forgetting her breakfast, and left the breakfast room. Lord Damion thoughtfully regarded her barely touched plate.

"Miss Webster chose a damnable time to take her departure," said Evelyn, frowning.

Dorothea nodded, sighing. "Yes, for I know that Victoria means to nurse Jessica herself. It is quite like her to do so. Of course she will have Eliza to help her, but Miss Webster would have been such a support to her just now. I only wish that I could offer my assistance as well."

Evelyn took her hand, pressing her fingers gently. "You are an angel, Doro," he said softly.

Lord Damion kept his own counsel, but he meant to keep a close watch on the situation in the nursery. The measles was a serious matter for a small child and Lady Victoria had every right to feel lively concern. When he finished breakfast, he ordered the butler to attend to Lady Victoria's every need promptly. He would observe Lady Victoria closely during Jessica's illness, for he had already seen that she would neglect her own needs if she was not reminded of them.

For days Jessica hovered between serious illness and recovery. She was fretful and petulant by turns and it proved a challenge to keep her comfortable. Each day Victoria had to coax her to take small amounts of rice or sago pudding, toast, and beef tea, but the tonic that Dr. Chatworth had left for her was the greatest challenge. Jessica detested the taste of it and Victoria felt exhausted after every session.

Victoria gradually became aware of a certain strained look about Eliza and began to wonder about it. She was therefore little surprised when the nursemaid came down with fever five days into Jessica's illness.

"I am that sorry, m'lady. I have failed you again," said Eliza fretfully. She lay on a narrow cot in her own room and, despite her illness, was embarrassed that her ladyship had seen fit to visit her.

"Never mind, Eliza. I've only come to tell you that Jessica appears to be on the mend. You need only think of yourself now." Victoria gently squeezed the girl's hand and rose to join Mrs. Lummington at the bedroom door. In a lowered voice she said, "I hope that we shall not be seeing an epidemic, Mrs. Lummington."

"Do not be worrying over that, my lady. I'll not have anyone around Eliza who hasn't had the measles before. And I shall have damp tea leaves scattered over the carpet each day before it is swept to catch up the contamination," Mrs. Lummington said reassuringly.

"I do hope that we shall be done with this before the twelve days of Christmas. Sickness in the household will certainly dampen the spirit of the holiday," said Victoria.

"To be sure, my lady. It would be a great pity," agreed Mrs. Lummington.

When Victoria wearily returned to the nursery, she was astonished to find Lord Damion seated comfortably in a wingchair before the fireplace with Jessica resting on his lap. "My lord!" she exclaimed uncertainly.

A glint of humor appeared in his eyes. "Your profound amazement wounds me, Lady Victoria. I must inform you that I am no stranger to sickrooms, though it is true I have visited patients a great deal older than Jessica."

"Mama, he is telling me about a great white horse," said Jessica happily. Her eyes were shining as she looked up at Lord Damion's face.

Victoria saw that Jessica was more contented than she had been in days and her heart softened toward Lord Damion. "I'm certain it is a splendid story, *menina*," she said gently. She looked at Lord Damion. "I am grateful, my lord."

Lord Damion's gaze was somber. "I intend this to be the first of many visits, with your permission, Lady Victoria."

Victoria was on the point of demurring when her daughter interposed. "Oh good, good! Lord Damion tells me many stories," said Jessica, clapping her hands.

Victoria smiled ruefully. "It seems that I have little choice, my lord, even though I have reservations about the propriety."

"Rest easy, Lady Victoria. I am a most proper gentleman when on an errand of mercy," Lord Damion said, grinning.

Victoria blushed. "Oh no, you misunderstand me. That was not what I meant at all!"

Jessica tugged impatiently at Lord Damion's coat. "Tell me about the horse now."

Lord Damion laughed at her. "I am reminded most strongly of my duty, young lady. Very well, I shall continue." He glanced once more at Victoria and his voice gentled. "Forgive me, ma'am, but you are perfectly hagridden. I shall look after Jessica so that you may rest."

Victoria made a gesture of dissent. "I could not possibly—"

"That is an order, my lady." Lord Damion's voice snapped like a whip. "And believe me, Victoria, I shall personally enforce it."

Victoria felt her face grow warm once again. The thought of Lord Damion putting her into bed was incredibly disturbing to her pulse. She had no doubts that he was quite capable of it and decided prudence was her best course. "Very well, my lord. But I shan't be gone more than an hour." At his nod, Victoria swept out of the nursery.

Victoria found that Lord Damion had meant what he had said about his visits to the nursery. Jessica looked forward to his daily appearances and was more cheerful about taking her medicine. Victoria, too, discovered that these were pleasant times and gradually grew accustomed to the easy rapport between Lord Damion and Jessica. When she thought about it at all, she decided that his lordship was one of those rare men who had a natural liking for children.

Lord Damion's thoughtfulness showed in a thousand ways, not the least of which were the lemon-water ices that he had sent up. Jessica squealed with delight each time the ices appeared. The little girl began to recover rapidly and Victoria forgot how difficult the first days without Eliza's help had been. Without consciously realizing it, she was learning to depend on Lord Damion for her comfort.

Twenty-five

Lord Damion made known his wishes that the Christmas traditions be observed and an air of suppressed excitement and goodwill could be felt in the house among family and servants alike.

Mrs. Lummington went by the old belief that it was bad luck to bring greenery into the house until December 24 and she instructed the household servants to wait until then. On the designated day garlands made from laurel and bay, rosemary, fir, and pine twigs appeared magically on the mantels and decorated the staircase.

When some of the family began to gather for breakfast, the general mood of all was uplifted by these visible signs of the holiday. Victoria, who had spent the early morning hours in the nursery, met Evelyn and Doro on the stairs on the way to the breakfast room. "Do you join us then, cousin? I thought St. Claire had mentioned that Jessica was much improved," said Evelyn.

Victoria nodded at him. "Yes, Jessica is quite recovered. Mary was good enough to sit with her so that I could come down to see the garlands. How beautiful they are! The hall is quite transformed."

"I so enjoy this season," said Dorothea happily, gazing around at the festive decorations.

"And I, too," said Evelyn, appreciatively sniffing the fresh-scented air. He glanced down at his lady with a wicked grin. "I am particularly partial to the kissing bough." Dorothea flushed with pleasure.

"I have not seen a kissing bough for years. My father was one to always keep up the old customs but after his death I missed the traditional signs of the holiday season," said Victoria.

"Then I must certainly reacquaint you with the kissing bough, Lady Victoria," said Lord Damion as he joined them in time to hear the exchange.

Victoria blushed furiously and decided immediately that she would avoid the drawing room, where the kissing bough would have been hung. She lowered her eyes as she accepted Lord Damion's escort into breakfast. As he seated her, his warm breath brushed her neck and Victoria could not suppress a shiver.

Lord Damion noticed it and thought he could guess the cause of her sensitivity. He knew that the attraction still existed between them. With a devilish concern, he asked, "Is there a draft, my lady? I would be happy to place a screen behind you."

Victoria sent him a sideways glance, suspecting him of toying with her. But his bland expression told her nothing. "That would be most helpful, my lord," she said, hoping that he would not press her further. She did not care to have him discover that his nearness affected her very breathing.

Margaret did not make an appearance at breakfast. She had taken to sleeping later in the mornings since Jessica's illness. Victoria had been seen but rarely downstairs for several days and Margaret no longer considered her serious competition for Lord Damion's attentions. She felt entirely secure in indulging herself, by having her morning chocolate served to her in bed, for Lord Damion would be hers to call upon the remainder of the day.

Lady Hortense and Sir Aubrey likewise did not come down but kept to their usual habit of taking breakfast in their own rooms. Later the two quietly took the carriage to the family chapel. There they laid a holly wreath bright with red berries on Lord Robert's snow-covered grave.

Lord Damion, who had already stepped outdoors to check the weather, remarked that it was a clear, cold day. "I should think it would make for good shooting if you would care to join me, Eve," he said.

Evelyn's eyes lit up. "That is a capital notion, St. Claire! A hot rabbit pie for dinner, would be just the ticket." He suddenly bethought himself of his wife and turned to her.

Before he could utter a word, Dorothea said, "Do go, Evelyn. You know that you shall enjoy the exertion."

"Then you shan't mind?" asked Evelyn.

"Of course not, especially as I intend to spend much of my day with little James," said Dorothea, a betraying softness in her eyes.

"That's all right, then," said Evelyn happily. He turned to Lord Damion and demanded to know when they were to start.

"After breakfast as soon as Cook is finished packing us a luncheon," said Lord Damion. He grinned at his cousin. "I gave orders an hour ago for the hounds and the beater, for I suspected that you would be as house weary as I."

"Too true. You have thought of everything," said Evelyn appreciatively. He began to whistle a lively air.

"I hope so," said Lord Damion, somewhat taken aback by his cousin's exuberance. He caught sight of Victoria's eyes, brimful of laughter, and shared with her a smile.

Victoria felt her heart turn over. She said briskly, "Well, I for one intend to be industrious and improve my mind in the library."

"You must be jesting, cousin," protested Evelyn. "Only a confirmed bluestocking would waste time with a book when the weather is this obliging."

"Evelyn is right, you know," said Lord Damion, looking at Victoria's unusually pale face. "You have nursed Jessica practically single-handed for nearly a week, my lady. You are in need of fresh air. I would be obliged to you if you exercised Starfire this afternoon, for she has become fat in these last weeks."

"If you wish, Victoria, I can sit with Jessica so that you will be free," said Dorothea eagerly. "Now that she is well I know that Jessica would be delighted to be introduced to James, and the dogs will keep her entertained."

Victoria began to laugh. "Very well, very well. I see that I must go riding. I suspect, however, that it is meant more for my benefit than for Starfire's."

So it was that Victoria found herself in the saddle. The mare moved smoothly beneath her, blowing steamy clouds in the cold air. Victoria kept her mount to the middle of the fields where the snow could be expected to be shallow under the brush of the wind. Soon she and Starfire were winging over frozen white earth. The cold wind caused tears to start from her eyes and her cheeks were numb, but Victoria laughed aloud for sheer joy.

After the initial wild gallop, she was content to allow Starfire to fall into a slower pace. They roamed freely through the winding dale, skirting the drifts at fences and around the scattered trees. Victoria looked up at the towering peaks that rimmed the small valley and thought that she had never seen any view quite as beautiful. It was sometime later when she realized that her gloved fingers were numb and she could no longer feel her feet. She turned Starfire back toward the Crossing.

On returning to the manor, she walked the mare around to the stables. Steam rose from the horse's wet back and Victoria started to rub her down with bunches of straw.

"Ere now! I'll be doing that," said John Dickens, coming into the stall.

Victoria laughed at him. "I well know that I am proving that women are a nuisance in the stables, John." She relinquished her task to him even as he grunted in reply. He threw a rare smile to her and nodded before he turned his attention to the mare. Victoria left the stables, knowing that he did not truly disapprove of her.

As she traversed the manor's halls, she discovered that she was more tired than she had realized. The two weeks of nursing Jessica had depleted her energy. When she finally reached her bedroom, she dragged off her wet outer garments and placed them carefully before the fire. Even as steam rose from the wet clothing, she fell into bed. Victoria slept dreamlessly and so deeply that she did not rouse at the sound of the luncheon bell.

Margaret was surprised to find only Lady Hortense and Sir Aubrey at luncheon. She inquired of Lord Damion's whereabouts and learned that he and Evelyn had gone shooting. She was more than a little miffed. Lord Damion would not be back until nearly dark and Margaret could see the long hours stretching before her.

"The road seems quite passable today. I believe that I shall order up the carriage and go into the village and do some shopping, for there is no knowing when we shall have such a clear day again," said Lady Hortense. "Would you care to go with me, Margaret?"

"I would be delighted," Margaret said promptly.

"Pray do not expect me to act as escort, Hortense," said Sir Aubrey. "This cold plays havoc with my gout and I refuse to subject myself to it any more than I must."

"Of course not, Aubrey. It shall be very cozy with just Margaret and me," Lady Hortense said placidly.

Sir Aubrey stared at her from under lowered brows,

uncertain if he had been insulted. When he saw Margaret turning away to hide a smile, he was positive of it. "Very well, madame!" he snapped, rising. "I shall be in the study if you wish to find me."

Lady Hortense and Margaret soon departed in the carriage, bundled under rugs and with hot bricks to their feet. They chatted like old friends. Sir Aubrey did not miss them. He whiled away the afternoon reading about the war and cursing the government's ineptitude. Inevitably the warmth of the fire worked its magic and Sir Aubrey's head began to nod.

When Victoria awoke, she immediately went to the nursery to check on Jessica. Dorothea smiled when Victoria entered the room and put a finger to her lips. "She fell asleep not a half hour ago, and my little James has just dropped off." Dorothea gestured at the two dogs lying in front of the hearth. "As you can see, it is truly peaceful here."

"Indeed it is," said Victoria, laughing softly. She seated herself in the wingchair opposite Dorothea. "This is so very comfortable. I feel incredibly content."

Dorothea glanced at her over the needlework in her hands. "I hope that you shall find the happiness you deserve, Victoria." When Victoria looked at her in astonishment, warm color rose in her face. "I shall speak freely because I am very fond of you. I know that you have been lonely without Charles and I know the depth of your heart. And I have lately observed a certain air about you when Lord Damion is nearby."

It was Victoria's turn to blush. "Lord Damion proved himself a steady friend while Jessica was ill. I am naturally grateful to him."

"You cannot hide so easily from me, Victoria. I know that you are in love with him."

Victoria read the absolute certainty in her friend's blue eyes and sighed. "It is so obvious, then?"

"Why the long face, Victoria? I think it wonderful. And I hope very much that Lord Damion will return your regard. I should like to see you a countess." Dorothea smiled teasingly.

Victoria obligingly laughed but as soon as she was able turned the topic of conversation. After a while she asked if Dorothea would mind if she went downstairs. "For I am positively famished after my ride and I have missed luncheon completely," she said.

Dorothea shook her head. "I shan't mind in the least. I fear I am a very domesticated creature. I cannot think of anything better than remaining here with the children and my needlework," she said contentedly.

Victoria went downstairs. The butler informed her that a cold collation of meats and cheeses had been left on the sideboard against the return of the hunters. Victoria thanked him and went on to the dining room.

Afterwards she wandered to the library. She knew that Dorothea would not be put out if she did not return. She was relaxed and in a pleasant mood and did not feel the need for anyone's company.

Victoria perused the titles on the library shelves. When she came across *Pride and Prejudice* by Jane Austen, she cried out in delight. She had heard a great deal about the novel when it had been published the year before but had been unable to obtain a copy in Lisbon. She settled herself in a wingback chair and was soon engrossed in the story of the Bennetts and Mr. Darcy.

Sir Aubrey found her sometime later. He greeted her and lowered himself into the chair opposite her. Victoria put aside the novel reluctantly.

"We missed you at luncheon, Lady Victoria. I hope Jessica continues to improve?" said Sir Aubrey.

"Jessica is completely recovered, sir. I missed luncheon quite on my own. I had laid down to rest and overslept, I am afraid."

"I am not at all surprised to hear it. Your devotion to duty has been commendable, my lady. Most women in your position would have left the nursing to someone in the household." Sir Aubrey studied her a moment, then said abruptly, "It is not in my nature to bestow compliments, Lady Victoria."

Victoria could not help smiling. "I am well aware of that, Sir Aubrey," she said dryly.

"Your insight into my character is wonderful, my dear," said Sir Aubrey with gentle mockery. "However, I do not mind telling you that I respect the manner in which you have attempted to raise your daughter. What little I have seen of her confirms me in my opinion. Jessica is a credit to you and the family and I believe that Charles would have been proud of you both."

"I am overwhelmed, Sir Aubrey," said Victoria with surprise. She had never expected to hear such commendation from one so cynical as Sir Aubrey.

Sir Aubrey leaned back in his chair at ease. His eyelids drooped slightly though his gaze remained sharp on Victoria's face. "What I really wish to tell you, Lady Victoria, is that I am all admiration for your handling of Lord Damion these past several weeks. I thought you had lost him with that quarrel, you know. But your performance has been superb and to interest him in the girl's welfare was a masterly touch."

Victoria had stiffened in her chair. "What exactly do you mean, sir?" she asked coldly.

Sir Aubrey waved his hand dismissively. "Pray leave off the outrage with me, Lady Victoria, for I am well aware that it is but a farce. We both recall our conversation on the first day of your sojourn here."

"Yes, and the outcome," retorted Victoria. "I have not altered my decision, sir!"

"Have you not?" asked Sir Aubrey softly, his eyes bright and hard. "Your conduct toward Damion has led me to believe otherwise. And he has responded most gratifyingly, has he not? Come, my dear, surely you cannot be so foolish as to insist the easy familiarity between you has arisen spontaneously."

Victoria colored and was on her feet in an instant, the novel slipping unheeded to the carpet. "Your opinion of my character has never been high, but this insinuation ... Indeed, allow me to be frank with you, Sir Aubrey. I find your thoughts disgusting!"

She turned on her heel, only to be brought up short by the sight of Lord Damion standing before her. "Oh!" She flushed scarlet, knowing that he had overheard, and fled.

Lord Damion looked over at his uncle with a certain grimness. "I believe you owe me an explanation, Sir Aubrey."

Sir Aubrey was as taken aback by the earl's sudden appearance as Victoria. He shifted uncomfortably. "I hardly think that there is anything we need discuss, Damion."

"I disagree," said Lord Damion quietly. He advanced until he towered over the older man. His eyes were hard. "I overheard enough to realize that Lady Victoria has every right to be disgusted with you." He had kept tight rein over his wrath, but it suddenly blazed forth. "Damn your eyes! How dare you suggest that she become my mistress!"

Sir Aubrey was startled. "What? No such thing. I never suggested it, but I assumed from your manner toward her that—"

"If my manner has been anything short of respectful toward the lady, I owe her an apology," interrupted Lord Damion.

"Perhaps I was mistaken in my observations," said Sir Aubrey, not entirely convinced. "It is more in the Giddings woman's style, after all. Naturally Lady Victoria could be expected to be more subtle in her methods."

"What the devil are you babbling about?" demanded Lord Damion.

Sir Aubrey looked up at him and said with irritation, "Pray sit down, Damion. I am getting a crick in my neck."

"I prefer to stand," said Lord Damion shortly. However he did move away to put his back against the mantel and fold his arms across his chest. "Now, sir, you will explain fully the reasoning behind your gross insult to Lady Victoria. I must warn you that we shall not stir from this room until I am satisfied of the truth."

"Spare me your threats, Damion. I am not one to tremble at your displeasure." Lord Damion stared at him, unmoved. "Very well. You shall have the truth and may it gall your damnable pride," snapped Sir Aubrey, dull red staining his sunken cheeks. "Lord Robert confided to me his wish to attach his son's memory to the earldom even though actual succession was to pass out of the March family line. He pensioned off Charles's widow, yes, and made provision to settle on her an additional, private income if she was ever to marry the heir to the title."

"So that was the substance of the unread codicil in Lord Robert's will," said Lord Damion slowly. He stared down at his uncle in disbelief. "And you made it known to Lady Victoria that first day."

Sir Aubrey nodded. His eyes glittered. "The moment I laid eyes on Lady Victoria I knew that she could match you fire for fire, Damion. I can yet recall the sparks in her eyes when you dropped her like so much wet baggage! My reservations against Lord Robert's wish evaporated in that instant. The next day I urged the woman to look after her own best interests, but she refused to consider it."

Lord Damion stared at him. "Did you say that she refused?"

"Ah, I see that my estimable nephew finds that of interest." Sir Aubrey smiled thinly, then gave his careless shrug. "I did not believe her, of course. What woman would turn down the chance of snaring riches and a title, especially when coupled with the Demon's much vaunted charm. But as you heard only a moment ago, Lady Victoria has once again done just that." He watched expectantly for Lord Damion's angry reaction. Sir Aubrey was amazed when Lord Damion threw back his head and burst into laughter. When his nephew's amusement had abated, he asked in disgust, "Have you gone mad?"

Lord Damion looked down at him with a grin. He felt as though he had been relieved of an immense burden. He had at last discovered the nature of

Lady Victoria's scruples. "I do not expect you to understand, sir, but you have provided the answer to a thorny question." Lord Damion strode from the library, leaving Sir Aubrey to stare after him.

Twenty-six

Victoria was unable to avoid Lord Damion, but when he made no reference to her interview with Sir Aubrey, she began to wonder if he had indeed overheard as much as she had feared. She hoped that he had not and she decided sensibly to put it out of her thoughts. But Victoria could not set aside so easily the faint unease that she felt whenever Lord Damion approached. She resorted to inviting Margaret into the conversation at every opportunity, thus successfully warding off any chance of private speech with Lord Damion.

When Dr. Chatworth paid a visit to check on his patients, he pronounced Jessica ready to resume her active life. Eliza was still in the process of recovering, however. He recommended gentle exercise as the best remedy for Jessica's weakened state and it was Lord Damion who first escorted the little girl downstairs.

Jessica was quickly tired by the exertion of climbing down the many stairs and was happy to lie on the drawing-room sofa beside Lady Hortense and watch her embroider. But she was soon up to chase Lucinda and Smudge. The little dogs raced madly around the entry hall, barking shrilly. Lord Damion quelled them with a stern command. Quieted for the moment, they waved their feathery tails and sat down to wait for Jessica to slide once more off the sofa.

The performance amused everyone in varying degrees. Even Margaret found something appealing in the little girl's exuberance. "I envy Jessica that renewable energy," she said with a smile. She glanced at Victoria. "I suddenly realize that a mother must be a very hardy creature. Dorothea is in for quite a shock, I fear."

"Not at all, sister I shall enjoy it most prodigiously," said Dorothea confidently. "It is Eve that I am anxious about."

Her husband looked up at her with laughter in his bright eyes. He was bent over the cradle and a tiny hand grasped his finger with surprising tenacity. "All very well, Doro. But I wager that James and I shall get along famously. See, he has already a manly grip. It will not be many years before I may teach him the sporting life."

The butler entered the drawing room to announce that dinner was served. Dorothea carried the baby into the hall and handed him to the waiting nurse, then she and Evelyn followed the others.

Jessica sat at the table, solemn in expression. She knew that it was an important occasion when she was allowed to take her dinner with the adults. Victoria, who was seated beside the little girl, gently squeezed her small hand. "I am proud of you, Jessica," she said softly for her daughter's ears alone. The little girl sat up as straight as she was able, her eyes bright.

It was Christmas Eve and the traditional dishes had been prepared. The butler took his place behind Lord Damion's left shoulder and removed the covers from the first course. Christmas dinner began with mince pies, to be followed by barley soup, stewed Spanish onions, and mashed potatoes and gravy.

The second course consisted of the meat entrees, garnished with greens and carved vegetable roses. "The roast beef and horseradish sauce are excellent. Pray convey my compliments to Cook," said Sir Aubrey, addressing the butler, who stood at the sideboard ready to serve the wines as he was called. The butler bowed.

The customary goose, seasoned with a heady combination of sage, onions, and port wine, was presented in all its golden-brown glory. Evelyn tasted the savory, tender meat with deepest satisfaction. "Doro, I truly pity you," he said.

"Pray do not assume that I shall abstain because I am nursing James," said Dorothea tartly. "I intend to taste everything. And I hope that there are still stewed Spanish onions in that dish, for they are far and away my favorite."

"I hope that our guests tonight also care for onions," murmured Margaret, watching in awe her sister's appetite for the pungent vegetable.

"I shall be more curious to learn little James's reaction," said Victoria dryly.

Margaret looked at her with instant comprehension. "Have you warned Doro?"

"Advice is never at its most effective until it is sought, Margaret. Perhaps Doro shall not need my words of experience. Infants never behave as one assumes they must." Victoria laughed in wry amusement at herself. "Do you know, all of a sudden I am full of hoary wisdom."

"But you are yet capable of errors in judgment, my lady," said Lord Damion. His gaze was intense.

Victoria dragged her eyes away, but she was acutely conscious that he regarded her still. Her heart pounded and she turned in relief to Lady Hortense when that lady addressed her.

"Victoria, you once mentioned that you held particularly fond memories of an English boiled plum pudding at Christmas. I have myself prepared one for dessert this evening. I hope that you shall enjoy it," said Lady Hortense.

Fresh plates had been placed around the table. The apple tarts, a rolled jam pudding, and charlotte russe were served, but the boiled plum pudding was voted the unanimous favorite. Jessica clapped her hands with delight. "My dear ma'am, it is wonderful! I have never tasted better. Whatever have you used to give it this delightful flavor?" asked Victoria.

Lady Hortense was beaming with pleasure at the enthusiastic reception of her plum pudding. "It is suet pudding, of course, with currants, raisins, eggs, bread crumbs, nutmeg, and ginger," she said.

"Make a clean breast of it, Aunt. Unless my taste deceives me, you have added a touch of something else as well," said Evelyn.

Lady Hortense laughed. "To be sure, but I shall not let a hint of it escape my lips. It is my own secret, you know."

"Come, Mama. Surely you cannot mean to deny us on this holiday," said Lord Damion teasingly.

"Certainly I shall," said Lady Hortense promptly, bringing on a general laugh. No one had yet learned her secret ingredient when the family dispersed after dinner to dress for the Christmas gathering that the ladies had planned so many weeks past.

It was eight o'clock when the first guests began to arrive. Lady Belingham, Sir Harry, and Miss Erica were among the guests, as were Reverend Pherson and his wife, the squire and Mrs. Terrell. Lady Hortense had invited sundry others, but Victoria did not know the other ten or so couples. Jessica was the only child present and Victoria thought she would be wise to enlist Dorothea's help in watching her.

A standing supper had been set out for the guests in the dining room. Beef, ham, and tongue sandwiches, lobster and oyster patties, sausage rolls and dishes of cut-up fowl, various jellies, blancmanges, and custards in glasses, tartlets of jam, sweetmeats, and a few plates of biscuits were offered in the buffet.

The guests were free to stroll from the standing supper to the drawing room, which had been elaborately decorated for the Christmas season. Garlands offset by huge red silk bows looped across the mantel and a fir and holly arrangement was displayed on the top of the pianoforte. Bunches of candles blazed everywhere and the bright light was reflected in the large gilt mirror over the mantel. The kissing bough was hung from the ceiling. Shaped like a crown, the fragrant greeenery was adorned with unlighted candles, red apples, rosettes of colored paper, and various ornaments. Suspended from its center was a bunch of gray-green mistletoe laden with white berries.

However, when the guests first entered the drawing room it was not the traditional holly and bay that drew exclamations of amazement. A small fir tree was set in a pot on an occasional table covered with pink linen. Red, blue, green, and white candles burned on its branches in three circular rows. Gifts of various kinds had been piled in front of the tree and the table was set against a wall so that the tree could be seen from three sides. "But how very unusual," said Lady Belingham, delighted.

Mrs. Pherson eyed the festive fir tree with disapprobation. "Indeed. A foreign custom, I feel certain."

Lady Belingham glanced sideways at the dour woman. "I think it vastly pretty. Hortense, pray tell us whose inspired mind gave birth to the tree?" Mrs. Pherson sniffed, but she waited to hear Lady Hortense's reply.

"You shall not believe this, but Sir Aubrey positively insisted upon the tree for Jessica's pleasure. He has developed quite a soft place in his heart for her, you know," said Lady Hortense.

"You are right, I do not believe it," said Lady Belingham. She saw Sir Aubrey passing and summoned him with a wave.

Sir Aubrey joined the three ladies, bowing to Mrs. Pherson and Lady Belingham with courtly grace. "Good evening, Lady Belingham, madame."

The ladies murmured a greeting, then Lady Belingham tapped him on the elbow with her fan. "Now, sir, you must tell us about the little tree. Hortense has related that it was your own idea."

"Lady Hortense compliments me unduly," said Sir Aubrey, bowing to his sister-in-law with mock formality. "The custom originated in Germany, I believe. During my grand tour as a young man I saw many such firs during the Christmas holidays."

"But what an utterly charming custom," said Lady

Belingham. She ignored Mrs. Pherson's disapproving cough. "Pray tell us how the Germans decorated their trees. Were they candlelit as well?"

Sir Aubrey inclined his head. "Indeed, my lady. The German tree is set up in the parlor with roses cut out of many-colored paper and apples, wafers and gold foil hanging from its branches. As you may guess, the children are greatly interested in the procedure and the tree is mainly for their benefit."

"Then perhaps I am still a child, for I am completely captivated, Sir Aubrey. I shall have a tree of my own next holiday," said Lady Belingham. Mrs. Pherson had had enough of her ladyship's shocking susceptibility to the frivolous and moved away. Lady Belingham watched her go with satisfaction and confided to her remaining two companions, "I have never felt at ease in that woman's presence."

"I compliment your insight, Lady Belingham," said Sir Aubrey gravely. He bowed once more and walked away, leaning lightly on his Malacca cane.

"Well! I have never known Aubrey to be so civil," said Lady Hortense, looking after him with surprise.

"The season apparently affects most of us favorably, Hortense," said Lady Belingham. "Oh, the candles on the kissing bough are about to be lighted. Come, Hortense, we must not miss it."

With due ceremony, the butler reached up a long smoking taper to each of the several candles nestled in the kissing bough. The onlookers laughed and clapped as each candle flared bright. The lighting of the kissing bough on Christmas Eve, an act to be repeated each night of the twelve days of Christmas, was a time-honored custom.

Victoria was as enchanted as the rest of the company. "I had forgotten how beautiful it was," she said, half to herself.

"Recall that I have offered to reacquaint you with this particular English custom, my lady," said Lord Damion, standing beside her. Since he had learned the contents of the codicil, he had made a point of being attentive. It was only a matter of time before

Lady Victoria once again spoke of the barrier between them and he meant to have an answer for her. He smiled down at her startled expression and lowered his voice. "I intend this to be a memorable Christmas Eve, my darling Victoria."

"My lord," protested Victoria, feeling warmth suffuse her face. She glanced about them, alarmed that someone might overhear him.

"Yes, my lady?" asked Lord Damion hopefully. But she only shook her head and made a smiling excuse to leave. He watched her cross the room to sit beside Dorothea, not at all discouraged by her reaction.

Victoria glanced about casually. "Where is Jessica, Doro?"

Dorothea's welcoming expression altered. "Did she not come to you, then?" she asked, dismayed. "She asked so sweetly if she could join you and naturally I allowed her to go. Jessica has been so good that I never dreamed—"

Victoria was canvassing the drawing room, but nowhere did she spot a small active figure in blue velvet. "Oh dear, I do not see her anywhere. Jessica can be such an imp when she wishes. I hope that she may not make a nuisance of herself."

"I am so sorry, Victoria!" said Dorothea contritely.

Victoria shook her head, smiling reassuringly. "Pray do not blame yourself, Doro. Jessica is learning how to get her own way, and with such originality that I am sometimes amazed. I shall go look for her. She may have gone into the dining room for a sweetmeat."

Victoria did not find Jessica in the dining room and as she returned to the drawing room she could not help but feel a certain anxiety. A little girl could go a great distance in a short time and Jessica was not familiar with the older, sprawling sections of the manor.

A window near the door had been discovered to be ill-fitting and a painted screen had been set across it to ward off drafts. Victoria had passed the screen without a glance when she went to the dining room, but now she paused. It would be very like Jessica to explore. Victoria stepped around the screen, only to stop short.

Sir Harry and Margaret were caught up in a passionate kiss. Nevertheless they heard Victoria's gasp and parted instantly. Margaret threw a defiant look at Victoria before she brushed past her.

Victoria and Sir Harry looked after her graceful form in silence. Sir Harry turned smiling eyes on Victoria. "Well, Vicky, you have never heard me say so before, but I am in love at last."

"Oh no, Harry!" Victoria exclaimed unguardedly. She was dismayed, for she knew that he spoke in all seriousness. "Margaret is a flirt of the worst kind. She will make you miserable."

"Don't I know it," said Sir Harry ruefully. "She'll lead me a dance and laugh as she does." He looked down at Victoria's troubled expression and laid his arm about her shoulders in a brotherly hug. "You needn't concern yourself so, love. I knew from the moment that I saw her what she is and I understand her character. She is restless and spoiled and wishes for the admiration of others. But she has a sterling quality as well. We are much alike, Margaret Giddings and I. She does not know it yet, but she will have me, and I shall make her happy. Meantime, I am contented to wait until she is ready."

"If you are right, Harry, she will make a splendid soldier's wife. Margaret has spirit enough for two," said Victoria, smiling up at him. She decided on the instant to keep her reservations to herself. Her friend was experienced enough to know his own mind. She only hoped that his ultimate decision would bring him happiness.

Sir Harry realized her tact. He raised her hand to his lips. "Thank you, dear friend. And I wish you joy of this glowering gentleman." Victoria turned her head swiftly. She blushed scarlet when she saw that Lord Damion had joined them. Sir Harry gave the earl a friendly nod. "A pleasant evening to you, my lord." He strolled out from behind the screen. Victoria's hand flew out to him, then dropped to her side.

Lord Damion took note of her blush and lowered eyes. "I perceive that Sir Harry is a most accomplished flirt. But I believe that I may claim some experience of my own." Before Victoria was aware of what he was about, Lord Damion turned her face up and kissed her softly. He raised his head to gaze deeply into her wondering eyes. "Merry Christmas and a happy new year, Lady Victoria."

"And to you, my lord," said Victoria. She did not any longer feel the least bit awkward with him. When he offered his arm to her, she accepted it with grace and they emerged together from behind the screen.

"Mama, Mama!"

Jessica flung herself at her mother and Victoria caught her up. "Jessica! Wherever have you been?"

The little girl brushed aside such an unimportant question. "Mama, you are to play carols!" she said excitedly, her eyes aglow. She tugged on Victoria's hand. "Come, Mama. Everyone is waiting for you."

"Then most assuredly she must come, and immediately," said Lord Damion. He reached down and swung the little girl up to sit on his shoulders. Jessica squealed with delight, clapping her hands. She was not at all afraid of the giddy height. With a flourish, Lord Damion offered his arm once again to Victoria. She laughed and put her hand through his arm.

Twenty-seven

Victoria was still laughing as Lord Damion escorted her across the crowded room. It struck more than one person that the trio looked to be a perfect family group. Squire Terrell nudged his wife. "Tibby, we must have them to breakfast after the wedding." His spouse stared at him. He blew out his cheeks. "Aye, madame, regard me with doubt. But I tell you that the neighborhood will see a wedding this spring."

Margaret stood nearby and was an unintentional eavesdropper. She stared in amazement at Lord Damion, with Jessica clinging to his shoulders, and Lady Victoria as they approached the pianoforte. Only the blind could have missed the warmth in the smile that the couple exchanged and it was brought forcibly home to Margaret that she had lost Lord Damion after all. Her feelings were mixed, but surprisingly enough she did not feel the rage that she expected. "Well, this has been a singularly unprofitable winter," she murmured to herself. Her gaze fell on Sir Harry's tall figure and she made a sudden decision. Margaret walked over to him without giving a backward glance to Lord Damion and Victoria.

Sir Harry welcomed Margaret with a quiet greeting. He had no difficulty in reading her mind. His chosen lady was feeling failure for the first time, but she was rising to the occasion like the thoroughbred he had known her to be. When Victoria called to her to join Lord Damion beside the pianoforte, Margaret graciously assented. Before she left him, Sir Harry caught her eye and made her a slight bow, allowing his admiration to show. Margaret's firmly held mouth softened and she went to the pianoforte with a light step.

Lady Hortense watched the scene with approval. "Oh bravo, Damion! I knew that you could persuade her," she said softly. Beside her, Sir Aubrey gave a start. He had been regarding Victoria and his nephew with great satisfaction and was already turning over in his mind how best to make the match acceptable to his sister-in-law. It came as a pleasant surprise to discover that he need not make the effort. His cynical face eased into a warm smile.

The first carol was the duet between Lord Damion and Margaret. Once again Margaret was in her element with the old song. Her eyes flashed like blue jewels and her voice soared in beautiful harmony with her companion's. When the carol was finished, the company was loud in compliments and entreaties for more.

Margaret laughingly declined a second duet and urged Victoria to play a time-honored carol that everyone might sing. Victoria obliged and the carol's bright hopeful words rose to fill the air with goodwill and cheer.

The caroling lasted the better part of two hours. When Victoria was at last free to rise from the pianoforte, she discovered that Jessica had fallen asleep. The little girl was curled on the sofa beside Lady Hortense, her tousled head in that lady's lap. "She looks like such an angel," said Lady Hortense softly, brushing a strand of light hair from Jessica's rosy cheek.

"I think it past time that I take her up to her bed," said Victoria, bending to pick up her daughter. Jessica was limp as a doll and did not stir as Victoria laid her over her shoulder.

"I do not think anyone will think you too beforehand for going upstairs, Victoria. Dorothea excused herself some time ago to nurse little James," said Lady Hortense.

"Then I, too, shall make my excuses. It has been a

very full evening. Good night, dear Lady Hortense," said Victoria. The older woman surprised her by reaching up to bestow a light kiss on her cheek. Victoria smiled and then began to make her way to the drawing-room door.

Margaret came up to her. "You are retiring then, Victoria?"

"As you see," said Victoria with a laugh as she nodded down at her daughter.

"You warned Sir Harry about me, did you not?" asked Margaret unexpectedly.

Victoria read the certainty in her eyes. "Of course I did, Margaret, for you are a terrible flirt."

Margaret nodded, and suddenly smiled. "You do realize that I do not care to be crossed. I shall probably do something outrageous now."

"You probably shall," agreed Victoria, returning her smile. They parted amicably, at last no longer antagonists.

Victoria was stopped several times as various people wished her good night, but at last she reached the hall. "Here, let me carry Jessica," said Sir Harry, who had followed her. Victoria relinquished her heavy burden with an exaggerated sigh of relief and he laughed. They went together up the stairs.

Victoria's graceful exit was taken as a signal by the guests to depart. There was a general exodus and calling for wraps and carriages. Good nights and compliments frosted the cold night air and the cheerful light from the manor door slanted over the white snow in the carriageway.

Victoria did not want to miss Lady Belingham and Erica and she returned downstairs with Sir Harry, who joined his mother and sister in their leavetaking. Victoria addressed Erica. "I did not spend as much time with you this evening as I would have liked, but I promise you that I shall ride over one day quite soon."

"I should like that. Harry leaves again for the Peninsula before long, you know, and it shall be very dull without him," said Erica with a laugh.

Lady Belingham overheard her. "Yes, and so it shall. Be sure that you do not desert us in our time of need, Lady Victoria. I still hope that you and Jessica shall come to visit with us at Belingham before you, too, return to Portugal," she said. Victoria laughed and promised her that they would. Lady Belingham turned to Lady Hortense and hugged her. "It was a marvelous gathering, Hortense. And I do believe that the gossip has been silenced. The Crossing's charming hospitality will be the topic for many a day," she said, chuckling.

"It did go off rather well, didn't it?" Lady Hortense said happily. The Belinghams did not tarry long in the cold and quickly entered their equipage. Lady Hortense waved to her friend as the carriage began to roll away from the steps.

As the host, Lord Damion remained at the door until the last of the guests had departed. But Sir Aubrey and Margaret had already gone upstairs, closely followed by Evelyn, who wanted to look in on his wife and son.

Lady Hortense was drooping when the door was at last closed. Lord Damion said gently, "Go to bed, Mama. I shall make the rounds."

"Very well. I need little persuasion, I fear," said Lady Hortense as she turned to the stairs. Victoria made to follow her, but Lord Damion held her back. She did not object, content for the moment to be with him.

Victoria and Lord Damion were left alone and she accompanied him as he gave a quick look in at the recent scene of festivity. The remainder of the standing supper had already been cleared away. The butler was tending to the hearth fires and Lord Damion gave him a word of thanks. The butler bowed, wishing his lordship and her ladyship a good night.

Lord Damion gestured toward the stairs. Victoria took his arm and they ascended as the servants were just putting out the guttering candles. Darkness swiftly engulfed the hall below and only the taper that Victoria carried lighted their way.

"I enjoyed this evening. I do not recall ever attending a more pleasant gathering," said Lord Damion.

"Nor I," said Victoria softly. "It can only be that the Christmas spirit infected us all. My lord, did you observe that Sir Aubrey and Evelyn did not exchange one cross word all evening? I was overcome with amazement, I assure you."

Lord Damion laughed. "We were all on our best behavior. And I, too, think it was due to more than the desire to impress the neighborhood with our family feeling."

They had reached Victoria's door and Lord Damion raised her hand to his lips. His eyes danced, inviting her to share his amusement. "I was told by my mother, who was quite heady with triumph, that my reputation as an unreformed rake suffered irreparable damage when I perched Jessica on my shoulders. We apparently presented quite the family picture."

Victoria blushed furiously. She gently withdrew her hand from his, suddenly trembling. "It will be a nine-day wonder, I have no doubt. I will bid you good night now, my lord," she said in a light tone.

Lord Damion took her face between his hands and gently kissed her. "Merry Christmas, Victoria," he said softly. He released her and walked away to his own room.

Victoria was hardly conscious of entering her bedroom. Her heart hammered erratically and as she leaned against the closed door she could hardly think for the happiness that welled up within her. She touched her soft lips, shaking her head in wonder.

Victoria knew in the back of her mind that she was going to be wretchedly unhappy when she left the Crossing, but she pushed aside the thought. For the moment it was wonderful to pretend that she was free to love Lord Damion.

She had given Mary permission to spend Christmas with her family and so undressed herself. Her fingers were clumsy on the gown's tiny buttons, but Victoria hummed as she prepared for bed. She blew out the candle that she had put down on her bedstead and started to slide between the sheets.

There was a scratching at her door and a loud whisper. "Victoria! Are you awake? It is I, Evelyn."

Victoria hurriedly put on a dressing gown before opening the door. "Evelyn, whatever can you want? It must be well after midnight!"

"Doro sent me to fetch you. We gave Nurse the night off and the baby—Victoria, he is screeching in pain."

"I will come at once."

They hurried down the hall, neither noticing when Margaret's door cracked open. Doro was sitting up in bed, rocking the pitifully screaming infant to no avail. Distraught tears ran down her cheeks. "Oh Victoria, I am so glad you have come!"

Victoria sat down on the bed and took the infant. She lightly laid her hand over his tiny abdomen and sighed. "Here, Doro. His poor little belly is tight as a drum. He has the colic," she said.

"Oh poor James," said Doro, softly stroking the baby's distended belly.

"But what can we do?" asked Evelyn, trying to make himself heard over his son's wails. "I don't mind telling you that he is driving me mad."

"Evelyn!" Dorothea exclaimed angrily.

Evelyn's jaw jutted. "It is true, Doro," he said bravely. "I am sorry for him and all, but I cannot stand much more."

"Evelyn, put some coals in the warming pan and bring me that comforter. Heat is what will ease him," said Victoria. Under her directions Doro settled into a wingchair. The comforter was folded securely around the warming pan and placed in her lap. Victoria laid the shrilling baby facedown across the warm comforter and Doro slowly rocked him, patting his back. Gradually his cries of distress lessened. When he had fallen asleep, Doro placed him back into his cradle.

Evelyn let out a sigh. "Thank God for that."

"He will be fine, until the next time that Doro has too many stewed Spanish onions before she nurses him." Victoria laughed at Doro's startled reaction. "I remember well how Jessica kept both Rebecca and me awake when I ate something which did not agree with her. I thought we should never quieten her, but warmth worked amazingly well."

"I do thank you, Victoria. And I promise you that I shall never touch another onion," Dorothea said feelingly.

Victoria laughed again and shook her head. "Oh, you shall. When James is bigger, he will not mind in the least what you eat." She turned to Evelyn. "If you will light my way, Evelyn, I desire nothing more than to return to my room and my lovely soft bed."

"Of course, cousin." As they walked down the hall, he said, "Doro and the baby are able to travel now, and when the Christmas holiday is almost gone, I think that we will shortly leave for home." He slanted a sideways glance at her. "My father has accepted our invitation to visit at Rosewood, at least until the London Season begins."

"I hope that it is a reasonably agreeable visit for all concerned," said Victoria.

Evelyn laughed heartily. "Oh, we shall quarrel. On that head I have no doubts. But we seem to get on better than we were used to and he positively dotes on little James, so that is all right." He fell silent again, then said, "I suppose that you and Jessica will be returning to Portugal shortly."

"Yes," said Victoria simply.

He found her hand and awkwardly squeezed her fingers. "Doro and I shall miss you both, you know. If ever you and Jessica are back in England, pray come stay with us at Rosewood. We would be delighted to have you."

"Of course we shall be back. We have family and friends in England now," said Victoria, giving him a quick smile through a fine mist of tears. She tucked her hand in his arm and they continued down the hall in companionable silence.

Suddenly they heard a woman's light coquettish laugh. "But you shall compromise me, my lord!" A man's deep voice made a low reply.

Evelyn and Victoria looked at one another. Victoria had stiffened at first hearing the voices and she murmured, "Perhaps it would be best if you went on alone. I shall await you here."

Evelyn took one sharp look at her face in the candlelight and grasped her elbow. "I believe you would do better to come with me, cousin." He firmly led her around the corner.

Upon their appearance the couple standing before an open bedroom door disengaged. Margaret fell back against the wall, her hand clutching the deep opening of her pretty negligee. Her eyes gleamed. "Oh! We are found out, my lord."

Lord Damion's dark hair was disarranged and he was in his silk dressing gown. He stood silent in the half-open doorway to his room and slowly put his hands into the dressing gown's large pockets. His expression was stern as he looked at Victoria with unreadable eyes. Victoria wished heartily that Evelyn had not dragged her in to witness this scene.

"Pray leave off this nonsense, Margaret," said Evelyn impatiently. "No one believes it for a moment."

"I am sure I do not understand what you are saying, Evelyn. Your appearance has come as a complete shock," Margaret cast a meaningful glance up at Lord Damion's impassive face.

"Allow me to be blunter, then. This shabby trick to compromise my cousin is wasted. Everyone in the place has known for months that your only reason for coming to the Crossing was to entrap the new Earl of March into marriage. And I for one am heartily tired of your games," Evelyn said roundly.

Margaret drew herself up as though stung. "How dare you insult me in such a manner!" she exclaimed, her eyes flashing.

"You have begged for it these many weeks. Go

back to your room before I am compelled to escort you, Margaret, for I promise you that I shan't be the gentleman about it," said Evelyn.

Margaret opened her mouth, but after glancing at Evelyn's implacable face she thought better of whatever it was she meant to say. Instead she brushed past him, her head high. Margaret met Victoria's eyes and startled her with a broad wink. "I did promise you, did I not?" she murmured for Victoria's ears alone, and gracefully went on without a backward glance.

Victoria realized in a flash that Margaret had indeed found an outrageous way to exact revenge for the warning Victoria had given to Sir Harry about her. A knot loosened inside her and she was able to look on the situation with far different eyes.

"I apologize for my sister-in-law, my lord," said Evelyn formally. "She sometimes allows her fancies to override her better judgment."

Lord Damion inclined his head. Evelyn glanced from him to Victoria. He handed his candle to Victoria. "Cousin, I wish you good night." Evelyn bowed to her and left the scene.

Margaret's shameless ploy appealed strongly to Victoria's sense of the ridiculous and she had difficulty meeting his lordship's eyes. "Pray excuse me, my lord. I wish to look in on Jessica once more before I retire."

"I should like to accompany you if I may," said Lord Damion.

Victoria nodded, feeling that it would be awkward to deny him. Together they walked the short distance and entered the nursery. Victoria placed the candle on the bedside table and bent to smooth the coverlet over her daughter's sleeping form. She smiled tenderly as she caressed Jessica's rosy cheek, then straightened.

"She is a beautiful child," said Lord Damion in a quiet voice.

Victoria gave him a quick smile. "So I think also, my lord."

Lord Damion took her hand. "And her mother is a very lovely woman," he said softly, drawing her into his arms.

Victoria began to tremble. She pressed her hand against his chest. "My lord—"

"Hush. You'll wake Jessica." His breath was warm on her upturned face. Lord Damion lowered his head and took possession of her half-parted lips. His arms tightened around her when he felt her response.

After several moments he raised his head, but his arms remained about her. Victoria let her head rest against his broad chest and sighed. She felt his hand softly stroke her hair.

"I hope you realize that little scene earlier was staged for your benefit," said Lord Damion.

"Yes, I knew," said Victoria. She was reluctant to spoil what she was feeling with words.

"Victoria, I love you. I want you for my wife. And you must know how I feel about Jessica." Lord Damion put his hands on her shoulders and held her away from him. "Victoria, I know the contents of the codicil. I had it out of Sir Aubrey that day." He shook her a little. "Damn you, did you truly think it would matter to me? I would gladly trade all I possess for you. Can you not—"

Victoria put her fingers across his lips. "Hush, or you will wake our daughter."

He stared at her and she smiled in sudden mischief. His eyes blazed and he caught her up in a none-too-gentle embrace. "Fair warning, my girl. I shall demand payment for every moment you have kept me dangling," he breathed, and his hands caressed her suggestively.

"You are no gentleman, sir!" said Victoria, laughing breathlessly. She slid her arms around his neck.

"I once told you that a gentleman born could play the rake better than any," said Lord Damion. He looked down at her, fire in his eyes. "And I mean to do so with you, Victoria." He swept her once more into his ungentle arms and Victoria raised her lips, willingly surrendering to his ardor.

Sometime later Lord Damion and Victoria settled themselves comfortably in a wingchair before the fire. Victoria rested her head on his strong shoulder and her fingers were entwined firmly between his. While Jessica slept, they spoke softly, contentedly of the bright future.

About the Author

Born in Kansas, Gayle Buck has resided in Texas for most of her life. Since earning a journalism degree, she has freelanced for regional publications, worked for a radio station and as a secretary, and is now involved in public relations for a major Texas university. She is the author of another Signet Regency, *Love's Masquerade*.